MORE THAN HE DESERVED

"You reckon God was sendin' us a sign in the way my boy died?"

The question hung there for a couple of moments before I realized Cleopha was talking to me. "Ma'am?" I said, trying to recall what she had asked.

"The way he died. Down where he was and covered in all that. You reckon the Lord took him like that to show us what happens to people like John?"

I shook my head. "No, ma'am. I don't believe the Lord has anything to do with this. What I think happened is that someone killed your son and dumped his body in there hoping no one would find it."

She nodded her head, thinking. "Yeah, that's what I think, too. He was not a good man. But he deserved better than that. You find him, Ray. You find who done this to my child, 'cause no mother should have to find her son that way."

Ray flipped his cigarette out through the door. "It'll be the sheriff what does the investigation, Cleopha. I'm just the constable."

She was shaking her head again. "No, sir! You do it, Raymond. You find him."

Ray nodded. "Yes, ma'am."

Books by Dean Feldmeyer

Viper Quarry
Pitchfork Hollow

Published by POCKET BOOKS

PITCHFORK HOLLOW

DEAN FELDMEYER

POCKET BOOKS
New York London Toronto Sydney Tokyo Singapore

This book is a work of fiction. Names, characters, places and incidents are products of the author's imagination or are used fictitiously. Any resemblance to actual events or locales or persons, living or dead, is entirely coincidental.

An *Original* Publication of POCKET BOOKS

POCKET BOOKS, a division of Simon & Schuster Inc.
1230 Avenue of the Americas, New York, NY 10020

ISBN: 0-671-76983-9

First Pocket Books printing January 1995

10 9 8 7 6 5 4 3 2 1

POCKET and colophon are registered trademarks of Simon & Schuster Inc.

Cover art by Teresa Fasolino

Printed in the U.S.A.

This is for

Ben Feldmeyer
and
Sarah Feldmeyer

"I have found the happiness of parenthood greater than any other that I have experienced."
—Bertrand Russell

PITCHFORK HOLLOW

1

"COME ON, DAN. WE GOTTA GO OVER TO PITCHFORK Holler. Someone killed John Wisdom in the crapper." Ray Hall speaking.

I suppose my reaction to Ray's outburst could best be described as one of partial confusion.

I was confused because I didn't know where Pitchfork Hollow was.

And I was confused because I didn't know who John Wisdom was. Had never heard of the man.

He had not been inside my church since I had taken the position as pastor of Baird Methodist two months ago. At least no one had introduced me to anyone by that name as they filed out, shaking my hand and nodding their heads in what I hoped was agreement with my sermon. Besides that, there were only about thirty people in church on any given Sunday morning, and I knew all of them.

So John Wisdom was a stranger to me. His name a complete mystery.

Confusion.

But only partial confusion.

I did know what a crapper was. I could thank my mother for that.

My mother is a fairly straightforward person. She calls things what she calls them and is rarely dissuaded from her personal jargon.

The vicissitudes of modern parlance affect her not a bit. When other people were saying, "Have a nice day," Mom said, "See ya." When black people insisted on being called black, and later, African-American, Mom was not the least bit disturbed by the changes. She still called them Negroes.

She is not always an easy person to live with, but she is always Mom.

I can distinctly remember her using the word "crapper" on at least two occasions.

When I was little we would visit my grandparents' farm in southern Indiana. It was a primitive place devoid of indoor plumbing except for a bathtub my great-uncle had insisted on putting in the master bedroom. The "comfort facilities," as my aunt Glenda used to call them, were to be found in a little, rundown shack that tilted precariously toward the east out behind the house near the garden. There was a little crescent moon, which purpose I have never understood, cut in the door, and that same door was loose at the top so that you had to hold it closed with one hand if you wanted any privacy. The roof leaked when it even threatened to rain.

Grandma called it a privy.

"Privy comes from the word privacy," Mom would

say to me. "Ha! They make you walk halfway across the county to get to the thing, carrying a roll of toilet paper all the way, and then you sit there exposed to the world, and they want to call it a privy. Baloney!"

Grandpa called it an outhouse.

"Any building beyond the main house can be properly called an outhouse," Mom would tell me. "I suppose your grandfather would be just as happy if we did our business in his toolshed?" She asked it like a question, but I never tried to answer it. A good son knows a rhetorical question when he hears one.

Uncle Maurice called it a WC, something he picked up in England during the Second World War. Mom just snorted. "Water closet? Where's the water?"

Aunt Glenda's "comfort facilities" didn't even get a snort. Mom always considered Aunt Glenda something of a dim bulb and rarely gave poor Glenda's ideas the benefit of contradiction.

"Your uncle Dave calls it what it is," Mom said one day as she guided me to the little shack, my hand in her left hand, a can of wasp spray in her right, and a roll of toilet paper tucked under her arm. "It's a crapper. And I daresay that if he could have his constitutional standing up, he wouldn't even go in there for that. We women don't have much choice, but while we are here visiting your grandmother, please do everything in your power to limit these trips to once a day."

It was a pretty high order for a seven-year-old, but I did my best and usually succeeded.

A good son tries to please his mother.

Anyway, from that day on, it was a crapper. Not a privy or an outhouse or a WC or, God forbid, a comfort facility. It was a crapper plain and simple.

That's my first recollection of the word.

My second is a later and more recent one, about thirty-two years following the first.

This was long after I had graduated seminary, been ordained, and become the golden boy of the conference. Long after I had completed my Ph.D. in systematic theology, written one book and begun another. It was after I had married and fathered two beautiful children. It was even after I had been appointed senior pastor of the largest, richest, and most prestigious Methodist church in the state at the tender age of thirty-eight.

It was also after I threw all of that away for a rather torrid affair with a woman who wore her raven black hair as short as a boy's, ordered her underwear from erotic catalog houses, and taught the third-grade Sunday School class in my church.

Did I say "torrid"? Maybe "sleazy" would be a better word. It ended after six months, when she announced her undying love for me to my wife and most of the members of the church.

And when the affair ended, so did my career.

The bishop, not satisfied to simply yank my credentials and throw me out of the church, had some very unflattering and, in all honesty, unbishoplike things to say to and about me. "Ungrateful," "stupid," and "insensitive" all stand out in my memory and, in retrospect, were probably accurate. "Little prick" was, I think, altogether uncalled for.

I responded with style and grace.

I got drunk. Stayed that way for a whole week, and when I came to, I was divorced and unemployed.

A friend from college helped me get a job teaching high school English in Louisville, Kentucky's, inner city, and I did that for two years. It was the kind of job that put bread on your table and despair in your heart.

It was in the second year of that job that I called my mother on the phone, hoping for a little emotional support. I was whining away, feeling sorry for myself and bemoaning the fact that I had been such an idiot, throwing away my career and my marriage and all, looking for a little empathy, a little sympathy from the woman who brought me into the world.

What she said was, "Yep. It's all in the crapper now."

Such a pillar of support, my mom.

But at least I knew what she meant. I knew what a crapper was. And I knew that my career was in one. If I was going to get it out, I was going to have to climb it out, starting at the bottom.

So I suppose you could say that it was my mother's use of the word "crapper" that was at least partially responsible for my being the pastor of a small Methodist church in Appalachian Kentucky a year later.

And I suppose you could also say that it was to her credit that I was only partially confused when Ray Hall made his announcement and beckoned me to his side on that third Monday of October.

"Come on, Dan. Someone just killed John Wisdom in the crapper."

While I may not have known who John Wisdom was, I most certainly did know, in no uncertain terms, what a crapper was. I had, in fact, been in one . . . figuratively speaking.

But Ray was not, as I would soon discover, speaking figuratively.

John Wisdom really was dead.

And he really was *in* the crapper.

2

FOR RAY TO MAKE HIS ANNOUNCEMENT TO ME IN PERSON, he had to walk all the way from the constable's office to the Baird Diner. It's a short trip. About a foot and a half. The Baird Post Office is just a little farther away—ten feet. And the Baird Store is just eight feet from the post office.

They all occupy the same building on the edge of Baird, Kentucky, just across Route 42 from the volunteer fire department. Ray is the constable and postmaster. His wife, May June, runs the store and the diner.

The store sells bread, bologna, candy bars, cigarettes, chewing tobacco, and soda. It has one of those big red soda coolers that has a slide-back top and about a hundred kinds of soda. The diner sells heart-attack breakfasts, hamburgers and fried bologna sandwiches for lunch, and a daily blue plate special for dinner. Grits come with everything whether you want them or not, and the place is tastefully appointed with card tables, metal folding chairs, and a soda fountain counter that's older than the town.

The post office serves the three-mountain township (third biggest township in Kentucky) and handles about fifty pieces of mail a day, which the people have to come and pick up. The constable's office is the smallest in the building. It's also the busiest.

Appalachia can be a violent place to live.

May June was wearing her usual uniform that morning—housedress, duster, running shoes, and sweat socks. Her hair was done up in a bun and she was standing behind the counter fixing my breakfast: two eggs over easy, country toast, ham, orange juice, coffee, and, no matter how much I protested, grits. The top of the counter came to just below her ample bosom.

"He ain't goin' no place, Dad," she said to her husband. "I'm just fixin' his breakfast. You want some?"

"Mother, a man's been killed," Ray started to protest. He stood six four and had steel gray hair combed straight back, going white around his ears. He, too, had a regular uniform—gray Sears work shirt and pants with black size fourteen work oxfords. "We really need to get goin'."

"Won't take but a couple of minutes. Siddown and I'll make you an egg-and-bacon samwich to take along." She cracked three eggs and broke the yolks as she spoke. "Now, what is this about John Wisdom being killed?"

Ray had been married to May June long enough to know that you didn't argue with her where food was concerned. He sat at the counter next to me and took a swig of the coffee that May June placed before him. It had been boiling just seconds before.

"Gilbert Carmack just called," he said. "That's all I know. He said I was to come over to Pitchfork Hollow on the double on accounta someone had killed Big John Wisdom in his crapper. Probably coldcocked him while he was takin' a leak."

"Oh, my Lord," May June said. She flipped the eggs on the griddle and shook her head.

Ray turned on his stool and spoke to me. "Gil said as how they got the call and figured it was ol' Cleopha needed them on account of her age, but when they got there it was Big John she'd called about. Mother, aren't them eggs done yet?"

"Drink your coffee, old man." She slid my breakfast in front of me and I dug in, trying not to think to much about my arteries. May June doesn't believe in arteries.

"Do I know Big John Wisdom?" I asked. "Or am I just going along for fun?"

May June folded Ray's eggs between two slices of Wonder bread and added four thick strips of bacon. "His mother, Cleopha, is a member of the church," she said. "She hasn't been to services since you been here, though. Too old. She's probably seventy if she's a day." I figured this didn't make her much older than Ray and May June, but they had never really told me their ages. Somewhere between fifty-five and sixty-five would have been close.

"Anyway," she went on. "She still sends a check every month. 'Bout twenty dollars, I reckon." She wrapped Ray's sandwich in a paper towel and started filling a thermos of coffee.

"Twenty dollars a month ain't nothin' to sneeze at

for a woman like Cleopha Wisdom," Ray said. "The Wisdoms ain't poor, exactly, but times can be hard for them what work in the mines."

"An' gettin' harder," May June said, handing Ray the thermos. "Now with John gone, it'll just be Charles feeding that whole brood. Last I heard, Eugene was outa work again."

They both shook their heads.

"Go warm up the Jeep," May June said to Ray. She picked up my plate and dumped what was left of the eggs and ham onto a slice of Wonder bread. "By the time you got it runnin', Dan'll have finished his breakfast."

I used their bathroom, stuffed the rest of my breakfast into my mouth, grabbed my Bengals jacket, and was out the door just as Ray started honking the horn.

Monday was supposed to be my day off.

I'd been in Baird for just a little over two months that October. After my mother's crapper revelation, I had applied for readmission into the ministry and was accepted on a probationary basis in the Kentucky conference. The bishop called the first week of August and told me to pack my bags, he had a church for me. I accepted it sight unseen, and eight days later I was preaching from the pulpit of Baird Methodist Church.

It was the first time I had preached in a church with fewer than five hundred members. And it was the first time in my life that I had been more than twenty minutes from a large metropolitan city. I arrived with a worn-out Bible, a worn-out Volkswagen, a manual typewriter, a suitcase full of clothes, and a mind full of misgivings. By October I was almost beginning to feel like a pastor again. The people helped. They were friendly enough, no worse nor better than any church

I had served. And Ray and May June had befriended me like a Prodigal returned. But it was all still more than a little bit awkward. I was, after all, a city boy.

But if anything can make you forget the city, it's autumn in Appalachia.

Baird, Kentucky, sits in a high valley nestled between three mountains—Clark, to the southwest; Pine Tree, to the northwest; and Devoux, the largest, which makes up most of the eastern horizon. Baird is to towns what a hamburger is to a whiteface steer.

Ray says you have to want to find Baird. Really want to find it.

You can drive through it in less than a second on Route 42 between State Route 106 and Perry, the county seat, thirty miles to the south. As you go through town heading north from Perry, you will pass, on the left, the Baird Store/Diner/Post Office/Constabulary.

Then there's Aunt-tiques, which is a building filled to the ceiling with old furniture and which has never, as long as anyone knows, been open for business. No one can even recall who owns the place.

A couple of dormitory houses for kids who come here to do volunteer work in the summers, Baird Methodist Church (my church) with attached parsonage, and the Weems place (Weems Hardware in Perry and Weems Sawmill on Pine Tree Mountain) complete the west side of town.

Across the road is the volunteer fire department (a cement-block building painted Florida green), the Mountain Baptist Children's Home (which is the reason Baird is here at all), the attendant outbuildings and dorms and so forth of the home, and the Baird School (K–12 in one building).

Basically, it was more like a bunch of buildings

sitting next to each other than a town, but it was home.

And in October it was a wonderfully beautiful home.

On the third Monday in October the first frost was yet to come and the leaves were turning out in all their multicolored grandeur. Gold, yellow, orange, red, and green all competed for attention, and each color succeeded moment by moment for those who paused to notice. Few had fallen to the ground, but those that had were just enough to make that comforting crisp, rustling sound when you walked through them.

And best of all, there were three big maples in front of the Children's Home that had each decided to turn a different color. One was gold, one was orange, and one was still green. It was a glorious, beautiful miracle and it made me pause every time I beheld it.

Every time except that morning when Ray was sitting in the Jeep, racing the motor and saying, "Come on, Dan! Get the lead out, will ya?"

I managed to jump into the passenger seat just as he spun the tires in the gravel of the church parking area and shot out onto Route 42. He took it up to sixty mph before we were out of town and all I could do was zip up my windbreaker and hang on to the roll bar. Ray's Jeep was so old, it didn't have seat belts.

We headed north on 42, then hung a right on County Road 3 and started across Mount Devoux. For the first fifteen minutes of the trip the speed, the road, and Ray's almost nonexistent muffler made talk impossible. Farther up the mountain, though, he had to slow down to forty or fifty to make the narrow twists and turns in the road without driving over a cliff or into a tree. I decided to try some conversation.

"So tell me about the Wisdom family," I shouted.

Ray shrugged. "Not much to tell. Cleopha's about seventy or so. Her daddy settled the holler and built the house she lives in. Her husband was Ahab Wisdom. Died about ten years ago. He was a harmless roustabout. Did a little moonshining, a little preaching, even some mining up on the mountain, I think. They had five kids. Two's dead. Other three still live in the holler with their momma."

I did some mental arithmetic and figured that these kids would have to be older than me if Cleopha followed the Appalachian pattern of starting her family in her late teens. "They all live in the same house?"

Ray took his eyes off the road only long enough to flash me a look that said, city boy. "No, hell no. Couldn't all of 'em fit in the same house. Hell, Dan, two of 'em's older than you. They all got families o' their own."

"Oh." I just let it sit there. Ray would say more when he was ready.

It took him about three minutes. "John was the eldest. He's the one's dead in the crapper. Charles is still there. Jimmy and Clara were twins, died in a fire when they was kids. Eugene's the baby. I think Charles's done some time. Have to check it out."

I assumed that he meant that he would have to check it out, not me. But I never knew with Ray. Since I'd come to Baird, he had sort of taken me under his wing and just naturally expected me to come along on these kinds of things. It wasn't really a bad idea. Sometimes it comes in handy to a cop, even if he's an unarmed, underpaid appointed constable, to have a clergyman riding with him.

In the past two months I had helped him with four traffic accidents, eight domestic quarrels (four with shots fired), and one death notification when a strip-mine blast went haywire up on Clark Mountain. I didn't mind going along. Those kinds of things are what we preachers are trained for. Besides, I liked Ray, learned a lot from him, and he never treated me gently or with deference just because I was ordained.

May June said it was because Ray considered me a "regular guy." You can do worse than being considered a regular guy by the Ray Halls of this world.

The rest of the thirty-mile trip took us about forty minutes and was made in relative silence. I thought about the coffee but decided it would be impossible to pour and drink it in the Jeep. I tried to light my pipe, but the wind burned the bowl so hot, I couldn't touch it. Ray drove with both hands, shifting gears and swearing as we worked our way across the mountain. You Whore, You Old Bastard, and You Rotten Son of a Bitch figured prominently in his monologue, and I didn't know if he was talking to the Jeep or the road. I assumed he wasn't talking to me.

Pitchfork Hollow sat tucked into a pocket in the side of Mount Devoux about thirty feet lower than the gravel road. A creek meandered out of the trees and through the little valley that must have measured about six acres and was cleared of all but a dozen trees. The grass was a little ragged around the house at the end of a dirt driveway, but it didn't mar the effect of a family community comfortably hidden from the outside world. Poor but nice was how I would have described it. A comfortable poverty.

The main house was a big two-story with a tin roof and peeling green paint. It had a porch that spanned the front of the house and was overhung with an open balcony upstairs. Half a dozen faded handmade quilts were hanging over the railing of the balcony, giving the house a sort of sad beauty.

No one answered our knock, so we walked around to the back. The rest of the hollow spread out behind the main house. About a hundred yards to the left and farther back toward the trees was a building that was more of a cabin than a house. Someone had started to hang siding but had run out of time, energy, money, or all three. The lapped cedar went up about halfway and then stopped, leaving particleboards exposed at the top.

Fifty yards directly behind the main house and across the creek was an almost new house trailer sitting on concrete blocks, with more blocks stacked as stair steps up to the front door. A smaller, older trailer sat about fifty feet to the right of the first, the only difference being that it didn't have the makeshift front porch.

A satellite dish sat incongruously in the middle of the big trailer's front yard, and several weather-beaten outbuildings were scattered around the hollow with no apparent plan in mind, as though they had been dropped accidentally from a giant airplane. Four big gardens, about a half acre each, were in the process of being turned over for the winter, but the remains of cornstalks could be seen sticking up through the soil in all of them.

Ray poked me in the ribs with his elbow and nodded at the gardens. "Shine patches," he said. "Onliest thing they grow is corn. Use it to make shine and buy their vegetables at the Piggly Wiggly."

Rusted pickup trucks were in plentious supply, and three muddy dune buggies sat in a row to the right of the half-finished cabin.

The only people in evidence were four men standing around a small building about a hundred feet up from the creek between the main house and the cabin. Two of the men wore the bright orange slickers and fire hats of the Baird Volunteer Fire Department.

The little building, I figured, would be the crapper, and the two orange fire hats would, of course, be Gilbert and Gaylord Carmack, the twin brothers who were cocaptains of the VFD.

"Hey, boys," Ray said quietly as we approached the group.

They each replied with his name. "Ray. Ray. Ray. Ray."

"This here's Reverend Thompson from over to the Methodist church," he said, nodding toward me.

The Carmacks, I knew, but the other two didn't bother to introduce themselves. They just said the one word again. "Reverend. Reverend. Reverend. Reverend."

Then we all just stood there. Smoking. Chewing tobacco. Spitting. Nodding our heads. Shaking our heads. As though the mystery of the thing, the horror of it, was just too damned much for words. Nothing left to say. Just had to stand here and absorb it for a few minutes, it was that bad.

I lit my pipe.

Gil and Gay folded their arms in front of them and spit at the ground simultaneously. They were identical twins, about sixty, and the ugliest two men I have ever seen in my life. About my height or a little more, put them at six one and thin as beanpoles. Pinched faces, long hook noses that curved down to where their chins ought to have been but weren't, and bowl-on-the-head haircuts that made their big ears stick out even more than they normally would have, which was considerable.

The other two men smoked cigarettes, hacked, spit, and shuffled their feet. One was in his mid-forties, beefy, clean-shaven with three little pieces of toilet paper in a line on his throat. About five ten and 220 pounds, maybe 230. He wore nearly new bib overalls and a flannel shirt. The other guy was in his mid-twenties, about five seven or so, thin and surly. His hair was blond and dirty, combed in a half-assed DA. He wore blue jeans, motorcycle boots, and a black Harley T-shirt with the sleeves cut off. He was smoking a joint or a hand-rolled cigarette. I was too far away to smell it.

Ray did what I call his cigarette ritual: take metal box from pocket, open box, remove cigarette, close box, tamp cigarette on box, lay cigarette on lip, replace box in pocket, take disposable lighter from pocket, light cigarette, take deep drag while absent-mindedly replacing disposable lighter in pocket next to metal cigarette box. The cigarettes were Camels.

Ray's cigarette ritual was a sign that he was looking and thinking. Finally he flipped the cigarette into a garden plot and spoke to the two men I didn't know.

"Why don't you boys go take care of your momma. Let us go about our business here." It was more an order than a suggestion, the way he said it. The two men mumbled something and shuffled off to the cabin.

"So whata we got here, Gil?" Ray asked.

"It's Big John, Ray," Gilbert Carmack said slowly, and spit. Gil always spit after he talked. Gaylord (pronounced Gay-lurd) spit before he spoke. That's the only way you could tell them apart. Oh, yeah, and Gilbert held his chew in his right cheek. Gaylord held his in his left. I know it sounds confusing, but you get used to it after a while: Gilbert (right cheek, after he talks), Gaylord (left cheek, before he talks).

"I know that, Gil. You told me on the phone," Ray said.

The twins looked at each other for a moment and shrugged at the same time, some silent communication taking place between them. Gaylord spit over his shoulder and said, "Maybe he better take a look."

"I reckon so," Gil said. Spit.

He moved up to the crapper and pulled the door open. Ray and I looked in. Ahab Wisdom must have been the Conrad Hilton of crappers, because this was the deluxe model. It was paneled in dark maple. The seat was a four-holer, the top hinged at the back with a little handle at the front so it could be opened by folding it up and leaning it against the back wall. Toilet seats had been fastened to the top around three of the holes, and the fourth was pear-shaped to be used as a urinal. There were two rolls of toilet paper stuck on wooden pegs on each side wall, and on the back of the door was a magazine rack holding six-month-old copies of *Reader's Digest, Guidepost,* and *Family Circle* beneath a handmade set of coat hooks. The roof of the structure was heavy, green-tinted, corrugated plastic. The whole thing stood about eight by ten feet with a nice solid oak floor. No wasps were in evidence. A coal bucket full of lime with a long-handled ladle stuck deep into the middle sat neatly in the corner. This was the Taj Mahal of crappers.

There were only two problems that I could detect. One was the smell. You can dress up a crapper all you want, but you can't disguise what it is. The smell gives it away. Same thing here. This may have been pretty, but it was still a shack standing on top of a pit full of human waste. It smelled, no, reeked, strongly of . . . well, crap! The smell rolled out of the door, hit me like a big, wet tennis shoe, and kept going, I presume, all the way to Perry. I tried frantically to relight my pipe.

The second problem was that John Wisdom was nowhere in evidence.

Ray and I looked at each other. Ray looked at Gilbert. Gilbert looked at Gaylord. Gaylord said to Gilbert (spit), "Show 'em."

Ray followed Gilbert into the crapper and quickly lit another cigarette, fanning it around as he went. Gil walked directly to the seat, took hold of the little handle in front, and opened it up. He didn't look down into the pit. He just stood there.

I finally got my pipe lit and caught up with Ray just as he was looking into the hole. I looked, too.

Big John Wisdom, all six-foot-three, 260 pounds of him was floating down there, facedown, the back of his head covered in what looked like blood. He was covered in the vile syrup at the bottom of the pit, and the flies had found him in spite of the lime powder someone had sprinkled over him.

"Oh, Christ," is what I think I said. I don't remember too well because by that time little silver specks had begun to float around in front of my eyes, I was sweating profusely, and my ears were ringing.

I heard Ray say something about getting the preacher outa here, he's gonna pass out, felt hands grab me under my arms and start dragging me out of the little room and into fresher air, and was nearly out cold when I distinctly heard Ray Hall mumble the only appropriate thing that could be said at a time like this: "Shit."

3

Mitral valve prolapse.

"What it is," Doc Pritchard, in Perry, had told me, "is one of the valves in your heart kinda, well, sags from time to time. Usually see it in women, but men get it, too."

"And?" I had asked, images of complicated open-heart surgery flashing through my mind.

"What? Oh, well, nothing really. You'll have chronic low-level chest pain. You'll have to take penicillin before you go to the dentist. Oh, and you may faint in extremely stressful situations." He smiled.

"What should I do about it?" I had asked.

He shrugged. "Stay out of extremely stressful situations?"

So I faint in extremely stressful situations. Like seeing a giant dead man floating in human excrement at the bottom of an outhouse. I used to get embarrassed and upset about it. Felt like a fool or a woosy or both. Now I try to plan on it. When I go on hospital calls where I'm liable to see something extremely stressful, I take smelling salts. Ray and May June know about the prolapse, so, consequently, everyone in town knows about it. May June thinks it's "cute."

I hate it. I even had the smelling salts right there in my jacket pocket. Didn't have time to get to them. Old Big John Wisdom just sort of snuck up on me.

I couldn't have been out more than a couple of minutes, because when I came around I was lying in the grass, staring at the clouds, and I was still sweating. My stomach felt a little upset, as it always does in situations like that, but other than that, I was okay. I lay there for a few minutes and listened to Ray and the Carmack twins talk.

"Well, I guess you better get him outa there. Christ, what a mess. Who found him?" Ray must have been smoking, because he was pausing at each punctuation mark.

"Ol' Cleopha found him," Gaylord said after spitting. "Says she come out to have her morning relief 'bout six or so and found him."

Gilbert cleared his throat. "Uh, Ray. She says she found him after." Spit.

"After? After what?"

"After she, uh, you know."

"No, Gil, I don't know what . . . Oh, Christ! You mean she peed on him?"

The silence that followed lasted so long that I sat up to see what they were doing. What they were doing was laughing. They were sitting on a log, holding their hands over their mouths, elbowing each other and laughing until tears rolled down their cheeks, and trying not to be heard doing it.

I was having trouble seeing the humor. Here was a man, a husband and, presumably, a father, dead, covered in shit and pissed on. What could possibly be funny about that? I asked as much.

"Well, look who has rejoined the living," Ray said, wiping his eyes with a bandanna. "Welcome back, preacher."

"Good thing he woke up when he did," Gaylord said without spitting. "Wouldn't want someone around here to mistake you for a corpse."

"Might get peed on!" Gilbert finished for him, and laughed so hard, he spit out his chew and fell off the log.

"Lighten up, Dan," Ray said. "You didn't know Big John. Fact is, he died in his element. He was a shit as long as I've known him. Beat on Charlotte like a punching bag, drove his sons off, spent more time in the Perry jail for fighting than you've spent in your shoes."

He stood and looked around the hollow, took a last drag on his cigarette, and flipped it after the others into the garden. Finally composed, he said, "You boys go ahead and get him outa there and into Perry. I'll make a report to the sheriff."

Gaylord spit to let us know he had something else to say. "Well, Ray, me and Gil was talkin' about that 'fore you got here. See, we was thinkin'. First thing, ol' Big John weighs nigh to three hundred pound, and we don't rightly know how we're gonna get him outa there."

"And when we do get him out," Gilbert added. "Well, Lord, Ray. We can't just put him in the back of the unit. He'll stink it up somethin' awful."

"What we was thinkin'," Gay went on. "What we

was thinkin' was maybe we'd just sorta hose him off here in the garden. That is, if the folks don't mind, and then they can lay him out here at the house."

Gil picked up the thread again. "Ol' Cleopha said that was what she wanted anyway. Said she wanted to bury him up to the family plot."

"So whataya think, Ray?" Gay finished for them.

Ray was already shaking his head. "Sorry, guys. He's not an obvious natural causes. Law says there's got to be an autopsy, so he'll have to go to Perry and come back. As for the rest of it, one of those pickup's got a winch on the front. You can probably use it to get him up and out. Hose him off and ride him to town in the truck if the brothers'll let you."

The twins seemed satisfied if not happy. "Anything else?" Gay asked.

"Yeah, bag the ladle outa the lime bucket. Someone used it to dump lime on the body. There may be prints on it. Take it with you to Perry. And the sheriff may want us to dip honey later on."

"Dip honey?" I asked. Nearly three months in Appalachia and this was a new phrase for me.

Ray nodded at the outhouse. "Clean out the pit. It's called dippin' honey. Guys what do it are called honey dippers."

Oh, my God. Who would do a job like that? What kind of poor, poverty-stricken, desperate, broken kind of person would resort to "dipping honey" just to put food on the table and a roof over his family's head? This had to be the lowest form of human life. "Who, in God's name, would do such a job?" I asked, more rhetorically than anything else.

The Carmack twins grinned and shuffled their feet as though they were embarrassed but proud, like they'd just been introduced as the coauthors of a book I'd just quoted. I should have known.

While the twins began working to get Big John back to the surface, we walked toward the half-sided cabin to talk with Cleopha.

The cabin was as half-finished on the inside as it was on the outside. The front door opened into a living room in which every single piece of furniture was burned, torn, or broken, with the exception of a nineteen-inch RCA color television on an old end table in a corner. The walls were covered with sagging Sheetrock that had been painted once a long time ago. Two dime-store landscapes hung crookedly above a dirty, worn nylon couch, and a matching easy chair at the end of the couch faced the television. A cane-bottom rocking chair sat in another corner, the cane broken and dragging on the floor as an old woman rocked slowly back and forth.

The two men who had been at the outhouse sat on the couch smoking and drinking beer, watching a game show on the TV. Ray knocked on the screen door and walked in without waiting for an invitation. The two men stood, and Ray took the opportunity of introducing me to Cleopha and her sons to remind me of their names.

"Cleopha," he said, gently, approaching her rocker. "This here's the Reverend Dan Thompson from over to the Methodist church in Baird. He likes to be called Dan. Dan, this here's Ms. Cleopha Wisdom. You already met her two boys here, Charles and Eugene."

Charles was the beefy one with the toilet paper on his neck. Eugene was the young, surly one in the Harley T-shirt. Ray had said that Cleopha was about seventy, but she looked twenty years older—big-boned, broad-shouldered, thick-legged, and stoic. Her face was heavily lined from a lifetime in the sun, and her hair was thick, gray, and pulled back into a bun. She wore a faded housedress and men's work oxfords. When I shook her hand it was callused and nearly as strong as Ray's. Her eyes were bright, serious, and clear. Only a trace showed of the tears she had shed for Big John Wisdom.

"Ms. Wisdom," I said. "I'm sorry about your son."

She sighed and nodded. "You want coffee?"

I looked at Ray and he nodded that we had time. "Yes, thank you. Sweet if you have it."

She waved her hand listlessly toward an inside door. "In the kitchen. Help y'self."

Ray said he'd get it and asked the boys if they would mind helping him. I sat down on the couch and tried to think of something pastorly to say. I know, all the experts tell us that you don't really have to say anything, just being there is enough. But that's only true if you're a layperson. If you're a clergyman, you're supposed to have something profound and wise on the tip of your tongue at any moment. You're supposed to be able to explain all of life's misery and pain and despair with a neatly composed, trite phrase.

I'm not very good at it. I don't have any magic phrases. So I just sat there and watched her rock back and forth. Finally, wondering what was taking Ray so long, I said, "John was your eldest?"

She nodded. "Eldest and worst. He was a caution, that boy."

"He gave you a lot of trouble growing up," I said. Good empathic response. Showed I understood what she said.

"Not just growing up," she went on. "He was trouble every minute of his life. Never done a good thing for another soul lest there was something in it for him. Beat up on his wife. Ran them two boys of his off soon as they were old enough to join the service."

"He was a hard man to live with," I said, trying to be helpful and feeling like an idiot.

"He was impossible to live with," she said, her voice becoming more strident. "He'd sass me. Cussed like a sailor when he was just a little skeeter. His daddy'd lay into him with a hickory stick, and do you think it'd do any good? Psh! He'd just sass his daddy for whippin' him. Like to beat that boy half to death and it never done no good." She shook her head, resigned. "It ain't our fault he turned out the way he done. We done our best with him and it never took is all."

"Ray says John had some trouble with the law," I said, trying to change subjects. When someone insists that something isn't their fault, it's usually because they think it is.

"Used to get in fights over to Perry . . ."

She was interrupted as Eugene Wisdom stomped through the room from the kitchen, hit the screen door with the heel of his hand, and stormed out, throwing his beer can into the yard as he went. Charles followed him out, shaking his head, and Ray entered the room carrying two chipped mugs full of coffee. He sat down on the couch next to me and handed me my mug. I took a sip and it tasted like road tar.

Cleopha had hardly even noticed the interruption. "Used to get to drinkin' and sassin' folks. Someone would take a notion to teach him a lesson. I reckon I could have told them some things about teachin' John Wisdom lessons. I haven't been to church lately. Ought to go more, I reckon."

Having completed her guilt catharsis, she changed

the subject on her own terms. I got the feeling that Cleopha Wisdom did a lot of things on her own terms.

"It's a right smart o' miles, Cleopha," Ray said. "Woman your age's got no business drivin' all that way by herself."

"I was thinkin' o' movin' to Florida," she said, apropos of nothing that I could discern. "But John, he said, 'Momma, you don't know a soul in Florida and your family's all here. What would you do with yourself in Florida?'"

Ray nodded his head as if he knew what she was talking about. I just sat there.

"Well, I told him that a person never knows folks till they meet 'em, and I guessed I'd just meet some folks down there. Down there in Florida I could go to church in the winter if I took a mind to go. I'd just get someone to drive me or I'd walk myself up the street to church. Wouldn't have to live a hunert miles from the place, like I do here."

Ah! There was a connection. Going to church.

"But," she went on, sighing again. "He said the family needed me here, for what, I don't know, unless it's to be their slave. Them girls is worthless. Don't know one end of a kitchen from another. I couldn't move myself and he wouldn't move me, so I just put Florida far from my mind."

Ray nodded again. Nodding and shrugging and spitting, I had learned, played an important role in Appalachian discourse. Even the way you hold and smoke a cigarette plays an active part in dialogue. I didn't speak the language, but I recognized it when I heard, or rather saw, it being spoken.

"Ms. Wisdom," Ray said after a moment. "I know this is a bad time but—"

"Most times is."

"—I need to ask a few questions about John's death. About yesterday and last night and all."

She just nodded. Sipped her coffee, which was probably cold by now.

Ray began his cigarette ritual as he spoke. "Did you hear anything last night? Anything odd?"

She shook her head. "I'm half-deaf. Didn't hear a thing."

"See anything? Anything at all?"

"Not a thing. Went to bed after the news. About eleven-thirty. Didn't wake up again until this morning about sunup."

Ray puffed on his cigarette. "You got up around six, six-thirty?"

She nodded again and rocked in her chair. "'Bout then. Had to get breakfast on. Shift starts at the mine at seven-thirty. Had to get my boys fed."

"They eat with you every morning?"

"M-hm. Their wives is too busy to feed 'em proper. I always fed my boys. Them girls ain't no good for nothin'."

"So what happened after you got up?"

"Well, I put the coffee on to boil and I went to the privy. And I found John. Then I came over here to John's house and sent Charlotte over to Charles's trailer and called the squad."

"You came from your house, the big house, to the privy and then straight here. Is that right?"

She nodded.

"Why did you send Charlotte away? Over to Charles's trailer?"

She tsked and shook her head. "She was 'sterical. Screamin' and wailin' till I couldn't hardly think. I needed to have my wits about me."

Ray nodded and got out his notebook and pencil.

"Maybe you could tell me about yesterday. What did John do yesterday?"

"Same as everyone else. All the men gathered over to the house to watch football and drink a sip. Then they got in them little car things and took off up the mountain."

"What men would that be, Cleopha?"

She looked up at him for the first time. "How's that?"

"You said, all the men. What men came over to watch the football game yesterday afternoon?"

"Oh. Well, there was John, o' course. And Charles and Eugene, though Gene don't have much truck with sports and such. And R.D. and the Eastman boy."

"Lester? Les Eastman?"

Her gaze settled back on the floor as she nodded again. "He'd be the one. And R. D. Miles."

"R.D. and Les go up the mountain, too?"

"M-m. Came over on them buggies of their'n. Loud enough to wake the dead, they was."

Ray continued writing in his notebook. "So they rode up onto the mountain in their buggies." It was a statement.

She kept nodding. I was beginning to wonder if maybe it was just the motion of her rocking chair rather than a true nod. Hard to tell. "They come back about dusk," she said.

"All of 'em?"

"Yeah. All of 'em. Come back and set out on the porch drinkin' till I run 'em off. I heard some more talk after that, so I allowed as how they'd gone over to John's or maybe one of the trailers. I went to bed."

Ray closed his notebook and stood, gulping down the rest of his coffee. "Well, we thank ya, Ms. Wisdom.

We truly do. I'll give my report to the sheriff and he'll probably be in touch."

"I want John to be buried in the family plot on the mountain," she said to no one.

Ray looked to me and nodded. I said, "Yes, ma'am. We can have the services right here in the hollow, maybe over at your house if you like."

She shook her head and looked up at me. "No services. Just words at the grave. That be okay?"

I nodded. "Yes, ma'am. That'll be fine if that's what you want."

"It'd be hypocritical to do more. He was a mean, hateful, vile person, Reverend. It's a terrible thing for a mother to say of her own son, but, God help me, it's His truth. Them that flees from the way of the Lord, they shall fall and perish. Ain't that what the Good Book says? Truth is, they ain't more'n a dozen people won't be glad to know he's gone." She looked at me again and a tear appeared in the corner of each eye. "Ain't that a shame?"

"Yes, ma'am. It is. I'll have a talk with the coroner in Perry and let you know when you can pick up John's body. Then we can talk about what you want said at the grave."

She started rocking again. "Talk to Charlotte. He was her husband. Let her decide what's to be said. If there's a good thing to say about him, she'll know it, I reckon. I'll send her to Baird to talk to you when she's up to it."

"That'll be fine," I said. She seemed to reign over the family like a queen. Best not to mess with a woman like that. Ray and I started toward the door.

She stopped us just as we got there. "Raymond."

Ray turned around. "Yes'm?"

"Why do you suppose he used the privy? He's got plumbin', you know. I never got it because Ahab built that privy for me special. But John had plumbin'. Hated the privy. So why'd he stop there when he was goin' straight over to his own house?"

Ray shrugged. "Guess we'll have to try to figure that out, Cleopha."

"You reckon God was sendin' us a sign in the way my boy died?"

The question hung there for a couple of moments before I realized she was talking to me. "Ma'am?" I said, trying to recall what she had asked.

"The way he died. Down where he was and covered in all that. You reckon the Lord took him like that to show us what happens to people like John?"

I shook my head. "No, ma'am. I don't believe the Lord had anything to do with this. What I think happened is that someone killed your son and dumped his body in there hoping no one would find it."

She nodded her head, thinking. "Yeah. That's what I think, too. He was not a good man. But he deserved better than that. You find him, Ray. You find who done this to my child, 'cause no mother should have to find her son that way."

Ray flipped his cigarette out through the door. "It'll be the sheriff what does the investigation, Cleopha. I'm just the constable."

She was shaking her head again. "No, sir! You do it, Raymond. You find him."

Ray nodded. "Yes, ma'am."

4

BEHIND THE BIG HOUSE GIL AND GAY CARMACK HAD ENlisted the help of the Wisdom brothers and were in the process of raising Big John out of the outhouse pit—the shit-pit, they called it.

Ahab Wisdom had, indeed, been a genius of crapper architecture. He had built it on tracks so it could be rolled aside, leaving the pit uncovered for the honey dippers.

"I thought, when an outhouse got too, uh, full to be used anymore, they just filled in the hole and built a new one," I told Ray as we watched from the porch of the cabin.

"Used to," he said. "You ever dig a ten-foot hole by hand?"

I hadn't. The deepest hole I'd ever dug was the two-foot dimples my mother transplanted shrubs into. I told Ray as much.

"Well, it's backbreakin', blister-raisin' work. Especially on a mountain like this. Mostly clay and sandstone. Someone figured out there was money to be made in cleanin' out the shit-pits. Save a man all that work o' diggin' a new hole."

"How do they do it?" I asked. "Clean out the pit, I mean?"

"Used to do it with a bucket an' a rope. Honey dippin'. Now they use a big tank truck with a vacuum pump on it. Same as to clean out a septic tank." Ray stepped from the porch. "Well, let's get back. I gotta turn in my report to the sheriff. For all the good it'll do."

He really was going to hand it off to the sheriff. I couldn't believe it. Ray had little use for Sheriff Fine. The spidery little man was Ray's second cousin and a consummate southern politician. "But you told Cleopha that you—"

"I told Cleopha what she wanted to hear. Two hundred dollars a month and a badge don't make me a homicide detective, no matter what she thinks. She'll get over it."

"Son of a bitch, Gil, you're gonna drop 'im!" That was Gaylord Carmack yelling at his brother. If you could call it yelling. I could barely hear it from twenty feet away. "Take it easy, will ya?"

They had somehow managed to get a hook onto Big John's belt and were dragging him out of the pit with the electric winch on the front of a pickup truck. I wondered if the belt could hold all that weight. Obviously Gaylord wondered the same thing.

If it didn't, I didn't want to see the result. Three hundred pounds of deadweight falling ten feet into a pit of human waste didn't conjure up a very pretty picture.

I hurried to catch up with Ray as he climbed into the Jeep.

It was midafternoon by the time we got back to Baird, and we were both surprisingly hungry. May June was pattying ground beef into Salisbury steaks, the Monday special, so she just fried up a couple into sandwiches for us. She also popped open a bag of potato chips and sat two cold Budweisers before me on the counter while Ray went into his office to call the sheriff.

He came back out a few minutes later, red around the ears and fuming. It was often that way when Ray talked to his cousin.

"Well?" I asked.

"He ain't there," Ray said incredulously. "Can you believe it? He ain't there. He's gone to Louisville to a sheriff's convention and won't be back till next Monday. He's left Elias in charge."

"Elias Knowly?" I asked.

Ray gave a look that said, *Do you know any other deputies named Elias?*

"Elias is a nice boy," May June said. "He'll know what to do."

"Mother," Ray said to her, grabbing a Budweiser out of the crisper drawer of the refrigerator. "Bein' a nice boy is a fine thing. But Elias couldn't find his butt with both hands."

"Oh, now." That was May June's answer to about half of what Ray said when he was mad. Oh, now.

"Well, it's true. What the hell does that little shit-for-brains gotta go to sheriff's conventions for anyhow? What? They givin' seminars on how to get reelected?"

"What are you going to do?" I asked, finishing my first Salisbury sandwich and starting on the other.

Ray took a bite out of his. "How the hell should I know? Goddamn little peckerwood redneck fart." I assumed he was talking about the sheriff. "I guess I'll do what I can. Try and figure out what happened up there. Who the hell's gonna run the post office while I'm playin' Dick Tracy? Will you tell me that?"

May June looked at me and winked. "Well, I guess I'll just have to do it. I guess I can squeeze it into my schedule. All that mail that comes in here. Ten, twelve things a day, not countin' the dirty magazines you steal."

"I only borrow 'em. They get where they're goin'. Eventually."

"I'll set 'em aside for you," May June said, smiling.

Ray picked up his sandwiches and took them into his office. I lit my pipe and traded beer for Diet Pepsi. The trouble with having a day off in a town like Baird was that it was not all that much different from any other day. My parishioners called me "preacher," and that's pretty much what they expected of me. I preached on Sunday. I also visited the sick when someone let me know that someone was sick. I sat in on as many church meetings as church rules required and no more. And I did my best to get around and see the old folks. But mostly folks wanted to be left alone until they needed me, and they'd let me know when that was.

The rest of my time I spent writing my sermons, trying to write a boring, scholarly book that I'd started nearly four years earlier when I was still married and successful but for which I'd lost most of my enthusiasm, and hanging around the Baird Diner, drinking

Diet Pepsi, smoking, and talking to whoever dropped in.

Darnell Kody dropped in.

Darnell was a big, pear-shaped guy in bib overalls, a Mail Pouch gimme cap, and the ever cheerful smile of Down's syndrome. He was also the town handyman. He was a savant where fixing things was concerned. Put a broken anything in his hands and he could take it apart and put it back together again in working order like magic. And he was never sure how he did it. It was Darnell who kept my ancient Volkswagen running.

We talked about my veedub while he ate a Twinkie and drank a Dr Pepper, and then he left to check out Bernard Weems's Wurlitzer organ.

"Gotta take a look at Mr. Weems's organ," Darnell said. Then he looked at me sheepishly and giggled. I often wondered if Darnell was as retarded as everyone in Baird thought he was.

Ludene and Coletta Frank dropped by, presumably for coffee. They were sisters, in their late twenties, built like tree stumps and plain as unpainted barn doors. They also had the reputation of being flirts with every preacher who had served Baird Methodist Church. Word was that if you flirted back at them, they spread the word that you were putting the make on them. If you didn't flirt back at them, they would accuse you of being gay. I wasn't sure which was worse for a Methodist minister, so I usually tried to avoid being alone with them. Actually, I usually tried to avoid them altogether, but they caught me at the diner.

"Well, there you are," Ludene said, as though I were hiding from them, which I would have been, had I known they were looking for me. "We've been looking everywhere for you."

"And you're just sitting here goofin' off," Coletta said, as though she had caught me flashing the school playground.

Then they both giggled and stepped in close. Ray stepped out of his office, made a U-turn, and went back in. May June cleared her throat and began to hum a hymn while she washed the lunch dishes.

"We just wanted to ask you about this fabric," Ludene said, displaying a swatch of bilious green fabric which she produced from a shopping bag. "What do you think? For the new curtains, I mean."

"I didn't know we had decided to buy new curtains," I said. A couple of months ago an old couple had died in a house fire and left the church a tidy sum of money. It was a curse. We had, since the will had been probated, held a dozen meetings and decided nothing. Mostly people argued. I had tried to stay out of it. It was their church. One day the bishop would call and tell me to move, and they would have to live with their decision. So let them make it.

It's a good theory, but it hardly ever works. There were now at least five factions in the church: the curtains-for-the-sanctuary faction; the new-furnace faction; the new-furniture-for-the-nursery faction; the repair-the-steeple faction; and the put-it-in-the-bank-and-wait-until-we-really-need-it-for-something-important faction. Oh, yes. There were a couple of people who had mentioned the possibility of using the money in some kind of ministry like feeding the hungry or setting up a clinic in Baird and paying a doctor to come in once a week for the mountain folks, but they had been shouted down so loudly and early that they hardly constituted a true faction.

And each group wanted the preacher on their side.

"It's a little loud," I said of the fabric. It was, in fact, awful. Lime green, shiny material that would have looked more at home on a Baptist tent revival evangelist. It would clash with everything in the sanctuary.

You would have thought I had taken it from her hands and wiped my rear end with it. Ludene's mouth fell open, she stepped back, breathed through her nose in a snort, stuffed the offending fabric back into the bag, turned on her heel, and walked out. Her sister followed.

"Now you done it." Ray walked out of his office and began unwrapping a Moon Pie.

"What?"

"You pissed off the Frank sisters. No minister pisses off the Frank sisters and lives to tell about it. They're ball busters, those two are."

May June refilled Ray's coffee cup and gave me a mug in place of my empty Diet Pepsi can. "Oh, now. They mean well."

"Well, Mother, I suppose you could say that of a rattlesnake, too. He don't mean no harm, he's just doin' what comes natural. But it don't make him nice to be around."

May June looked at me and dismissed Ray with a flick of her wrist. "Don't you worry about them girls. I'll fix it with 'em. They just need a mother figure to sit 'em down and have words. Their mother died when they was little, and they ain't had no one to teach 'em right."

Ray watched her walk back to the stove and shook his head. "Fact is," he whispered to me. "She can't stand them two. She sure must like you." He finished his coffee. "Well, I gotta sort mail. I'll be goin' back out to Pitchfork Holler tomorrow. Get all their statements. You wanna come?"

"Sure," I said. I could work on my sermon in the afternoon.

"We'll have to get there 'fore Charles goes to the mine, so I'll be leavin' about six."

"Six. Okay, fine." I wished I'd said no.

"That means you'll have to get up early, you know. Like five-thirty or quarter to."

"Yeah. I know. I'll be here."

"Have to go to bed early. Get plenty o' rest."

I drank some coffee. Ray grinned.

"Or maybe I should just pick you up over to Naomi's as I go by. Ain't but a couple of minutes outa my way."

"I'll be here, Ray."

"Suit yourself. No need to make that long drive, though. I'll be glad to pick you up. But it's up to you."

"I gotta be back early tonight anyway. I have work to do."

"Oh, well, you got work to do, so you'll probably call it an early night. Be home early. Ten, eleven."

"Whatever."

"Well, that's fine, then. You tell Naomi we send our love."

"I'll tell her." Sometimes Ray Hall could be a pain in the ass.

The church, my church, the Methodist church, has ruled in General Conference assembled and written in the *Book of Discipline* that all good Christians should observe "celibacy in singleness and fidelity in marriage." It was also widely held that the clergy, as the especially visible representatives of the faith, should hold to this standard even more seriously than anyone else. And, generally, in the abstract sort of way that such decisions are usually reached, I agree that the world would be a much better, more peaceful, easier-to-live-in place if everyone held themselves to that moral code. Especially the second half, the fidelity in marriage part. Certainly my life would have been a whole lot easier, smoother, and nicer—if not necessarily better—had I done so.

I did not, however, live in an abstract world. The world in which I lived was very real indeed and it was filled with temptations and opportunities, depending on how you viewed them, that made that strict moral standard somewhat problematical in practice.

Not to put too fine a point on it, I was in love.

Madly, passionately, frightfully, achingly, hormonally in love.

And the object of my passion was no less a beauty than Naomi Taylor, daughter of Hebrew Taylor, the richest, meanest man in the county.

Naomi was sixteen years younger than me and the prettiest, most sought after woman in eastern Kentucky. She stood about five-ten with shoulder-length black hair and ocean blue eyes and a generous mouth. She had a smooth, well-curved, yet athletically feminine body that she kept in shape by hiking three to five miles a day in the mountains. She was smart, college-educated (B.S. in finance from U.T. Knoxville), articulate, passionate, and though raised a Baptist, she had no problems with attending a Methodist church if I was doing the preaching. The small cleft in her chin and a bump on her nose were her only physical flaws. She worried constantly that both were too big. I thought they were cute.

And yes, there are such things as miracles. She was in love with me. Love handles, blond hair going gray, bad left knee from an old football injury, less than honorable reputation, and all the other physical, moral, and emotional imperfections—she loved me.

Naomi viewed sex with a kind of ain't-this-the-damnedest-thing-you-ever-saw exuberance, and thought that the *Kama Sutra* was one of the lost books of the New Testament. She just didn't want to get married right away.

After college, she had surprised everyone by coming back to Appalachia to work for her father, who was dying of black lung disease. She spent her time working as his accountant, transferring all of his accounts to her computer, and balancing his books, which took about fifteen hours a week. The rest of her time she spent cooking for her six brothers and stepbrothers, hiking in the mountains, and fixing up the mountain cabin her brothers had built for her as payment for coming home until Daddy died.

She liked her life and she loved me, but she couldn't see giving up one for the other.

It has been said that a Methodist minister must be ready to preach, pray, die, or move on a moment's notice. The bishop could call tomorrow and order me to another church anywhere in the conference. And, if I was married, it would be expected that my wife would joyfully follow me to my next appointment.

As much as she loved me, Naomi wasn't sure she was ready to join me in my oath to serve at the bishop's pleasure.

So, for the past ten weeks, since my first visit to her cabin, we had settled into a pleasant, if nerve-racking, charade in which we tried to appear as a properly courting couple to the members of my church and snuck off together for the more intimate pleasures of the flesh whenever we could manage it.

For my part, I was convinced that Hebrew Taylor

would one day give us all a break and die, Naomi and I would get married, and we would settle into a happy, domestic routine of nonstop sexual congress. So, if we were not obeying the letter of church policy, we were honoring its spirit by at least intending to get married. It seemed reasonable at the time.

My parishioners, however, would not have understood. Celibacy in singleness is always a reasonable demand to place on others when you yourself are married, sleeping on opposite sides of the bed, and having sex once a month whether you need to or not.

With my record, the last thing I needed was one of the Frank sisters running to my district superintendent and telling him that I was boffing one of my parishioners. He was one of the old-school theological liberals, true, but he wasn't that liberal.

So we were . . . careful. Naomi called it discretion. I called it sneaking around.

This Monday night, however, was not to be one of our sneaking-around nights. The third Monday of every month was reserved for dinner at the Taylor house on Clark Mountain. Naomi cooked and, at her insistence, we all gathered around the big dining room table and tried to get along with each other.

After only two attempts, I had come to hate the third Monday of the month.

Hebrew Taylor, her daddy, didn't have much use for preachers and he hated my best friend, Ray Hall, for sending his two eldest sons to jail a few years ago on a drug bust.

The two ex-con sons, Joshua and Jacob, who were now out of jail and back working for their daddy, pretty much shared their father's feelings on preachers and Ray Hall.

Thirty-year-old Amos, the third boy, never said anything.

Adam, nineteen, was taciturn and moody, still grieving over the death of a girlfriend he had hoped to run away with last summer.

David, fifteen, was a Nintendo junkie and talked of nothing but his prowess at the video screen.

Five-year-old Isaiah was the only saving grace of the evening ordeals. He talked nonstop and usually got me to tell him a story by telling me one or asking me ingenious questions like: "What's the scariest thing that ever happened to you, Dan?" He was a cute, lovable kid, and I thought he took after his older sister a lot.

So it was to this ordeal that I was headed, not to Naomi's mountain cabin with its breathtaking view and great balcony and bubbling hot tub on the side of Mount Devoux, that Monday night.

I left the diner and walked to the parsonage, showered, shaved, changed into clean jeans, running shoes, and a flannel sport shirt, threw an old, gray tweed sport coat in the backseat, and was in my Volkswagen headed toward Clark Mountain by quarter to six.

It was still early and I had hoped to miss the spit-and-whittle club that gathered on the porch of the diner every night, but as with everything else on this Monday, it did not go according to plan. The Carmack twins were already there, sitting on two old plastic and steel kitchen chairs, rocking back on the hind legs and watching the road. With them was Ray Hall, Darnell Kody, and three old guys I didn't recognize. I waved as I drove by and cursed under my breath.

By tomorrow morning, everyone in the township would know where the preacher went last night and, more important, when he left and, probably, when he got back. I could almost hear the conversation as I drove south on Route 42.

—There goes the preacher.

—Yeah. In kind of a hurry, ain't he?

—Course he is. Wouldn't you be? Pretty little thing like that waiting for you?

—What, you mean Naomi? She still seein' him?

—(Knowing nod of the head. Maybe a spit to punctuate it.)

—Never could figure out what she saw in him. What is he, twenty years older'n her?

—At least.

—Well, he's goin' the wrong way. Naomi lives up to Devoux, don't she?

—Yeah. But old Hebrew don't. He lives up to Clark, yonder.

—You mean he's goin' to Hebrew Taylor's house? Voluntary?

—Ain't enough pussy in the world make me go to Hebrew Taylor's house voluntary. That man's mean as a mile a rattlesnakes.

—Preacher's got to be the pussy-whippedest man in the world to go up there. That girl's got him by his short hairs.

—Shame to see a woman do that to a man.

—Him? He's a preacher. Preachers ain't like other men.

—Whataya mean, ain't like other men? You mean they ain't got the same 'quipment? Same needs as any other man?

—No, I just mean preachers got more control than most. That's why they's preachers. An' besides, preachers are masters of their houses. They don't let women do that to 'em.

—I don't know. I might let her do it to me. She's a fine-lookin' lady.

—You keep talkin' like that, you're gonna die like a mouse.

—How's that?

—Shook to death by a pussy.

Loud, raucous laughter to follow. One coughs. One spits. And on it goes.

Or maybe not. Maybe I was just being paranoid.

Well, I would just have to be discreet, that's all. Discreet and careful. Dinner and a smoke, then home. I had to get up early in the morning. Naomi could drive herself home. She'd understand.

Wouldn't she?

5

HEBREW TAYLOR AND HIS SONS LIVED HALFWAY UP CLARK Mountain in a two-story colonial house that would have been comfortable in any suburb of Louisville or Lexington. The driveway was full of Fords: two pickup trucks, a Bronco, a Pinto, and Naomi's old LTD. There was also a dune buggy like the ones I'd seen in Pitchfork Hollow.

I was only ten minutes late, but it was enough to keep me from having to make small talk while Naomi finished setting the table. She was wearing a lightweight, soft sweater, blue jeans, and high-top sneakers, and still managed to look sexy as hell. She kissed me on the cheek, gave me a pinch on the butt and push toward the dining room.

Dinner was ham loaf and sweet potatoes, homemade bread, string beans, and apple pie with Cheddar cheese. Sweet iced tea for the kids and strong coffee for the adults.

I had just eaten two sandwiches in the midafternoon, so I wasn't really hungry, but I nearly floundered myself taking two helpings of ham loaf and a huge piece of pie. Nerves, I guess.

Dinner conversation was pretty much the same as always. The two ex-cons held their forks in their fists like knives and shoveled the food into their faces as though it might be their last meal. Their left arms encircled their plates, a trait, Naomi told me, they had picked up in prison guarding their food from other inmates. Occasionally they would grunt or groan at something their daddy said.

Amos the silent was silent as usual, and Adam was still grieving for his girlfriend, LeAnn Bertke, who had been dead for three months.

David, the Nintendo freak, Isaiah, the youngest, Naomi, and I did most of the talking, trying to sound cheerful and full of enthusiasm. Little Isaiah asked me what I'd done that day, so I told him.

"An' you fainted?" he asked when the story was finished. "You really fainted?"

"He passed out," Naomi corrected. "Boys don't faint. They pass out."

"I fainted," I told him with a wink.

"It musta been really gross," he said, delighted. "Was it?"

It was, but I had told as much as I dared at a dinner table. "Yeah, pretty gross," I said.

"When you gonna get that thing fixed?" Hebrew Taylor interrupted. Hebrew's dinner conversations were a phenomenon in their own right. His black lung disease was walking him slowly to the grave and had gotten only a little worse in the past weeks, but he seemed to use his oxygen mask more when the weather got cooler.

At this meal he would wear it when he was chewing and lift it up to talk or take another mouthful of food, letting it snap back into place quickly when he was finished speaking or filling his mouth.

"What thing's that, Hebe?" I asked, around a mouthful of pie.

"That mitral thing. Your heart."

Of course, he knew. I had told Ray and May June Hall. May June had told Dora Musgrove, the church pianist and chief busybody, and from there on, it was in the public domain.

"Well, Hebe, it's not a thing that needs to be fixed," I said. I had, at first, believed that it would be easier to let people know the reason for my fainting. They would realize that it was a "heart thing" and let it go. Wrong. Now I found myself explaining mitral valve prolapse every week or so.

"Passed out, didn't ya? Made you faint dead away. Sounds like something needs to be fixed to me. Lest maybe you like passin' out." He let his mask snap back into place. The ex-cons chuckled.

"Well." I sighed. "I guess they could go in and replace the valve or something, but we're talking about open-heart surgery here. Doc says all I have to do is stay out of stressful situations and I'll be okay."

Hebrew harrumphed into his oxygen mask.

"It can't really be fixed, Daddy." Naomi jumped to my defense. "It's chronic. He's had it all his life and he'll keep on havin' it. Besides, I think it's kinda cute."

Sometimes Naomi's help wasn't all that helpful.

"Somethin's broke, it oughta be fixed. It was me, I'd get it fixed," Hebrew replied from under his mask.

Naomi looked at me and shrugged. What's the use?

"What kinda OTRs them boys got?" Adam, the nineteen-year-old, asked quietly.

I was so shocked to hear him talk, and glad, too, that I nearly fumbled the ball. "Uh, OTR?"

"Off the road," he said, just as quietly.

"Oh. You mean the dune-buggy-looking things? Well, I don't know. They look pretty much like the one you have out in the driveway. But theirs don't have license plates."

"They ain't roadworthy," Adam said. "Probably Volkswagens, stripped down and charged up. They say where they went to on Sunday?"

"Well, I didn't really talk to any of the boys. Just Cleopha. She said they went to drive over the mountain. Were you up there, Adam? Did you see them?" I didn't want to pry, but this was the first time since August that Adam had shown any interest in anything except his own grief. I wanted to keep him talking. Besides, if he saw something up on Devoux on Sunday evening, it might help Ray in the investigation.

"Nah," he said, killing my hopes. "Me and Benny was gonna ride over there. They got some good mountain trails. But Benny heard how Price Deaver and his buddies was gonna be up there, so he said we'd best not go."

Hebrew's mask came off with a flourish. "Benny Kneeb? I done told you I don't want you hangin' around with that white trash anymore, didn't I? I want you to stay away from him. He's trouble."

Adam came out of his chair like a shot. "I just said I didn't do nothin' with him, didn't I? Didn't I just say we didn't go over to Devoux on Sunday? So whataya gettin' your ass all in the air about?" He threw his napkin on his plate and stormed out the front door.

Thank you, Hebrew Taylor, you old fart. The first

time in nearly a year that Adam says more than ten words and you jump on his case.

Hebrew stood as though he was going to go after Adam, and I held up a hand. "I'll talk to him," I said, and stood to follow the boy out.

"Pussy," one of the ex-cons said to my back. The other one snorted a laugh. Then something about crying, but I couldn't make it out.

Adam was sitting on the front porch smoking a cigarette. I sat down next to him and started filling my pipe.

"I didn't mean to get you into trouble," I said, meaning it.

He shrugged. "Ain't nothin'. He's always mad about something. Black lung, mostly, I guess."

"How you doing?" I asked.

Another shrug.

In the city you ask that question and people say, "Fine," whether they mean it or not. It gets everyone off the hook. In the mountains you ask it and people shrug. Oh, you know, it seems to say. Things are good and bad and usually more bad than good, but we've seen worse. We'll get through this (mine closing, layoff, car wreck, hangover, divorce, beating) just in time to be ready for the next one. And then, somehow, we'll get through it, too.

"So tell me about you and Benny," I encouraged.

"Oh, Daddy don't like him since we got in that trouble last summer. That's all. Just like he didn't like LeAnn, you know. He don't want me seein' him's all."

"But Benny still works for your daddy?"

"Yeah. Daddy says just 'cause he's white trash don't mean he ain't a good driver."

"Your daddy likes that phrase, doesn't he?" I asked. " 'White trash,' I mean."

Adam shrugged again. "I guess. I ain't even sure what he means by it except we ain't supposed to hang around with anyone he describes that way." He examined the ash on his cigarette. "That's what he called LeAnn. White trash."

"But you kept seeing her," I said.

He shrugged again. "I usually do what he wants, though. He's dyin'."

"Usually." I made it a statement, not a question.

"Yeah, usually. Sometimes me and Benny have some beers together, you know. I don't flaunt it in front of Daddy, though. Ain't no use, is there?"

"I guess not. So what'd you do Sunday?"

"Nothin'. It was like I said. Him and me was gonna go over to Devoux and ride the trails, but he heard how Price Deaver was gonna be over there with some of his boys, and we decided to stay out of it. I just hung around here and watched the game. Benny done the same. Stayed home, I mean."

"Who's Price Deaver?" I asked, trying to get my pipe relit.

"Lives in Perry. His daddy's on the city council or something. He's got this OTR club. I mean, they don't have meetings or nothin', they just ride together. Got this half-assed clubhouse up the mountain somewhere."

"Did he know John Wisdom?"

"Oh, hell, Dan. Everyone knew Big John. And most wished they didn't. He musta beat up half the county at one time or t'other."

"He ever beat up Price Deaver?"

Adam flipped his cigarette into the driveway. "I wouldn't be surprised. Ol' Price, he ain't the kind to back down from a fight. Even one he knew he couldn't win."

"Roughneck?"

"Well, not mean, like Big John. But crazy, you know? Kinda thinks of hisself as an outlaw. Wears his hair long like Willie Nelson and hangs out at the honky-tonks in Perry."

"So he's a crazy, half-assed leader of a half-assed OTR club that happened to be on the same mountain the night John Wisdom was killed," I said, more to myself than to Adam. "How many in that OTR club, Adam?"

He shrugged again. "Depends. It changes around. Was pretty big a couple years ago, but most of the guys got tired o'Price's bullshit, you know? I guess maybe two or three is all there is left."

I just sat there smoking and thinking about how convenient it was. Two or three half-assed punks being there at the right place at the right time.

"You think he done it?" Adam asked, quietly.

"Did what?"

"Killed him. You think Price Deaver killed Big John? 'Cause Price is crazy and all, but he ain't never killed no one."

"How do you know?" I asked.

"Well, Price ain't the kind o' guy to keep a thing like that secret. He'd have to tell someone. Brag about it. Show what kinda balls he's got."

"M-m-mh," was all I could think to say.

"You still think he done it, don't you?"

"Who done what?" Naomi asked from behind the screen door.

"Ate all the pie," I said, innocently. "I think Isaiah probably ate all the pie by now, and I missed a second piece." I patted Adam on the shoulder as I rose to go back into the house. He didn't move to get up.

I didn't blame him.

There was still some pie left, so I had another piece and some more coffee, thinking about jogging or hiking or something. Tomorrow. We all sat around and watched television for a while and smoked and tried to ignore each other until about eleven when I got up and made an elaborate show of stretching and yawning.

Naomi offered to walk me out to my veedub, and I took her in my arms as soon as we were beyond the reach of the porch light. I kissed her hungrily and she leaned into me.

"You going to leave soon?" I asked.

"In a minute or two," she said. "Why? You got somethin' in mind?"

"I thought I'd follow you home and make sure you got there safely. It's late, you know."

"I been driving these roads for a sight longer than you," she added. "Maybe I ought to follow you home. Just to make sure you get there safely."

"I like your place better," I argued. It was more secluded and more romantic and more private. And she had a water bed. And a fireplace. And a hot tub.

"How will you get back?"

"Drive. I'll follow you up the mountain, then drive back later."

She shook her head. "Someone will see you come in and they'll see the direction you came from and know you were up to my place until all hours."

"We could leave my car at the church and I could ride up with you." I hugged her close and kissed her on the sweet spot below her right ear.

"Stop it. I'm thinkin'. How would you get back down the mountain?"

"You'd have to drive me home," I said, not really thinking much about logistics.

"No, that would be worse. Someone'd see you comin' back with me in my car. All hell'd break loose."

"Why don't you just come back to the parsonage with me?" I asked, moving to the other ear.

"Oh, yeah. The Frank girls would love that. They'd be on the phone before daylight. 'Do you know what that Baptist hussy done? Why, she spent the night at our minister's house, that's what.'" She did a frighteningly realistic impersonation of Colette Frank.

I reached under her sweater and discovered she was wearing one of those sheer little bras that don't do what a bra is supposed to do but excite the hell out of men who see women wearing them. I groaned.

"I think it's too late," she said, groaning along with me as I explored the bra. She leaned into me and I leaned back against the veedub. "It's too complicated. I don't think we're going to be able to pull it off tonight."

Considering where my hands and mind were, the pun was too obvious to merit comment. I kissed her softly and felt like I would explode if this went on for another moment. The kiss lingered forever, our mouths brushing against each other, licking, tasting, breathing each other in.

"I have an idea," I said.

"What?" she breathed.

"Marry me."

"Oh, Dan." She sighed. "Please don't . . ."

"The district superintendent could be here by Wednesday, perform the ceremony in the afternoon, and by dinnertime we could be ensconced in the tackiest honeymoon suite in Gatlinburg," I said quickly.

She leaned her head on my chest. "Daddy needs

me," was all she said. It was enough. I'd heard it a hundred times and I was frustrated and aching and tired and mad and I said what I felt.

"Bullshit!" I stood straight up and turned, laying my arms on the roof of the car. "He's got six boys and men in there at his beck and call, ready to kiss his ass every time he bends over. What does he need you for?"

"I'm his only daughter," she said, laying her hand on my back.

I didn't respond to her touch. "It's not like I'm going to chain you to my porch and never let you see him again. You'd still be his daughter even if, God forbid, you should marry a preacher!"

"But what if the bishop calls?" There was fight in her voice now. "What if you get transferred next summer? What am I supposed to do? Just pack up and leave? Screw you, Daddy, but the bishop has called."

I turned to face her but stayed at arm's length. "The bishop isn't going to call, damn it. With my reputation I'll never get out of these hills."

"You don't know that!" she said. "Yeah, you screwed up in your big church with your big salary and all. But that's not the only reputation you got. You're a Ph.D. You wrote a book. You—"

"Got divorced! Had an affair with a Sunday school teacher, for Christ sake. A Sunday school teacher! Got drunk and told my bishop to go fuck himself—"

"You're the kindest, gentlest, most sincere, honest minister I've ever known. And you're a damned good preacher, too. That all's part of your reputation, too, Dan. And sooner or later that part's gonna catch up with you again. And when it does, where does that leave me? When they want you to take some big church in a city somewhere, what are you gonna do with your little hillbilly wife then?"

Hillbilly wife? What was she talking about?

"You were called to the ministry, Dan. I really believe you were called of God. You have every gift you need to do the job. You believe and you want other people to believe, too. But . . ."

Now she was crying. Her accent was getting thicker. I tried to reach out to her, but she stepped back. She was Hebrew Taylor's daughter and she would have her say or be damned.

". . . but I wasn't. God didn't call me to no ministry that I can tell. I'm just an ignorant little hillbilly gal, and no college degree can ever change that. You got it so easy. You're sure of your callin'. You know what you gotta do. But it's hard for me. If I was to marry you, I'd be marryin' your career, your ministry, too."

It was bullshit, of course. I could feel the specter of Hebrew Taylor hanging over this long discourse, his parental tentacles snared around her heart, his anti-clerical tirades burned into her psyche. And it pissed me off.

"I need time, Dan," she went on. "Can't you love me enough to give me some time? I need time to say good-bye to Daddy. I need time to think about what my life will be like. I love you, Dan. I really do. And I want to marry you. But I need some time. Won't you give me that?"

A frustrated erection can make a man say stupid things. "Sure," I said. "Take all the time you need. You know where to find me." I climbed into the veedub, slammed the door, and kicked it to life. She was standing on the porch as I drove away.

Not two miles down the road, I felt like an asshole.

For two thousand years, Christianity has aspired to only one goal. We preach it to our congregations. We study examples of it in the lives of the saints and in the legends and records of the Bible. We worry about it and fret over it and most of the time we fail at it.

In the old days they called it "grace." Amazing Grace.

Unconditional love. Love that requires nothing of the beloved. Love that is a gift, given for the sake of giving. Accepted, rejected, abused, refused, it doesn't matter. Here it is, it's yours, do with it as you please. There's more where that came from.

So difficult is it to give that when we see it, we often have trouble believing it.

Cleopha Wisdom had it, as parents often do for their children. She didn't much like her son, John. She certainly didn't approve of him and the way he lived and behaved. But she loved him. You could tell by the look on her face and the sag in her shoulders as she talked about him.

When she looked down into the bottom of that crapper, she didn't see Big John Wisdom, the bully bastard that everyone else saw. She saw the fat little boy who grew up in poverty, without shoes, and sassed his ma and pa, and cried when he hurt his knee, and with whom she sat up all night when he had the fevers. She saw the baby she rocked and nursed and cuddled and sang old hymns to.

And she loved him. Unconditionally. "You find the man who did this to my child," she had told Ray.

Ray and May June had it. For each other. You could tell by the way they finished sentences for each other and thought each other's thoughts. You could tell in the way they looked at and teased and pinched each other. "Say what you will, old woman or old man, you can't make me not love you."

And they had it for their son whose name I didn't know and who had "died in the war." You could see it in the "guest room" they kept just as it was the day he went away to boot camp.

And yet, somehow, I, their pastor, couldn't even manage to give it to the one person in this world whom I loved more than any other. When she needed me to love her unconditionally, I had been more interested in making my point, making her feel bad because she couldn't let go of her bigoted, narrow-minded father and join me in a life of uncertainty.

Some pastor.

So when I got home, about midnight, I did what any man does when he has made a fool of himself and needs to hear that he's still okay. I called my mother. Mothers are supposed to be bottomless fountains of unconditional love. I was sure that she would understand my feelings even if no one else would.

"Daniel," she said. "That girl is the best thing that has happened to you in three years. I like her. Be patient with her. If you fuck this up, I will never speak to you again."

I went to bed exhausted. My head swimming from the events of the day. Monday. My day off.

All in all, it had been the day off from hell.

6

I WALKED OVER TO THE DINER AT SIX ON TUESDAY MORNING to find May June behind the counter, coffee already brewed and the smell of buttermilk biscuits and maple syrup permeating the air.

She poured me a big mug of coffee and slid two saucer-sized biscuit sandwiches with egg and Canadian bacon in front of me. "Might as well sit and eat," she said, sipping her own coffee. "His nibs's on the phone. So how'd it go last night? Tell me everything except the dirty parts."

"There aren't any dirty parts," I said, sighing.

"Oh," she said. "You wanna talk about it?"

Two coal truck drivers crashed through the door, shivering and yawning and saying hi to May June. I shook my head and she moved off to take their orders. The coffee was good and strong and hot, just what I needed with five and a half hours of sleep. The frost had still not come, but it was in the mid-forties outside, and after the summer we'd had, it felt like forty below zero. I was not looking forward to a long ride in Ray's open-air Jeep. I'd dressed in blue jeans, work boots, flannel shirt, and a down vest. The corduroy Bengals gimme cap would keep my head warm, but my ears would suffer and I still couldn't find my gloves from last winter. I drank the rest of my coffee in a gulp, trying to build up some extra warmth.

May June cracked some eggs on the griddle, topped off my coffee mug, and hung there for a few seconds. She had something on her mind, but I didn't push her. She would say it or she wouldn't.

Finally she sighed. "Thanks for goin' with him today, Dan. I know you got other things you could be doin'."

I shrugged. "It's nothing."

"The Wisdoms is hill folks. I don't hold nothin' again' 'em, but you should know just the same," she said, sipping her coffee and watching the door to Ray's office.

"What do you want me to know, May June?"

"Well, hill folks is different, is all. Oh, I don't mean it's like *Deliverance* or anything. You're hind parts is probably safe." She smiled, then became serious so quick, I almost didn't see the smile. "Thing is, those of us around here have come down from the hills. It's more'n where you live. It's kinda how you take things. You know, values and all."

"Hill people have their own way of doing things," I offered.

"That they do." She turned and stirred the eggs on the griddle, scrambling them with a twist of the wrist. "They don't trust the law and they got their own code."

"And Ray's the law," I said.

"He wasn't always. That's why they tolerate him. He's known most of these hill people since he and they was kids, so they tolerate him. But he's the law now. And he's moved outa the hills."

"Baird is hardly a metropolis."

"Don't matter," she said, shoveling the eggs onto biscuits. She took them over to the truckers and refilled their coffee. When she came back she brought me a glass of orange juice poured from a carton. "Musta been ten years ago we had a county prosecutor," she said. "Local boy from Perry went off to law school, come back and ran for CP, and got himself elected.

"Well, he was a city boy. I know Perry ain't much of a city, but it's a right smart of miles from the hills, too. Anyway, he decided he was gonna stop the marijuana bein' grown in the hills and brought down and sold in town. Got hisself all worked up and arrested some kids in town said they got it from some hill people.

"So this CP, Terry Parkus his name was, he goes to the sheriff and says he has the names of three families he wants investigated. Wants the menfolks brought in for questionin'.

"The sheriff says nothin' doin'. He ain't about to go up in them mountains and get his head blowed off because some kids is rollin' reefers out behind the school gym. He don't even want to know the names. But Terry, he's got a bee under his blanket and so he gets hisself a pistol and a badge and puts on a pair of jeans and gets in his car and drives up into the hills all by hisself to arrest some people."

She stood up abruptly and hollered across the room, "You boys okay? You need anything else?" They shook their heads, so she leaned her breasts back down on the counter.

"He never come back."

I didn't follow. "What? Who didn't come back from where?" I asked, a little confused.

"Terry. The CP, he never come back. Never found a trace of him. 'Cept his car. It had been rolled off a ravine up on Mount Devoux. But they never found nothin' else, not his badge, not his gun. He just disappeared. The sheriff finally got off his butt and took some of his men up to look for him, but he really didn't know where to look. Sheriff back then was even more worthless than the one we got now, and I don't reckon he looked all that hard, but nobody's ever seen anything of him since."

"How long ago was this?" I asked, feeling a little chill go up my back.

"'Bout ten, fifteen years ago," she said.

"Well, that was a long time ago, May June. And you said yourself that it's not like *Deliverance* or anything on Mount Devoux. Do you really think Ray might be in danger?"

"It ain't me that thinks it," she said, shaking her head like I had missed the whole point of the story. "It's Ray." She looked over both shoulders and back at his office door. It was still closed. "He put his shotgun in the Jeep, under that blanket in the back, just before you got here."

"Oh."

"I'm just glad you're goin' with him. Those folks don't trust the law and they don't like it. But they have a high degree of religion. They'll think twice't before they try somethin' with a preacher."

I thought a moment about how I was dressed. I didn't usually cultivate a preacher look.

"You look fine," she said. "Folks around here don't expect the preacher to wear a frock coat. But that's why Ray always introduces you as a preacher. May not mean much in the city, but up here it still carries some respect."

Ray chose that minute to come out of his office and announce that I was late. "Get plenty o' sleep, Preacher?" he asked, winking at May June.

"You lay off him, now, you old coot." May June jumped to my defense. "He was up to Hebrew Taylor's house last night. Weren't no night for romancin'."

I had been right. The grapevine had done its work. Everyone in Baird knew where I'd been last night. Naomi had been right, too. Had I gone home with her or she with me, everyone would have known that, too.

Ray took half his mug of coffee in one gulp. "You sat down at table with Hebrew Taylor, voluntary? You must love that girl somethin' dear."

"You know he does," May June said, handing him a biscuit sandwich wrapped in a paper towel. "Now, go on with you or you'll be too late to catch Charles before he goes to the mine."

I tried to call Naomi from the diner before we left, but there was no answer at her cabin. She was probably already hiking in the woods trying to figure out how to tell me to stay out of her life forever. Why is it that being an asshole always seems like such a good idea at night and such a bad idea the next morning when it's too late? Wouldn't life be a whole lot easier if it was the other way around? You could be hateful and mean in the morning then you would still have all day to repair the damage you'd done.

Ah, well. I'd try her again when we got back. Ray had the Jeep warmed up and was honking the horn by the time I hung up. May June caught me before I could get out the door.

"I didn't tell you the worst part," she said, handing me a thermos of coffee.

"Worst part of what?" I asked, thinking she was somehow talking about my fight with Naomi. She wasn't.

"About that prosecutor disappearin'," she said.

I looked at her and let my face ask the question.

"Well, there weren't never any proof, you understand. Terry never let on who the people was he was goin' after. He was like that. Didn't trust folks. Kept things close to the vest."

"May June . . ."

"It's just that, well, there ain't no proof or nothin'. But folks have always said that one of those three families he was goin' after? One of 'em was supposed to be the Wisdom family."

"Great." I wished she had put something a little stronger than coffee in the thermos.

Ray drove even faster than usual, taking the mountain road like a maniac. Most of the coal trucks weren't out on the road yet, so it was a little safer and he could cheat the blind curves a little wider than usual.

We passed the Viper cutoff just as the sun broke over the mountain, and by the time we reached the nameless road that led up to Naomi's cabin, it was full daylight. Ray honked the horn as we passed the road, but Naomi's cabin was another two and a half miles up the mountain. She wouldn't hear it unless she was hiking nearby.

By the time we got to Pitchfork Hollow, my hands were frozen stiff and my feet were numb. I stomped and flapped beside the Jeep for a few minutes while

Ray went up to the big house and knocked on the door.

"Have to pay our respects to the matriarch before we go talkin' to her kin," he had said.

I saw the door crack open, he talked to someone for a few seconds and then waved me up to the rickety porch. "You remember Reverent Dan, Ms. Cleopha," he said, indicating me with a nod of his head. "We're in luck, Dan," he said to me. "Charles and Eugene are here havin' their breakfast with their mother. She's invited us in for coffee and pone."

I said, "Thank you, ma'am," and meant it. Hot coffee and corn bread with maple syrup might help thaw me out some.

Charles and Eugene were seated at a big kitchen table that would easily seat ten. Eugene looked like he hadn't changed clothes or attitudes since I saw him last. Same black T-shirt and dirty jeans. Same sullen, pissed-off look. Charles was clean-shaven and smelled of Old Spice this morning. He had traded the three pieces of paper on his neck for one on his chin. He was dressed for the mine in gray coveralls, and his lunch tin sat on the kitchen counter, the thermos next to it, standing open.

Ray took a seat across from Charles and around the corner from Eugene. I sat next to him. Cleopha poured chicory-laced coffee for everyone, filled Charles's thermos, and excused herself to "do some chores."

"You find 'em yet?" Eugene asked with a challenging tone.

"Who's that?" Ray countered, calm as a summer day.

"The shits what killed my brother, who else?"

"Well, that's what I come to talk to you about, isn't

it? No, I haven't caught anyone. Ain't even tried, to tell the truth."

Eugene snorted and leaned his chair back on two legs. "What'd I tell ya?" he said to Charles.

Charles ate a piece of corn bread with his fingers.

"Thing is," Ray went on, "I'm just a constable. I check things out and if it seems an investigation is needed, I'm supposed to report it back to the sheriff."

"Sheriff don't give two shits about us hill jacks," Eugene snorted again.

"Watch yer mouth," Charles said evenly around his corn bread.

Ray went on as though he hadn't been interrupted. "But the sheriff's out o' town on official business. So I just found out that I'm the investigatin' officer, so to speak. So here I am." He took a swig of his coffee and smacked his lips. "Your mother makes a fine cup."

"So whata ya doin' here?" Eugene asked. "Why ain't you out investigatin'?"

"Eugene," Charles said. There was something of a warning in it.

Eugene came down on all four feet of the chair. "This is bullshit! Our brother's dead in the shitter, murdered, and the law's sittin' here drinkin' coffee. What'd I tell ya?" He stood to leave.

"Siddown, Eugene," Charles said, just as evenly.

"I ain't—"

"I said siddown."

Eugene sat. Tilted his chair back and lit a cigarette. Crossed his arms over his chest.

"Now, shut up your mouth and listen for a change. Whataya need to know, Ray?"

Ray took another sip of his coffee. "Well, I got to know where you boys was Sunday night—"

"Oh, fer chrissake!" Eugene bellowed.

"—and if you saw or heard anything suspicious, out o' the ordinary, during the night."

"What time?" Charles asked.

"Well, I talked to Doc on the phone 'fore we come up here. He says that Big John died between one and two in the morning, give or take. What about then?"

"We was both in bed," Eugene said. "Where'n hell would we be?"

Ray shrugged. "Have to ask. Hear anything? Anything wake you up?"

Charles shook his head.

"Yeah," Eugene said. "A hard-on. Got me a ragin' boner in the middle o' the night an' had to wake up the ol' lady. Gonna arrest me for that?"

The tops of Ray's ears were getting red. That was a bad sign. Not that I blamed him. In the past five minutes he had lied to defend his worthless second cousin, the sheriff, and he had taken more lip from Eugene Wisdom than I'd ever heard anyone give him.

"Charles," he said. "Your brother's got a ugly mouth on him."

Charles nodded and shrugged. What can you do?

"Not that I mind," Ray went on. "I was in the service. MP. I heard worse and I been called worse than he could ever think up. But this here is a preacher. A man o' God. Wouldn't you think that even a skinny little brainless peckerwood like Eugene would show some common decency?"

Now Eugene's face was red.

"Fuck you, lawman! I don't have to take that from—"

He didn't finish his thought. Ray grabbed him by the front of his T-shirt and dragged him up onto the table, flipped him over onto his stomach, and pressed his face into the wood. Then he leaned over and spoke very quietly into Eugene's ear.

"You listen to me, you little butt lick. I don't give a shit about you or your big-assed dead brother, but I made a promise to your momma. No woman deserves to find her child like that. Now, all I'm doin' is askin' some simple questions so's I can find the man what killed her child, and you're gonna sit in that chair and act civil and answer my questions nice and polite or I'm gonna kick your ass all the way down this mountain and have you locked up for obstructin' justice. And on the way down I'm gonna step on you like a giant on a pissant, do you understand me?"

Eugene's face was beet red under the viselike grip of Ray's hand, but he managed to nod his head.

"What'd you say?" Ray asked.

"Yessir."

Ray lifted him up off the table, and Charles and I put our mugs back down. Charles, I noticed, had not missed a bite the whole time.

"Tell me about Sunday," Ray said to both men.

Charles shrugged. "I worked in the garden and put the snow tires on the truck in the morning. Around noon Les and R.D. showed up and we all went over to John's to watch the game."

"What game?" Ray asked.

Eugene sighed, no doubt wondering what possible difference this could make in the investigation, but he didn't say anything. I wondered the same thing myself.

"Cincinnati and Pittsburgh," Charles said.

"So what happened?"

"Cincinnati won. Kicked Pittsburgh's butts for 'em. Boomer was twenty for twenty-four. John was happy as a pig in slop. R.D. and Les is Pittsburgh fans for some reason, and we always been Bengal fans, so John, he took off on them two like he had thrown all them passes personal. Wouldn't let it go, you know?

"Well, we'd had a few beers during the game and we were all a little shit-faced and it got kinda ugly. Ol' Les come after Big John, which, I think, is just what Big John wanted, someone to whip. Me and R.D. pulled them off'n each other, and John was laughin' and Les was still pissed.

"So I suggest we take a ride up the mountain, seein' hows them two rode their ORVs over and all." He stopped and sipped his coffee. It was cold, so he walked to the sink, poured it out, and poured another half cup for himself. He leaned against the sink and kept talking.

"Anyway, we get up on the mountain, just cattin' around, you know. And then Big John says he's outa chew and thought he'd go on over to Devoux to get some Mail Pouch on accounta ol' Mat usually keeps his store open on Sundays to sell beer to the football fans.

"Then Eugene here says why don't we race. Everyone take a different track path and see which one is fastest."

"Weren't me what suggested it," Eugene said, trying his best not to be too truculent. "Was Les."

"Well, it was someone. Anyhow, we done it. Raced over to Devoux to get John some Mail Pouch."

"Who won?" I asked.

They all looked at me as though I had just walked through the door. Then Charles said, "I guess I did. John come in second by about two minutes and was pissed as hell. John had to win at everything he done.

"R.D., he come in third about fifteen minutes later on accounta he don't give a damn about racin'. He just likes to bust around the mountain and don't even like to go all that fast. Eugene here got stuck down to Stinkin' Creek, and Les flipped his ORV over on its top back up one o' the trails. He walked in and we had to go help him tip it back. Tell the truth, I think he was a might drunker than the rest of us."

"Was he hurt any?" Ray asked.

"Les? Oh, hell no. We all got harnesses and all in them ORVs. Onliest thing hurt was his feelings. Ol' John weren't done with him over the football game and then he took off on Les for turnin' his rig over. Just rode him all the way back."

"Les get pissed off again?" Ray handed his mug to Charles, who filled it for him and handed it back. Ray began his cigarette ritual.

"Naw. By then he had cooled off and was laughin' about it hisself. We come back here, had a few more beers, then I drove over to Melrose in my pickup, had a chew and whittled a bit with the boys. Got back here around eleven-thirty or midnight."

"Union meeting?" Ray asked.

"Naw, nothin' like that. Just talk, you know. Union talk. Bitchin' about the mine and the foreman. Talkin' about the last strike and the next one. Shittin' each other along."

Ray nodded. He'd been a union miner, years ago. He knew the importance of the brotherhood, the fellowship those guys had with each other. Chewing tobacco and whittling together were sacraments in the sacred and secret order of the UMW.

"See anything when you got back?" he asked Charles.

Charles shook his head. "Naw. It was dark. Les and R.D.'s ORVs was gone. I figured they left before dark, havin' to go by night across the mountain and all."

Ray had made a few notes in a little notebook as Charles talked. Not so much for his own memory as to encourage Charles. Ray's memory was nearly flawless, but, he told me, people were always more willing to talk when you took down notes. It showed you were really listening to what they said. It seemed to work with Charles.

Ray turned the page in his notebook and looked at Eugene. "What about you, Gene? How'd you spend the day?"

7

EUGENE SHRUGGED HIS SHOULDERS AND LIT ANOTHER cigarette. Somehow, he had lost his desire to talk. He looked at Charles, who nodded and got up to pack his lunch tin.

"I slept in. Got up and went over to watch the game. Drank some beers and watched Big John and Les get into it and Charles and R.D. tryin' to break 'em up. Went up on the mountain like Charles said."

"Where'd you get stuck?" Ray asked, taking notes.

"Stinkin' Creek, just like he said."

"I know that. Whereabouts in Stinkin' Creek?"

Shrug. "I don't know. 'Bout a mile and a half from Devoux. Maybe two mile."

"How'd you get out?"

"Used the winch on the front of my ORV. Looped it around a big oak tree and pulled myself out. I come in last except for Les. They was all down turnin' him back over when I got in."

"They were gone when you got to Devoux?"

"Yeah. I drank a couple o' beers and waited for 'em. They come back and we all was funnin' Les, then we drove back here and had some beers."

"Then what?"

Eugene rolled his eyes and sighed. "I went home and went to bed. Beer musta made me sleepy. Anything else?"

Ray closed his notebook and shook his head. "Not for now. Thanks for your help. I'll be talkin' to R.D. and Les later on. Gettin' their statements."

Eugene shrugged and Charles started for the door, anxious to get to the mine. I couldn't imagine why unless he would get docked if he was late. There's nothing to be anxious about when it comes to a coal mine.

"Can I ask something?" I asked Ray, and everyone stopped and looked at me. Ray tilted his head toward the Wisdom brothers. Go ahead.

"Did you see or hear anyone else up on the mountain when you were running your ORVs?" I asked them both.

They looked at each other and both of them shook their heads. "Nah," Eugene said. "No one up there but us. Just us an' the mountain like Big John liked it. Not another soul for miles around."

"Do you guys know a fella named Price Deaver?" I asked.

Charles grinned. "Sure. Blond-headed pretty boy from Perry. Everyone knows Pricey. Why d'you ask, Reverend?"

"I heard he was up on the mountain with some friends on Sunday. And I heard he didn't like your brother very much," I said, looking from one brother to the other.

"Nope," Eugene said. "Just us."

"Well," Charles said, scratching his nearly bald head. "The truth is, Reverend, even I didn't like my brother much. Can't say as I know anyone who did except maybe Eugene here. You wanted to have a hard-on, excuse me, a mad-on for Big John Wisdom, you had to wait in line."

"I heard that Price Deaver has a clubhouse of some kind on the mountain," I went on. In this far, might as well keep going.

"Yeah, I heard that," Charles said, moving for the door now, anxious to be on his way. "Little cabin he uses for drinking and smoking pot and screwing, excuse me, sexual escapades."

"Any idea where it is?" Ray asked.

"Somewhere above Devoux is all I know. You ever seen it, Eugene?"

Eugene shook his head again. He still didn't want to talk.

"Sorry," Charles said. "I gotta go or they'll dock me." And he was gone, out the door and gunning his pickup toward the road.

"Not goin' to work this morning, Eugene?" Ray asked. "Takin' the day off?"

Eugene looked like the top of his head would explode. His cigarette wasn't a quarter of an inch long, but he was still smoking it, holding it like it was a roach. A practiced pot smoker.

"Oh, that's right. You don't have gainful employment, do you?" Ray said, baiting him. I wondered why.

"I ain't gonna throw my life away in the bottom of some mine, lettin' my lungs turn to stone," Eugene said, defensively. "I'd rather starve first."

"Or let your brothers feed you. And your wife and

kids." Ray stood and walked to the kitchen window that looked across the creek toward the two trailers.

"I take care of my own," Eugene said, rising, stubbing out his cigarette roach.

"Oh, yeah," Ray said, looking out the window. "I can see they're living' in high style." He shook his head. "Mind if we have a look around the holler for a spell?"

"Would it matter if I did?"

"Not a bit," Ray said, stepping out the back door of the kitchen. "Just bein' polite is all. You comin', Preacher?"

I followed Ray into the backyard of the big house. He stood there and stretched for a moment. The sun was warming the ground, and the temperature was in the mid sixties. It felt good and the air was clean as we walked toward the outhouse where John Wisdom had died.

"You got anything else you want to share with your local constable?" Ray asked me.

"Yeah, I'm sorry about that, but I didn't have a chance to tell you about Price Deaver before we got here. Then I forgot about it until they started talking about being on the mountain." I started loading my pipe as Ray lit a cigarette.

"What's the whole story?" he asked.

"What you heard in there is about it," I said. "Adam Taylor and that friend of his, Benny Kneeb, were going to take their ORVs up on Mount Devoux last Sunday, but Benny said he'd heard that this Price Deaver kid was going to be up there with some buddies of his and they decided against it."

Ray nodded. Smoking. Thinking. "Adam told you this?"

I nodded.

"Funny," Ray said. "Ain't like Benny Kneeb to be afraid of someone like Price Deaver. You remember Benny, don't you? Big kid, stretches out those triple XL overalls he always wears. He's the one I cold-cocked that time over in Hebrew's garage."

I remembered. It had been more than two months ago, but the memory was vivid. Ray had taken Benny, and I had taken Adam. It took Ray one shot to put the big Benny on his knees. Adam had tried to run over me, and I had stopped him with a nose-in-the-numbers tackle my high school football coach would have been proud of. Adrenaline. I'm usually a very peaceful man. Adam and I had made up and were on speaking terms, thanks to Naomi. I hadn't seen Benny since then.

"Adam said this Deaver kid's supposed to be some kind of a wild hard-ass or something," I said to Ray. We had stopped in front of the outhouse, and Ray was walking back and forth looking at the ground.

"M-mh," was all he said, so I joined him, walking back and forth, looking at the ground.

"What are we looking for?" I asked.

"Drag marks."

"What got dragged?"

"Big John."

I stopped and looked at him. Let the silence ask rather than saying it out loud.

"That talk I had with Doc this morning?" Ray said, not looking up. "He gave me more'n the time of death. Gave me the cause of death, too."

I just stood there, relit my pipe. Ray turned and started back, still looking at the ground.

"Doc says there weren't no prints on the lime ladle. Nothin' on the body to help either, after Gil an' Gay hosed it off. Says we ought to look around outside the crapper, though." He looked up at me, then down at the ground again, indicating that I should be doing what he was doing.

"Uh, Ray?"

"M-mh."

"He was hit on the head, Ray. Remember? We already knew that."

Ray shook his head. "Didn't kill him. Hurt him a right smart, I reckon, but didn't kill him."

I stopped looking at the ground again. "What did?"

"Suffocation."

"You mean someone overpowered Big John Wisdom, suffocated him with something, and then hit him on the head? Why?"

"No, no. You got it backwards."

This would go on all day if I didn't drag it out of him. Ray loved knowing things.

"You going to share it with me?" I asked, using his own words.

"He was still alive when they threw him in the crapper." He looked at me and smiled. "Whacked him over the head, lifted the seat, dropped him in. He come to, splashed around, and suffocated down there tryin' to climb out."

"You mean he drowned in all that . . ."

"No, he suffocated. The fumes got him. Pretty nasty way to go, huh?"

I didn't feel very good. My pipe tasted bitter and foul, and all this looking down and walking back and forth was making me dizzy.

"Don't see any drag marks, do you?" Ray asked.

I shook my head.

We stood there looking at the ground, then at the privy for a long time, smoking, thinking again. "Ner nothin' else. Too many people walkin' around here, I guess. Still, though, you'd think there'd be some drag marks," Ray said. Then, "Well, let's go, then. We'll stop by and tell Cleopha she can claim Big John's body when she's ready. Doc says it's stinking up the morgue. Can you imagine that? A morgue smelling worse than it already does?"

I couldn't, but I didn't say as much. I sat in the Jeep and sipped coffee from the thermos while Ray talked to Cleopha. When he came back down off the porch, he told me that she would send Charlotte, John's widow, down to Baird to make arrangements for the funeral. I nodded and finished the coffee.

"Well, it's about break time," Ray said, looking at his watch. "You want somethin' to eat?"

Melrose was not really a town. It sat on the east side of Mount Devoux, about halfway down the mountain on winding County Road 3, the main road over the top. It took us another twenty minutes winding back and forth over the cutbacks and turns before we got there, and when we finally did, I didn't know why we had bothered.

There was a little church on one side of the road with a cemetery and a sign that said MELROSE PENTECOSTAL HOLINESS CHURCH OF GOD in the front yard. Rev. Clyde Harland, Pastor, Sunday school 9:00 A.M., Preaching 10:30 A.M. and 7:00 P.M., Prayer Meeting Wednesday night 7:00 P.M. Across the road was a store. Its sign was not as forthcoming as the church's. It said STORE.

That was all of Melrose.

Ray slid his Jeep to one of his roaring stops in front of the store and we went up on the porch and in through a slamming screen door. The old man behind the counter wore bib overalls and a dirty white T-shirt. He was about seventy and toothless. He put down his *American Hunter* magazine and looked up but didn't say anything.

"Henry," Ray said, walking around the racks of groceries, used paperbacks, beer, bread, and pop.

"How do, Ray," was all the old man said. He didn't sound too glad to have customers.

"Got any Moon Pies?"

"Over by the bread, yonder."

"They fresh?"

"No such thing as a fresh Moon Pie," the old man said. He picked up his magazine and went back to reading.

"How about the coffee?" Ray asked.

"Fresh an hour ago," Henry said, not looking up.

Ray came around the corner and handed me a Styrofoam cup of coffee with cream and sugar and a Moon Pie. Ray loved Moon Pies—little gobs of marshmallow, surrounded by stale graham cracker and waxy chocolate. I was less enthusiastic.

"What do I owe you?" Ray asked, stepping up to the counter.

"On the house."

Ray threw a dollar on the counter. "Les Eastman or R.D. Miles been around lately?"

Henry shrugged. Magazine still in front of him, leaning over the counter with his elbows on it.

"How about Price Deaver and his buddies?"

Another shrug.

"You know Price, don't you, Henry? Nice-lookin' boy, wears leathers and acts like he owns the place?"

Nothing. Not even a shrug.

"You still rentin' them videotapes under the counter there?"

That got him. He closed the magazine and stood up facing Ray. "What do you want, law?"

Ray ignored the question. "This here's Reverend Dan Thompson, from over to Baird. He's a Methodist."

Henry looked at me like I was something he'd just discovered on the bottom of his shoe. Said nothing.

"He hears about a man rentin' dirty videotapes," Ray went on, "why, he's likely to take a notion to raise some hell like that Methodist preacher down to Mississippi. Or Louisiana. Wherever it is. You know who I mean, don't you, Henry? Why, that Methodist preacher don't like dirty films one bit. Methodists are like that, aren't they, Reverend?"

I just stood there. What the hell was he doing?

"I axed you what you wanted, didn't I?" Henry said.

"Les Eastman been by here? Or R.D. Miles?"

Henry shook his head. Oh, yeah, Ray. Great improvement. Real cooperation here.

"How about Price Deaver? He been in here? Nice-lookin' kid, long blond hair, wears leathers and has a cabin hereabouts?"

Henry stared straight at Ray. "I know him. He ain't been in here either."

"How about Charles Wisdom? He been around lately?"

"Seen him Sunday night. Him and some of his union buddies sat out on the porch and whittled a might."

Ray began his cigarette ritual and considered all of this. Then said, "Well, that sounds like a good idea. I reckon we'll sit out on the porch and finish our coffee and Moon Pies." He turned and walked out, and I followed.

There were four bent-branch rocking chairs on the porch of the store, and we each took one. I heard the back door of the store close and looked around the corner but saw no one.

"Going to call Les and R.D.," Ray said. "Warn 'em that the law is lookin' for 'em."

"Warn 'em?" I asked, sipping my coffee. He hadn't put enough sugar in it.

"Hill folks. They don't trust the law. Figure if I'm askin' questions, I must be after 'em. Idjit."

"So you're not after them?"

He looked at me like I'd lost my mind. "Hell, no. Oh, I got to get their statements, but I got no reason to be after 'em that I know of. All old Henry's doin' is stirrin' up trouble. Now they'll go shut down their stills and hide their pot till I'm gone."

"Ray," I asked, looking into my coffee. "Just what was this all about?"

"Just checkin' on Charles's alibi. He said he come up here and met with the boys. I'm checkin' it out. He probably stayed until closin'. If he didn't stay that late, he wouldn't have said he did. Coulda stayed later, though. No way of knowin'."

"You think Charles killed John? His own brother?"

Ray shrugged and dragged on his cigarette while he chewed his Moon Pie. I never did see how he did that, eat and smoke at the same time. "I don't know," he said. "Still could have, I guess. He said he left here at midnight. It took us twenty minutes to drive over. Even goin' back in the dark at normal speed, it wouldn't take him over half an hour. Doc says John died between one and two in the morning."

"But why? Why would he want to kill his own brother?"

"Said he didn't like him, didn't he?"

"People don't like each other all the time, Ray. It doesn't mean they go around killing each other," I said. I wadded up my Moon Pie wrapper and looked around. Stuffed it in my pocket.

Ray lit another cigarette from the first one. "Couple years ago, 'fore you got here, there was this fella up on the mountain made corn whiskey. Merciful Prim, his name was." Ray was looking out over the Pentecostal church with a glassy look in his eyes. Storytelling posture.

"Merciful Prim?" I asked.

"I swear to God. That was his given and real name. Anyway, ol' Merci sold corn that was the sweetest, smoothest shine on Pine Tree Mountain. Got a good dollar for it, too.

"So he sells ten quarts to this old boy from Perry's givin' a barn dance, see. Old boy, he gets home and opens up a quart just for a taste, to see if it's as good as everyone says it is. Next thing he's loaded it all back into his pickup and haulin' ass back up Pine Mountain.

"He gets up there and tells Merci he ain't never paid for doctored shine before in his life and he ain't about to start now. Ol' Merci, he gets his ass in the air on account o' this old boy is accusin' him o' cheatin' him on his shine *and* on account o' he's insultin' the shine, to boot.

"So Merci, he takes a sup, and sure enough, it's been doctored. Got grain alcohol in it been added, not raised natural. Now he's pissed, see? He goes stormin' into the house, gets his shotgun, and heads on up to the still with this feller from Perry followin' along.

"They get up to the still and . . . now, this is as best we can figure it . . . there's this nephew of his been helpin' him out sittin' there by the still smokin' a joint, and Merci, he just hauls off and shoots that boy big as you please. Hell of a mess. Then he turns around and shoots that feller from Perry, too.

"Then he just sat down there by his still and got drunk as a lord. And that's where we found him, passed out by the still. Claimed the boy was drinkin' the shine, or stealin' it to sell himself, and toppin' off the jars with store-bought alcohol, so he needed killin'. Claimed the feller from Perry was a mealy-mouth complainer woulda ruined his reputation, so he needed killin'. Don't that beat all?

"And you know he was right? You mention Merciful Prim's name up on Pine Tree Mountain and all anyone talks about is that wonderful shine he used to make, not them two old boys he killed. And him servin' two life sentences in Lexington right now. Killing them boys didn't hurt his reputation a bit, but waterin' his shine sure would have."

Ray smiled at the recollection, pleased with the story and his telling of it.

"So," I said. "The point is . . ."

He shook his head. How could a preacher be so dense? "The point is, these are hill people and they got a different code about what's important and what ain't."

"Charles doesn't seem like hill people to me," I said. And he didn't. Clean-shaven, soft-spoken, articulate. He seemed different from the others.

"He did two years of a six-year sentence for belting a police officer up to Cincinnati," Ray said, evenly.

"Really?" was all I could think of to say. It surely didn't seem in character for Charles.

"It was thirty years ago, but he done it. By all accounts, he wasn't too ashamed of it either."

"What was he doing in Cincinnati?" I asked, finishing my coffee, cold now.

"Tryin' to get his family outa these mountains. Workin' in a factory. Got drunk at a union meeting and belted a cop. Cop was off duty, doin' security work, but in Cincinnati, a cop's a cop."

"Thirty years was a long time ago," I said.

"He done time, Dan. Doin' time puts a mark on a man. You see where he went when he came back, don't you? Big John and Mother Cleopha took care of his brood whilst he was in the can. Now he's payin' off his debt." He lit a third cigarette without the ritual.

"Thirty years is a long time to pay off a debt."

"They're hill folks, Dan. That's what I been tryin' to tell ya. They're different."

"That why you got that old single-shot under the blanket in the Jeep?" I asked, not looking at him.

"May June told you?"

I nodded.

"Thought she would. That woman loves me somethin' dear. I don't know why."

I laughed. He really didn't. "What was all that about the videotapes?" I asked, changing the subject. I couldn't stand the thought of Ray Hall getting sappy on me.

He laughed. "Nothin' really. Ol' Henry gets pirated porno tapes from somewhere and rents them out to the locals."

I smiled. "Really?"

"Really," Ray said, nodding. "Old stuff, mostly. Your basic fuck and suck, pretty nasty."

"People up here got VCRs?" I asked.

Ray continued to nod, looked up and down the

road. "Years ago, you'd drive along these mountain roads and you'd see three things in or around every house, no matter how run-down or shabby it was. You'd see a smokehouse, a pickup truck, and a radio. Now'days, you see a Deepfreeze, a pickup truck, and a satellite dish. Them what can't afford satellite dishes buy VCRs. Rent tapes from guys like Henry. Porn ain't the onliest thing he rents. He's got Disney stuff, too."

All I could do was shake my head and try to light my pipe. People, especially mountain folks, are never what you expect them to be. They break their backs working in coal mines, filling their lungs with black dust, and what do they spend their money on? Pickup trucks and satellite dishes. And fuck-and-suck movies for Mom and Dad and Disney movies for the kids. Amazing.

"Problem with these pirated tapes is that the quality's so poor. There's this ol' boy in Perry, though. His are pirated, too, but they're first copies." He threw away his cigarette butt. "Well, Les and R.D. have had enough time to clean up their acts. Let's go see 'em," he said, heading for the Jeep.

The image of Ray and May June Hall lying in bed watching a porno movie was almost more than I could handle. On the other hand, he hadn't said it was porno movies he was getting from that "ol' boy in Perry." Maybe it was the Disney movies he and May June were watching.

No. That was even more ludicrous than porn. Ray Hall and Bambi didn't fit into the same frame of reference. Not as long as Bambi was a baby deer. Now, on the other hand, if the Bambi in question was a fetching young California blonde with big boobs and she was with, say, a Chad or a Tom with nice buns and a tattoo on his bicep, well, maybe.

I climbed into the Jeep and was tempted to ask Ray about this guy he knew in Perry, but there are some things you don't share with your parishioners, even if they are your friends.

Besides, Naomi could find out from one of her brothers. They'd know and she'd ask them. She'd like the idea. Think it was a kick. Probably. If I hadn't been such an asshole the other night. I made a mental note to call her and start patching things up as soon as I got home.

8

THE WAY TO LES EASTMAN'S HOUSE WAS SO ROUNDABOUT, the gravel and dirt roads so narrow and full of potholes, that I didn't even try to follow the route. I just held on and worked at trying to figure out what was going on in Ray Hall's mind.

The first and most natural suspects, Ray always said, were the family members. Kin killin' was almost a recreational sport in Durel County. Something like ninety-five out of a hundred of the homicides in the past ten years had been perpetrated against family members by other family members. Of the remaining five, four were committed by friends. The other was usually an acquaintance or a stranger in a bar who mouthed off at the wrong time. So, mostly, these folks killed kith and kin.

That meant that Eugene and Charles Wisdom had to be at the top of the list. They both had plenty of opportunity—they admitted to being in Pitchfork

Hollow at the time of the murder—but they lacked motive. Oh, sure, Charles didn't like his brother, but it didn't seem to be the kind of dislike worth killing someone over, and Charles just didn't have the temperament of a killer, Ray's story notwithstanding.

Eugene had the temperament, but he, too, lacked motive. From all indications, he worshiped Big John. Lord knew why. Every account of Big John Wisdom was worse than the next. But little brothers have a way of seeing only the big brother who once was. Besides, Eugene didn't have the balls to go up against Big John. He was mostly air.

We were on our way to meet R. D. Miles and Les Eastman. They were friends, so that made them suspects in Ray's book. And Les may have had motive if he and Big John had gotten into it over the football game.

Granted, a football game isn't much to kill someone over. But murder has been done for less. I remembered standing in the emergency room of a large urban hospital, talking with the family of a man who had just been stabbed because he and his kids had cut in line in front of another man and his kids. They were waiting to see Santa Claus. And hadn't Ray just told me a presumably true story about a man killing two people over some doctored moonshine? I supposed it was possible that murder could be done over a professional football game.

Except the Wisdom brothers had said that Les was laughing about it by the time they finished the ORV race to Devoux. Old friends, I have found, are often even more forgiving than family. If they really were old friends of John Wisdom, they had taken his teasing and meanness before and probably were pretty used to it. Besides, Charles had said they were gone by the time he got home at midnight, and John had been killed between one and two in the morning.

Well, we were on our way to meet them now. I'd have to reserve any further opinions until after we'd talked to them.

And then there was the elusive Price Deaver, town boy, pretty boy, rich kid, and wild man who wore leathers and acted tough and may have had it in for John Wisdom.

Jesus, the whole thing was giving me a headache. It was like a theology class I'd had in seminary. The professor used to say that trying to come up with a systematic theology that explained everything in the universe was like trying to keep the flies out of a twelve-window house when you only had eleven window screens. Only you didn't know you were one screen short. You kept insisting that all the windows were screened, but the flies kept coming in, so you kept moving the screens around, and all you managed to do was exhaust yourself and piss off everyone else in the house because they just wanted to take a nap and forget about screens and flies.

I think that professor sells computers now.

Ray wasn't about to give up and start selling computers. He was bouncing us toward Les Eastman's house like it might be burning and we were the VFD.

"I think they live right next door to each other," he yelled over the Jeep's Swiss-cheese exhaust system. Next door to each other could have meant anything from trailers ten feet apart to cabins separated by a mountain.

"How do you know?" I asked.

"Don't. I asked Cleopha. She said she thought they were neighbors on accounta they always come over to her place together, cross-country in their ORVs. When they come by road they ride in one pickup truck."

I coughed some dust out of my mouth. "She give you the address?"

"Just the general direction." He indicated the front of the Jeep with his finger. "Up this road somewhere. She said look for an old red Chevy pickup with the rocker panels rusted completely out and a dirty bumper sticker."

And there it was. A big red Chevy three-quarter-ton pickup truck with no rocker panels to speak of and a "Shit Happens" bumper sticker. It was parked at one end of a dirty, dented, old Airstream trailer that sat about a foot off the road, surrounded by heaps of aluminum cans.

Ray nearly passed it, backed up and nosed the Jeep up behind the pickup, said, "Mating position," to me, and winked. "Looks like he's home. Let's have a look."

We approached the front door and Ray knocked.

Nothing.

Ray knocked again. Harder, rocking the whole trailer. "Les? You in there? It's Ray Hall."

The door opened a crack and the smell of unwashed human body rolled out. A pale, yellowish eye and a vein-riddled nose poked out of the crack. "Ray? What you want?"

"Wanta talk, you crazy no-account. Whata you got a girl in there or what? Let me in."

Les hesitated a moment, then pushed the door open and turned back in to the trailer. I saw enough of him to see that he was about six feet tall, rail-thin, and his skin was the same color as his eye. He was in boxer shorts so big that he should have worn suspenders to keep them up. The trailer smelled oppressively of unwashed body, rancid meat grease, stale cigarette smoke, and beer.

Nice.

"I thought you might be out," Ray said. "Didn't see your ORV. You got coffee in here?" He started rummaging through the tiny kitchen while Les pulled on a pair of bib overalls that were as dirty as the rest of the trailer.

"Instant," Les said, yawning. "In the cabinet yonder. No, over the sink. I take mine black." He sat down across from me at the eating table, and I introduced myself as Dan Thompson.

"He's the minister over to Baird Methodist," Ray said. "We just been up to see Cleopha. Gettin' things set for Big John's funeral."

Les shook his head. "Terrible thing."

"I reckon," Ray said, putting a pan of water on the gas stove.

"My ORV's over to R.D.'s. Got stove up pretty bad on Sunday. I rolled him." Less licked his lips and looked around the trailer, no doubt trying to remember where he had put the hair of the dog.

"Still run?" Ray asked, shaking the water pan, trying to get it to boil quicker.

"Yeah. Needs some work, though. R.D.'s supposed to come get me this morning. We been workin' on it. He just lives about a mile up the road, there. He's got tools."

"Jean Ann take your tools, too?" Ray asked. "Jesus. Don't that just beat all." Then to me, "Les here hurt his back in the mine a couple of years ago and had to go on disability. His wife left him and took the kids as soon as the checks stopped rollin' in, ain't that right,

Les? Looks like she took damn near ever'thing else, too."

Les was shaking his head. "Nah, I sold 'em. Sold the other trailer, the tools, ever'thing, bought this pigsty, and then I drank and smoked the rest of it up." He smiled to himself, black and yellow teeth showing. "Fuck 'er."

A truck pulled up outside the trailer, and Ray poured coffee into two cups. He knew I'd rather drink molten lead than instant coffee, so he didn't even offer me any. R. D. Miles walked in without knocking.

He stopped a moment, not knowing me, looked around the trailer, saw Ray, and stopped again. Then it dawned on him. "Ray Hall, right? Constable." He looked at Les but got no help there.

Ray put his coffee cup down on the counter and extended his hand. "Right as rain," he said. "And this here's Reverend Thompson. He's a Methodist."

R.D. shook my hand. He was a pleasant-looking man of about fifty. About an inch shorter than me, which would have made him five ten or eleven. Hair the same blond as mine, only thinner. He had a gold tooth in the front of his broad smile, but it didn't ruin a generally open expression.

"I come to get this here no-account outa this shi . . . stink hole and come up and work on his car," he said. "That truck o' his hasn't run for a week, but all he cares about is his ORV. He talk any sense to you?"

Ray smiled and went back to his coffee. "Nah, we only just got here. Need to ask you boys some questions about the other night over to Wisdoms' place. You heard about Big John, didn't ya?"

R.D. nodded, serious now. "Oh, sure. We heard

about him. Sorry thing. John was a hard man to like, that's for sure. But he didn't deserve that. Everyone either hated or loved him. No in between for ol' John."

"What did you fellas do on Sunday?" Ray asked, getting right to it. He tasted his coffee and threw it out, took out his notebook.

"What time on Sunday?" R.D. asked.

"All day," Ray said.

"Well, I got up and come down here and picked up Les and dropped him off at my place. Then I took Loretta and the kids up to church in Melrose and waited for them at Henry's store. Les here worked on his ORV while we was gone, tuning it up and all." He picked up a chair and shoved it up to the table, took a packet of Red Man Chewing Tobacco out of his pocket and filled a jaw.

"I got home and we ate a sandwich, then took our ORVs cross-country to John's to watch the game." He looked around for something to spit into, found an unwashed coffee cup, and set it in front of him on the table. I tried to figure out how to move away from him. Smoke, I can stand. I even contribute my own. Tobacco juice is in a league all its own.

"What game was that?" Ray asked.

"Cincinnati, Pittsburgh," R.D. said. He looked at me when he said it and nodded at my cap. "Me and Les are Pittsburgh fans. Sorry, Reverend."

I smiled and shrugged. You live in the mountains long enough, you pick up the language.

"Good game?" Ray asked. Ray was a Cincinnati fan. He'd given me the cap. He knew damn well it was a good game, for Cincinnati.

"Pretty good," R.D. said.

Les muttered, "Shit."

"Well, we lost. Boomer was a throwin' fool. Couldn't miss, and the Steelers looked like they all had the flu or somethin'," R.D. said, clearly embarrassed by Les's lack of manners in front of a preacher.

I've never had a problem with people expressing themselves in the way they're most comfortable. But I can't get people to believe it.

"Got their butts kicked," Ray said. He was talking about the Pittsburgh Steelers.

"Ol' John, he had some fun with us about that for a while. Then we took out the ORVs. Drove around and ended up racin' to Devoux."

"How'd you do?"

"Oh, I don't care much for racin', you know. I just like bangin' around. I got there third or fourth. Les here flipped his and we had to go help him flip it back."

"Big John give you hell about that, too?" Ray asked Les.

"Fuck him," Les said, smiling again. I thought it might be easier to look into R.D.'s coffee cup full of tobacco spit than to look at another of Les Eastman's smiles. It was truly gruesome.

"How'd Eugene do?" Ray asked.

"He got stuck somewheres," R.D. said. "He was in Devoux when we got back with Les, covered with mud and shit." He realized, too late, what he had said, looked sideways at me, and seemed relieved that I hadn't fainted or stormed out.

"See anyone else while you were cuttin' around them trails?" Ray asked.

R.D. thought for a moment. "Hard to tell," he said, at last. "All that noise. Coulda been someone else up there tearin' around. Never occurred to me. You hear an engine, you just allow as how it's one of your group, you know? But I guess it coulda been someone else. I never saw no one, though. Les?"

Les shook his head and looked around for his bottle again.

"What about after you come back?" Ray said.

"We had a few beers, talked for a while, and then it was gettin' close to dark, so me and Les took off. Our ORVs ain't road-legal, so we had to go home cross-country. Didn't want to do it in the dark."

"You don't have lights?" I asked, remembering Adam Taylor's ORV with two headlights on the front and two more on the roll bar.

"Lights don't make it safe, Reverend. Best to travel the mountain in daylight." He said it like he was talking to a nine-year-old.

"Only safe way to drive one of them things," Ray said, closing his notebook. "Thanks, fellas. We'll be talkin' to ya."

R.D. got up to walk us out the door, and Les, his path finally clear, made a dive for the cabinet under the kitchen sink. He was pouring a drink for himself as I closed the trailer door. R.D. had come out with us and was walking Ray to his Jeep.

"I just wanted to say this where Les couldn't hear me," he said. "I don't want you to get the wrong idea about him. See, me and Les, we grew up in these hollers together and we been good friends, him and me and John, all our lives. It's just that his wife leavin' him hit him pretty hard. That and him gettin' hurt."

Ray just stood there looking at him, waiting for him to spin it out.

R.D. obliged. "See, Les an' John got in to it after the

game on Sunday. Couple o' years ago, little thing they got into wouldn't a meant a thing. Ol' Les, he woulda let John's ribbin' just roll off his back. But he'd been drinkin' and John was in a worse mood than usual and, well, Les kinda lost it. But he was all over it by the time we got back from the ride. He was laughin' it up and all."

Ray nodded.

"I just wanted you to know that," R.D. said, somewhat aware that he was explaining things that didn't really need to be explained. You often do that with the police. You just figure they think you're a suspect, so you start telling them things they don't even care about knowing.

Ray smiled. "Thanks for tellin' us, R.D."

R.D. shrugged.

Ray started to get into the Jeep and stopped, turned back. "R.D., can I ask you a personal question? Got nothin' to do with John Wisdom."

R.D. shrugged. "Sure, Ray."

"Why ain't you workin'? I mean, it's Tuesday, what, noon? Why ain't you at work?"

R.D. smiled in a small, self-deprecating way. "Laid off," he said. "I was workin' over to Weems's Sawmill until about two weeks ago. Then they let me go. Me and about eight other ol' boys. Just not enough work, they said."

Ray nodded. "Sorry to hear that, R.D. You got anything else?"

R.D. shook his head. "Couple o' things, maybe. Maybe not. Uncle Sam, o' course. And my wife works for Henry sometimes, over in Melrose. And we got vegetables she put up last summer. We'll get by."

Ray climbed into the Jeep and started it, gunning

the engine enough to send us into orbit if he happened to slide into gear by accident. "I reckon you will," he said to R.D. "What choice you got?"

"Ain't it the truth," R.D. said. He spit near the Jeep's front tire. "Ain't it the truth."

The ride back to Baird took only about thirty minutes because Ray knew some back roads that went through but gave me permanent kidney damage.

Ray called the potholes "thankyouma'ams." I called them Grand Canyon East. We hadn't tried to talk during the ride. I was afraid to interrupt Ray's concentration, assuming the stern look on his face was due to an extreme effort to keep us on the road without killing us.

It wasn't.

"Well, that was interesting," he said as he began his cigarette ritual. We were parked in front of the diner.

"It was terrifying is what it was," I said. My back was screaming and my nerves were shot.

"Naw, not the road. The talk," he said, chuckling and lighting his cigarette at the same time.

"It was? I thought it was all rather droll." An attempt at city humor that didn't penetrate Ray's thought process.

"We learned a lot this morning," he said.

"We did?"

"Sure we did. Lot of interesting stuff."

"Like what?"

"Well, we learned that Charles, Eugene, Henry, and R.D. are all lying," he said, smiling. "Boy, for a preacher, you sure don't read people very good."

"What? Not Cleopha, too? How do you know they were lying?"

He smiled again. Go on, ask me, the smile said.

"Okay," I said. "What are they lying about?"

"Well, Charles is lying about not likin' his brother John. Fact is, he probably hated Big John's guts."

"How do you know that?"

"Well, Charles is a union man, right? Lotta union talk. Big union man up in Cincinnati before he done his time. Even goes to the unofficial meetings in Melrose of a Sunday night."

"What's that got to—"

"John was a scab. Back about four years ago there was a wildcat walkout over to Boyer Coal. Everyone walked out for three days on accounta unsafe conditions, they said. Everyone but Big John Wisdom. Big John said he had to feed his family and fuck anyone who didn't like it."

"He mined coal all by himself?" I asked, realizing how silly it sounded the minute I said it. I guess it was his name. Big John, like in that Jimmy Dean song that was popular about a million years ago.

Ray laughed. "Oh, hell no. He drove a truck. Hauled mined coal to Perry till the strike ended. Got some threatening calls and the road in front of his house got spray-painted. You know, scab, in great big letters. But no one messed with him. I reckon they was afraid of him. He cut a pretty wide swath, you know. And everyone liked Charles, too. But it caused a right smart of embarrassment for Charles, I guess."

"You think Charles would kill John because he scabbed on a strike four years ago?" I asked.

"Possible," Ray said, blowing cigarette smoke toward the sky. "Or that may have lit the fuse that just now exploded over something else. Important thing is, Charles is a liar."

Well, maybe not a liar, I thought. Maybe he was just soft-pedaling the truth a bit. Or maybe he really had softened in his dislike of his brother. It was possible. "What about Eugene?" I asked.

"Well, Eugene knew there was someone else up on the mountain on Sunday. Probably seen 'em."

"Oh, come on . . ."

"He answered too quick. No, R.D. gave the right answer to that question. He said he didn't know. Too much noise. Too many trails to know for sure. But not ol' Eugene. He just says, 'Nope. No one but us chickens. An' that's a fact.' How'd he know for sure? He couldn't. So he lied when he didn't need to, see."

"But why?"

"Probably protectin' someone. Maybe he got him a little on the side. Maybe he was threatened. Who knows? The important thing is that—"

"He's a liar, I know."

"Right." He lit another cigarette from the butt of his first. He was really thinking now. "Then there's R.D. His was just a little bitty lie. That's what makes it so interestin'. Why tell one at all?"

"What was his little bitty lie, Ray? I missed it."

"Ain't surprised. He said he came in third or fourth, remember? He came in third, plain and simple. Big John woulda been there keepin' score and woulda made sure everyone knew their position. That's the kinda guy he was. You're first, I'm second, you're third. Onliest ones left were Les, who rolled his ORV, and Eugene, who didn't come in until they were gone to help Les get his ORV picked up."

"That doesn't make sense," I said, lighting my pipe. If we were going to sit here, I might as well join him. "Why would he lie about something so simple and stupid?"

"That's what makes it so curious," he said.

"Henry," I said, after a minute.

"Oh, Henry ain't no big deal. He's hill people. They lie to the law just to stay in practice. Probably thought he was protectin' R.D. Said he hadn't seen R.D. lately. R.D. said he had been there on Sunday morning while his wife and kids were at church across the road. R.D. couldn't deny it because he knew I could check it out. He didn't know we'd already had a talk with Henry. Henry, he lied just in case R.D. wanted to, he would be covered."

This was all getting confusing. "What about Les?" I asked, just to be saying something.

Ray shrugged. "Who the hell knows? R.D. wouldn't let Les say anything. Soon as he saw my Jeep, he hotfooted it down there. Les didn't have a chance to lie. R.D. saw to that."

"Protecting his buddy?" I asked.

"Protecting their still, probably. Thought I was there to bust their still and didn't want Les to get to drinkin' and blurt out where it was. Either that or their stash. Marijuana is the new moonshine, you know."

I knew.

"Probably got a crop hid up on the mountain somewhere and he wanted to protect his investment. Need to get Les alone. Might be a good idea to get him about three sheets to the wind and let him talk. He might know something that would be useful. Hell, he mighta killed Big John hisself. He don't look like a man can take much ribbin'."

"You going back?" I asked, a little worried. My job didn't require much of me, but it did require something. May June was worried, so I had agreed to ride around with Ray and his shotgun. I was beginning to worry a little about my own responsibilities, though. There was the Administrative Council meeting that night and a sermon to prepare for Sunday and John Wisdom's funeral, whenever that was going to be.

"Me? No, you are," Ray said evenly.

"I am what?"

"You're gonna go up and talk to Les. Ask him about Sunday evening. Take a little taste with you. He'll open right up."

"Oh, Ray, come on. I know you go around calling me the deputy constable, but it's just not so. I'm a preacher. I can't go up on the mountain carrying a jar of moonshine to a drunk. Besides, I wouldn't know what to ask."

"Just call on him. You're a preacher, ain't you? You're supposed to call on folks in trouble. And Les Eastman's in more trouble than most around here. So call on him. And take a little medicinal tonic with you. I'll have May June put some in a jar with a frilly thing on the top for you."

"Why can't you do it?"

"I gotta go into Perry tomorrow and fill out my reports. Besides, I'm the law. He ain't gonna say a thing to me. And R.D. will be down there 'fore I can get my notebook open."

"Ray, do you understand the seal of the confessional?"

"You ain't Catholic," he said. "Besides, I doubt he'd confess anything."

"No, probably not, but if I undertake the role of pastoral counselor, I'm protected by the same law," I said, stiffening. This was my turf.

"The law ain't real clear on that," he said.

"I'm not talking about the law of the Commonwealth of Kentucky," I said. "I'm talking about Thompson's law. I don't break the seal. For anyone or anything. God knows I haven't been a model minister.

Before the big fall, I broke nearly every rule there was for preachers. But that one I kept. I'm not going to break it now." Nice speech, I thought. Passionate. Articulate. Short. Maybe a little heavy on the indignation, but at least it came from the heart.

"Not even for a murderer? A murderer who might go out and do it again if he ain't caught?" Ray looked straight ahead. I hoped he wasn't getting mad. Naomi was already mad at me. I didn't think I could stand it if he was, too.

"Not even for a murderer, Ray. I'd do everything I could to get him to turn himself in. I'd hang by him every minute. I'd hound him and badger him until he gave himself up just to get rid of me. But no, I wouldn't turn him in. I'm sorry."

He flipped his cigarette into the driveway and smiled at me. "That'll do," he said. "That'll do just fine. You go talk to him after Big John's funeral. I'll still have May June put up some of that tonic I confiscated for Les. God knows he needs it worser'n I do." He started to get out of the Jeep, then stopped and turned back to face me. "Oh, and that talk we had about videotapes?"

I just looked at him.

"I reckon this seal of the confessional would cover a thing like that, wouldn't it? It's not for me that I care, you understand. Hell, I don't give a damn what folks think of me. But May June's kinda fragile, you know."

"You're covered," I said, smiling. "May June, too."

"There ya go," he said, returning the smile. "Remind me and I'll give you that feller's name and address. You don't patch things up pretty soon with Naomi, you're gonna need 'em."

How did he know about Naomi and me?

Before I could give it any thought, the screen door

slammed and May June came out onto the porch. "Well, are you two gonna sit out here all day or come in and have some lunch? You ain't had lunch yet, have you?"

We said we hadn't.

"Well, come on in, then. And hurry. You got just enough time to eat a sandwich, then Dan here's got an appointment."

"Appointment?" I said, mentally going over my calendar for the week. I didn't remember any appointments for Tuesday afternoon.

"The girls was here a little after noon and I fed them and the children and said you'd be back directly. They went up to the thrift store to shop around, but they'll be back down here directly, so come on and eat." She turned to go back into the diner.

"What girls, May June?" I shouted.

Her voice carried out from the diner. "The Wisdom girls. They come about John's funeral. Now, come on and eat."

9

The Wisdom girls turned out to be Charlotte, John's widow, and Bethabelle, Eugene's wife. They returned from the thrift store at the Mountain Baptist Children's Home across the road just as I was finishing my fried bologna sandwich.

Charlotte was a tall, thin, frail woman with what had to be waist-length hair, braided and wound up in an elaborate bun. Her face wore an expression that was full of pain and sadness, more than the death of Big John could have brought on. It seemed to have been stamped on her face a long time ago. Her long hair and shin-length dress identified her as a Pentecostal, probably a member of the Melrose church across from Henry's store.

Bethabelle was everything Charlotte wasn't. She looked to be in her mid-twenties and she was poured into a pair of blue jeans that pretended to be old and a black T-shirt like the one her husband wore, only he didn't fill his out nearly as well. Her breasts were smallish, but the nipples seemed to have a life of their own, straining to burst through the fabric. They were the kind of nipples that should have names of their own.

Her hair was chestnut brown and fell straight just past her shoulders from the part in the middle. It wasn't quite dirty, but it could have used a shampoo. She licked her lips constantly and wore a practiced pouty expression that, I was sure, was a hit at the VFW dances in Perry.

She also had three kids with her. Two boys and a girl, all preschoolers, dirty-faced, snotty-nosed, and cute in the sad way that neglected Appalachian kids often are.

The minute they walked in, May June whisked the kids away into the store and gave them candy and soda and marbles to play with.

"Y'all go on over to the church where you can talk," she said, waving us away. "I'll watch the young 'uns for a spell."

I picked up what was left of my Diet Pepsi and introduced myself and off we went, down the road to the church. When we got to my office, which is the connecting room between the church and the parsonage, they sat in the two folding chairs. Charlotte straight and tall, still sad, and Bethabelle leaning forward, her hands on her knees.

It's usually best to start an awkward meeting with a little small talk, so I indicated the grocery bags they were carrying. "Find some bargains up at the thrift store?" I asked.

"Did we ever," Bethabelle said, opening her bag. She stopped and looked at me. "Was it really your idea to start that thrift store?"

"Well, it was the whole church, really," I said. It was a lie. It had been my idea, but a good pastor doesn't toot his own horn. He shares the credit and takes all the crap. "We thought it would be a help. Folks from churches all over the county send stuff their kids have outgrown and folks here can use. The Home lets us use their basement, and we charge enough to cover the extra electric bill and pay for the shelves and hangers."

"Ain't just kids' stuff up there," she said, digging in her bag again. Her accent was trying hard to be Scarlett O'Hara, refined and seductive, but there was too much hard Kentucky in her to pull it off. She sounded like a briar trying to be something she wasn't.

She held up a man's sport coat. It was five years out of style. "Won't Eugene look good in this," she giggled. I couldn't tell whether she was kidding or not. "And look at this!" She held up a pair of women's panties, pink, with a little devil standing beside the crotch, leering. How in God's name had those gotten in there? The ladies of the church would have a fit if they knew.

Bethabelle stood and held them in front of her. "What do you think, Reverend?" she asked, trying on the pout again.

What I thought was that it would be extremely embarrassing if I had to stand up at that moment. An image of her in nothing but those pink, see-through panties had crashed into my brain, and the effect had been immediate and heart-stopping. She was quite a package.

"And look here!" Now she was holding up a white teddy against her breasts. "Only fifty cents. Does it look cheap?"

It did. But it was a really good kind of cheap.

"I think you got a real bargain," I managed to croak. "Eugene should thank his lucky stars."

The mention of her husband's name seemed to drain some of the enthusiasm from her. The pout stayed, but it spread up into her eyes a little. "Oh, him." She sat down, stuffing the things back into her grocery bag, and crossed her arms across her marvelous chest.

If not Eugene, who the hell had she bought these things to wear for? Then it came to me.

Several weeks ago I had driven Ray to Perry to get a part for his Jeep. While we were in town he took me to a roadhouse that was supposed to have the biggest tenderloin sandwiches and the coldest beer in the state. They did. The sandwiches were as big as dinner plates, and the beer gave me a headache every time I took a swig.

What was really amazing, though, wasn't the food. It was a couple who were playing pool in the corner. He was about thirty, bearded and thick across the chest with what Ray called work-muscle, as opposed to workout-muscle. The girl he was playing pool with was about his age and marvelously built, wearing a see-through blouse and no bra. She was hanging on him like a glass bulb on a Christmas tree.

That in itself was no big deal except that the guy's wife was sitting at the bar three stools down from us, getting loaded on boilermakers, not seeming to give a damn that her husband was playing grab-ass with a girl in a peekaboo blouse.

I pointed this out to Ray on the way home, and he said it was called Kentucky courtin'. He said it was just generally accepted by a lot of folks that it was a woman's job to keep her man if he was worth keeping, and every man was fair game for every woman. If a woman saw a man worth getting, she went after him, and it was up to his own woman to keep him if she wanted him. "That ol' gal at the bar musta figured he weren't worth keepin', 'cause she sure as hell weren't doin' nothin' about it," Ray said.

The other side of the Kentucky courtin' ritual was that it was a man's responsibility to keep his wife if he thought her worth keeping. And the way a man kept his wife was to bring home a paycheck regularly, sleep with her pretty much exclusively, and not beat up on her or the kids. If he reneged on any of these, she had a license to go shopping for a new man.

"It ain't written down nowhere that I know of," Ray said. "But that's how it works."

So Bethabelle Wisdom was shopping. And today she was checking the prices at the local Methodist church, where the pastor happened to be single and available and reliable in the paycheck department even if he was a little old for her.

With this insight my swelling ego, and other parts, went immediately flaccid and I could feel sweat start to roll down my back. According to Ray, if a shopping woman decided you were worth going after, nothing could stop her. Not a wife, not kids, not anything.

"They're like bulldogs," Ray had said, and gone on to tell about a time May June had taken his shotgun and run a woman off who had decided to go after Ray.

He ended the story by saying, "It's the poverty. People get poor and hungry and desperate enough, they'll break any law, commit any sin, just to get a ride down off the mountain."

That's what it was that spread to her eyes with the pout. It wasn't disappointment, it was desperation.

And a desperate, pouty, pretty girl with great boobs and a white teddy are dangerous things for a preacher to have around when he's alone. I made a mental note.

"How about you, Charlotte?" I asked, trying to slide the conversation away from Beth, and my mind away from her breasts.

Charlotte hadn't moved a muscle throughout Bethabelle's little underwear number. Now she set her mouth primly and said, "Just some things for the children."

"Children? I thought your kids were grown and in the service."

"Her children," she said, nodding her head sideways toward Bethabelle. "Lord knows someone has to look after their needs."

"Here we go," Bethabelle said, sighing.

"Any mother, any good mother, would tend to her children's needs rather than buy harlot clothes for herself." She turned to look at Beth and said, "By her plumage and the clothing of her body shall the harlot be known. Thus saith the Lord."

She said it so confidently that I nearly assumed that it was scriptural, then it occurred to me that I had never heard anything like it. No, it wasn't from the Bible. It was the word according to Charlotte Wisdom, couched in King James English to give it weight. Nice trick if you can pull it off.

Bethabelle wrinkled her nose and looked straight ahead. "Kisseth my ass. Thus saith Bethabelle." It didn't have the ring of biblical authority that Charlotte's did, but it was worth serious consideration, I thought.

"You all wanted to talk about John's funeral?" I said, trying to bring the conversation around to something constructive before it broke down completely.

"No funeral. Just words at the graveside. John wasn't saved, and I won't have him mourned over and prayed over like he was some kind of saint." Charlotte gave a little nod to punctuate her statement.

"He weren't no saint!" Beth said, astonished. "Lord, that's like sayin' Mount Devoux ain't no hill. He was a prick is what he was."

"You don't know—"

"He beat you, he run off his kids, he terrorized everyone in the county, and he scabbed for the mine owners. Shoulda left him where you found him, Reverend. Onliest fittin' place for him to be buried." Now Bethabelle nodded to punctuate her statement, and it made her whole body sort of jiggle. Pleasantly, I thought.

Charlotte directed her attention back to me. "I think it's only fair to tell you that I didn't want you to do this funeral. My first choice was Reverend Harland from my own church. But he is forbidden from burying anyone who hasn't been saved. I don't mean no offense, but I thought I should tell you."

"No offense taken," I said. "I understand completely." Which was absolute bullshit of the deepest kind. Didn't bury anyone who wasn't saved? What were we supposed to do, just let the unsaved ones lie around the yard until the Second Coming? Try as I might, I could not begin to understand some of these independent mountain denominations.

"Well, we'd like the Lord's Prayer said, of course. And the Twenty-third Psalm and a few words from you. Not about John, but about the Lord. Maybe you'd sing a hymn. I hear you have a passable voice?"

She tilted her head slightly and waited for confirmation.

In fact, my voice is quite good, especially when I'm singing one of my favorite hymns. Naomi says it's a confident voice. I guess that's good. "I'll try to find something appropriate," I said.

"Fine," Charlotte said, and rose to leave. "Tomorrow morning at ten."

"I got to get a couple things from the store," Bethabelle said to Charlotte, but smiling at me over her shoulder. Nice. A butt shot with a smile over the shoulder. And not a bad butt at that, though the smile could use some work, what with the teeth and all. Stick with the pout, Beth.

She hurried after her sister-in-law. "I don't know what's wrong with that husband of mine. He's in Melrose practically ever' day and he can't even remember to pick up a can of condensed milk. I'll swan!" She wiggled her way out the door, into the sanctuary of the church, and a moment later I heard the door close.

I called Naomi's number and got a busy signal.

I wrote down some notes about the funeral for John Wisdom.

I wrote down a note to talk to May June about being more careful when she and the ladies sorted the clothing that went up to the thrift shop.

I tried Naomi's number again and no one answered.

I checked my calendar and saw that the church Administrative Council was meeting tonight at seven-thirty P.M., and immediately got a stiff neck and chest pains.

So I took a nap on the couch in my living room. It was threadbare, scratchy nylon, donated by the Children's Home, but it was a heck of a nap couch.

But I couldn't sleep. I kept thinking about pink panties with devils on them and white teddies and Naomi's hot tub and . . .

And why was Eugene Wisdom going up to Melrose every day? Looked like Henry, the storekeeper, was a bigger liar than we had figured.

The ministry does not usually require you to be an early riser, so I was out of practice. Usually it's out of bed around eight, into the office by nine, coffee and paperwork, then lunch. After that, well, a friend of mine used to say the thing he liked best about being a preacher was that all he had to do was "pay the bills," then he could do whatever he wanted. What I usually wanted was to hang out at the diner for the rest of the day or meet Naomi at her cabin for fun and games.

Getting up before dawn that morning had taken a heavier toll on me than I realized, and I slept like a log on the couch. Right through May June's fried chicken dinner special and fifteen minutes into the meeting of the Administrative Council of the church.

I arrived in the church basement panting and apologizing that "a counseling thing took longer than I expected."

They bought it.

But the damage was done. They were already fighting. The meeting, which should have taken no more than an hour, took two and a half. Fully nine-tenths of the time was given to heated debate over how the money left by McHenry and Ernestine Martin should be spent.

The savings account faction seemed to be gaining ground, and the fix-up-the-nursery faction was slowly dying, though they didn't know it yet. They were falling victim to essentially the same argument that was doing in the fix-up-the-steeple faction. It went like this: "Why do we need to fix the steeple? We don't ring the bell anymore!" When I mentioned that we didn't ring the bell because the steeple was broken, they just looked at me like I was butting in where I had no business. It was much the same with the nursery: "Why fix up the nursery? We don't got any younguns in the church to speak of." I thought of telling them that we didn't have any children in the church because the nursery looked like a crypt and the furniture was moldy and stinking. But I didn't.

Preachers should stick with preaching. Let businesspeople run the church. Or so they say.

I was glad to see that the Frank sisters had managed to alienate nearly everyone else on the Council with their fabric ploy, and their curtain-for-the-sanctuary faction now numbered only those two. The furnace faction was still gathering steam and looked to be a contender when the primaries were through, meaning a pitched battle between the furnace faction and the savings-account faction. I couldn't wait.

The three people who had offered the ministry and mission suggestions tried again and were shouted down again, but not quite as loudly or as quickly as before, and no one said, "Charity begins at home," so I thought there still might be a chance of getting some of the money for missions if I was willing to add the weight of my ecclesiastical authority and a little old-fashioned born-again guilt to the cause. I would give it some thought. We really needed that medical clinic in Baird. It was over and hour to the nearest doctor in Perry, and the Children's Home across the road had plenty of space.

Having spent two hours and fifteen minutes arguing

about the money and deciding nothing, we got down to real business.

June Ann Crabtree wanted to know why I had served Communion to Darnell Kody, the retarded handyman around town, two Sundays ago when "everyone in the church knows for a fact that he hasn't been saved."

It wasn't the question that pissed me off. It was the how and why of it. She had asked the same question of me in private last week, and I had given her a kind, gentle, pastoral answer about Holy Communion in the Methodist church being inclusive and open to all who seek it and how we are enjoined by Scripture not to judge others, etc., etc.

She had accepted it with a polite smile. Or seemed to.

Now she was showing me that she didn't accept it at all and was going to use her not insignificant influence with the members of the Council to overturn two hundred years of Methodist polity.

So I blasted her. The full broadside. This was Thompson's second rule, and I held it no less dear than the first one. I would not break the seal of the confessional and I would not deny Holy Communion to anyone who sought it.

It took only two minutes, but it was well done and it shut her up on the subject for good and left icicles hanging from the furnace ducts in the ceiling. Yes, preachers are supposed to be kind and gentle people. But there are some things worth fighting about.

The room got so quiet, I could hear a dog barking outside. Everyone was looking at me with their mouths hanging open, so since I was already the center of attention, I changed the subject.

"I noticed today," I said, gravely, trying to act embarrassed, "that there were some ladies' underthings in the ladies' bin up at the thrift shop."

They all looked at each other and then at me. So what?

I plunged on. "What I mean is, these were what might be considered risqué. Things that were kind of, uh . . ."

"Sexy?" May June Hall said, deadpan.

"Well, yes," I said. "Even, uh . . ."

"Dirty?" Now everyone was interested.

"Yeah."

They still looked around the table at each other. So what?

"Well, I was just wondering if maybe the ladies who sort the clothes that come in might not want to be a little more thorough, that's all. Some of the folks who shop in the thrift store aren't as, uh, broad-minded as we are and might find those kinds of things, well, offensive."

They still looked around the table at each other and then at me. But this time their faces said, *You poor, naive thing.*

May June, having taken the role of spokesperson, spoke again. "So what you're sayin' is the only people who should have the chance to buy panties with little devils on them is rich, broad-minded, liberal city folk, and we ought to be protecting these poor, ignorant, narrow-minded hillbillies from such wickedness."

"No, that's not what I meant," I began.

"I'm glad to hear it," May June finished for me. "Because there were five of us here around this table who sorted those things, and we thought it would be a nice Christian gesture if we left them in there and allowed those poor hill folks a little fun like the rest of the world. In fact, we put them right on the top of the bin so's they'd stand out."

Several heads nodded in enthusiastic assent, and those that didn't seemed to nod as if this was something that should be taken for granted. Poor hillbillies like, and should have the opportunity, to wear sexy underwear the same as everyone else. Only a fool or Satan himself would even think of denying them such a harmless, simple pleasure.

Before I could defend myself with another word, Hayden Smith, the chairman, brought down the gavel, ending the meeting, and everyone headed for the brownies and coffee that May June had brought.

I munched a brownie and sipped coffee and mingled and made small talk and laughed and joked with them, and they teased me about ladies' underthings. The ladies reassured me that while they had no intention of censoring the clothing bins at the thrift shop, they would put the delicate things on the bottom so as not to offend my sensibilities. The men said off-color remarks they thought would shock me. I didn't act shocked, but I shook my head and put on my you-guys-are-awful, tolerant preacher's expression.

God, I really did like these people. Loved them. But I sure as hell didn't understand them. How could they be so selfish and conservative and even mean when they argued about the Martin money, and then, in the next minute, be so kind and softhearted and gentle when talking about sexy women's underwear?

Even now May June was giving out assignments, telling different women what to bake and when to have it at the diner so I could take it up to the Wisdom place when I did the funeral tomorrow morning. May June was part of the fix-up-the-nursery faction, and the fact that these same women had, just fifteen minutes ago, told her that her ideas were silly and ridiculous bothered her not a bit. There were hurting souls on the mountain who needed the ministrations of the church, and she was going to see to it that they got it.

And speaking of hurting souls on the mountain, hadn't I better start patching things up with Naomi? I hugged May June, arranged to pick up the food in the morning, and went through my office to the parsonage to call the love of my life and beg her forgiveness.

10

WEDNESDAY MORNING HARDLY DAWNED AT ALL. A COLD front had moved in from the northwest over Pine Tree Mountain and mated with the warm front that had kept the temperatures mild for nearly a week. That mating brought forth round, black clouds that met in groups, broke up, and met again in ever-changing configurations. Jacob's ladders of sunlight reached down through the holes in the clouds and touched the tops of the mountains, and if it hadn't been so damned cold and threatening eventual rain, it would have been beautiful.

My veedub was filled from floor to ceiling with food. Casseroles, cobblers, salads, fried chicken, ham, pies and cakes, and homemade bread. On the floor were four one-gallon jars of iced tea which, even though sealed with wax paper and lids, managed to slosh on my ankles and cuffs as I tried to shift gears going over Mount Devoux.

My winter clothes were still in the boxes I'd moved them in, so I was wearing my tan wash-'n'-wear preacher suit, white shirt, and black tie. The tan pants would not be too severely damaged by the tea if I could get them rinsed out quickly, but it was still a pain in the neck. It would still need to be pressed after rinsing. Maybe I could get May June to do it.

Older women in the church love nothing so much as a helpless young preacher. May June refused to let me pay even a cent toward any of the meals, snacks, and coffee I had eaten at the diner. "We don't pay much, but the food's greasy, fattening, and full of cholesterol," Ray had said with a smile as he dug into his biscuits and gravy.

Ray had tucked a quart jar of water-clear moonshine under the seat of my Super Beetle just before I left. "Just say you found it on the front stoop when he opens the door. He won't believe you, but it'll save you from any embarrassment," he said.

"Ray, I don't—"

"I know. You won't break the seal thing," he said. "I ain't askin' you to. Just talk to 'im. If he done it or knows who did, see what you can do."

"But he was gone by the time Charles got back," I said.

"Yeah, I know. But we still ain't sure how late that was. I ain't got that part figured out yet." He slapped the rear fender of my car like it was a horse's rump and I was off, sloshing iced tea and trying not to slide the cherry cobbler into the sweet potato casserole.

The trip took longer than I had planned, what with the food crashing around in the car and my having to take the turns slower than Ray had. So I didn't have time to stop by at Naomi's place like I had planned.

There had still been no answer at the cabin last night when I called. Worried, I called her father's house.

"Ain't here," Jacob, one of the ex-cons, grumbled. "Thought she was with you. Ain't seen her since Monday night."

Now I was really concerned. Where could she be? Perry? Why there? You could spend an afternoon in Perry, but certainly not two days. Shopping in Lexington? She would have told her father if she was doing that. Where the hell could she be?

I slowed down even more as I passed the Viper cutoff and crawled to a stop when I came to the road that wound up toward her cabin. I sat there straining my eyes, trying to make her appear with the intensity of my gaze. Maybe I would be lucky enough to catch her when she came down the trail to get her mail.

Then it struck me. Check the mailbox. See if she's picked up her mail yet. If she had, then she just wasn't answering her phone, or I had just been unlucky enough to call when she was out hiking in the woods. I put the veedub in neutral, set the parking brake, and cracked the door open to get out. The unmistakable thunder of a coal truck coming down the road rumbled from around the blind bend just ahead. In a minute he would come around the bend, not knowing I was there, and I would be dead meat, sitting in the center of the road.

Shit.

I shifted into first gear, forgot about the added weight of all the food, popped the clutch, and stalled the engine. And, of course, the VW decided to take its time restarting. I ground it and cursed it and prayed to God to make it start—a prayer that my theology professors would have scoffed at—and finally, just to keep me in my place, it started. Reluctantly.

By that time the coal truck could not have been more than a hundred yards around the bend, barging down on me like a runaway locomotive, because I no sooner lurched to the shoulder of the road when it screamed by, blasting away on the air horn.

One of the gallons of iced tea had turned over and was slowly dripping into my shoe, the cherry cobbler was sitting squarely in the middle of the sweet potato casserole, and I had nearly gotten killed because Naomi Taylor was giving me the silent treatment.

Fuck the mail. I drove on, slowly, to the Wisdom place.

John Wisdom was laid out in all his fat glory in a homemade casket in the living room of the big house. He had on his Sunday suit, which was about a size too small and twenty years old. He still smelled bad, but the dry ice packed around him was helping to keep that bearable. They had told Doc that they didn't want him embalmed, so he had packed the body in dry ice for storage until they came in the pickup truck to retrieve it.

The fog rolling off the ice added a nice touch, I thought. I'd have to remember that for Mom. She would like the effect.

My arrival sent everyone into action. Charles, who didn't have any toilet paper on his chin or neck today, introduced me to his wife, Marie, a short, fat, pretty lady with a port wine birthmark that covered the right side of her neck and stretched up to her ear. Her smile was so endearing, and her manner so gracious, though, that I didn't even notice the birthmark until the second look. She hid it beneath a layer of charm.

Funny how people react differently to things like that. Another woman would have become bitter and indignant at having been saddled with what most would see as a disfigurement. Marie had become charming. I loved her instantly and thanked her for the coffee she offered me even though I didn't really want or need it.

Eugene and Bethabelle were sitting on the porch smoking cigarettes. Eugene was still in his T-shirt and jeans and looking angry. Bethabelle was in a tight, black dress with a leg-slit cut nearly to paradise. Her version of Sunday dress-up clothes.

John's widow, Charlotte, was sitting in a rocking chair in the living room reading her Bible, and Mother Cleopha was in the kitchen setting out the food that a whole herd of kids were bringing in from my car. I recognized two of the kids as Bethabelle and Eugene's, but I'd never seen the other three. Neighbors, maybe. Whoever they were, they seemed happier to be out of school than they were sad to be saying good-bye to John Wisdom.

In fact, the only person who seemed to regret seeing Big John go was his mother, and she cried silently the whole time she worked in the kitchen. Charles, not knowing what else to do, kept saying, "Mom. Mom."

I walked up to her and said hello, and she looked at me with eyes that were red-rimmed and tired and heartbreaking. I set down my coffee cup and did the easiest, most natural thing a minister can do. I opened my arms and invited her in. She fell against me and wept loudly, and I hugged her and patted her back and said nothing.

Charles seemed to realize that he had missed something and sidled up next to us, hesitated, and then reached out and took her from me and hugged her to himself, engulfing her in his big arms. She was nearly as tall as Charles, but she seemed to melt into him, and I wondered how long it had been since anyone had hugged this hard old woman who had bathed and diapered and nursed and fed and raised these people.

A long time. Maybe longer.

It took her a good ten minutes to cry herself out and then another ten to "fix up her face," and then we were ready to go. They all filed in around the casket and held hands, and I said a prayer, and Charles and Eugene nailed the lid on with quick, deft strokes of the hammer.

That done, we loaded the casket onto the bed of a pickup truck parked in the yard. "Lard-ass is too big to carry," Charles said in the cab of the truck, his wife, Marie, sitting between us. She elbowed him in the gut and they both chuckled.

We drove slowly down through the yards in the hollow, across the creek on a temporary bridge, and then started up a path into the woods behind Charles's big house trailer, the family all walking silently behind the truck. "Watch out the back window, Reverend," Charles said. "Wouldn't want to lose him goin' up the mountain. Big John slides outa this truck and starts down the mountain, he won't stop till he reaches Stinkin' Creek. Dam it up and we'd have to go around by the road every time we went to Devoux."

Marie elbowed him again and they chuckled again and I got the idea that the passing of Big John, while a sober experience, had not necessarily plunged them into the pit of despair. On the other hand, I had conducted more than one funeral where the entire family laughed and joked together even in the middle of abject grief. We all handle it in our own way.

The family plot was just a flat place on the side of

the mountain. About a dozen stone markers were scattered around and the grave was freshly dug, about four feet deep with two large boards across it. Eugene, Charles, the women, and I wrestled the casket out of the truck and laid it on the boards and then the family gathered around the grave as they had in the house, holding hands. I had the feeling that there were family rituals, hill people things, at work here that I knew nothing about, and I felt like an interloper.

I stood at the head of the casket and did what they had asked. I noted the beauty of the mountain, the colors of the trees that die so they can live again, the Jacob's ladders of light, symbolic of God's constant contact with His creation. I read from the Bible. I said a prayer and started to ask Cleopha if the family would like to sing a hymn, being somewhat hesitant to sing a solo, but willing if the occasion required it.

I didn't have a chance to finish my question. Without introduction or comment, a female voice so clear and pleasant, so pregnant with feeling and melody that I nearly melted at the sound of it, began to sing. It was not soft or loud, but it filled the woods, and even the birds on the mountain seemed to fall silent in the presence of a greater talent than their own.

And it was slow. Not like a song. Not even like a hymn. But like a prayer:

"When the trumpets of the Lord shall sound
and time shall be no more,
When the morning springs eternal bright and fair,
When the saints of earth shall gather over on
the other shore
And the roll is called up yonder, I'll be there."

I looked at Marie Wisdom, standing next to Charles, holding his hand on one side and a child's on the other. The birthmark seemed to be fading, even as she stood there in the shade. Her eyes were closed and her face was filled with a kind of contentment and assurance that I, with all my seminary education, had never come close to knowing. Tears rolled out of the corners of her eyes as she sang.

Charles stood next to her, his eyes closed, his head bowed, and he, too, cried silently. As did everyone around the circle except Eugene and Bethabelle. I cried, too. I don't know why. I hadn't known John Wisdom and probably wouldn't have liked him if I had. I had nothing in common with these people and couldn't even begin to know what their lives had been like.

I guess it was the song. And the woman singing it, maybe. Disfigured at birth, poor, saddled with a family, not to mention a life, that was cruel and violent and often mean. Of all the hymns she might have sung, this one seemed to apply in some special way. I certainly hoped it did for her sake. As if to emphasize that hope, when she came to the chorus, I sang out and the rest of the family joined in, too:

> "When the roll is called up yonder,
> When the roll is called up yonder,
> When the roll is called up yonder,
> When the roll is called up yonder, I'll be there."

We sang it slowly like the prayer that it was, and when it ended, we just let the silence hang there for a moment. Eugene broke first, in anger or grief, I couldn't tell. He just turned and stormed off through the woods, back to his trailer.

The mood was broken and we all climbed into the front and back of the truck and headed back down to the house.

"We'll come back after dark and bury him," Marie said. Another family ritual? "You'll stay and help us eat some of that food you brought," she added as an afterthought. It wasn't a question, it was a statement. I am a Methodist preacher, after all.

Years ago, when my grandparents were young, Methodists weren't allowed to have fun. They went to church on Sunday and then they went out to the farm and ate and talked and they played Rook. The Rook deck didn't have face cards, so it was okay.

Dancing was out. As were movies. Smoking and swearing were not acceptable, and the drinking of strong spirits was anathema. They signed a little card once a year to remind themselves about all the stuff they couldn't or wouldn't do because it was too sinful.

They knew it was sinful because the people who did do these things seemed to be having so much fun.

Things have changed since then. It was a gradual thing. First we stopped signing the cards. Then we stopped hiding the fact that we were doing all these things. A Catholic priest friend of mine used to say that it never shocked him to see Methodists drinking. What shocked him was to see them drinking in front of each other.

Except for the clergy, of course. The more lax the laity got about their own prohibitions, the more strict they seemed to become about those of their pastors. Smoking, drinking, foul language, debt, doubt, and sexual promiscuity were all grounds for expulsion. We clergy learned, and for the most part, accepted, that the things that caused headaches and embarrassment for laypeople caused unemployment and poverty for us. All those sinful, self-destructive, pleasant things that the laity seemed to take for granted were forbidden to the clergy.

All those things save one.

Gluttony.

Parishioners don't just tolerate gluttony in their pastors, they seem to enjoy it. They require it! No meeting ends without brownies and coffee being served first. No group gathers without everyone bringing a covered dish. Whether you come to the church to be married, buried, or baptized, you will be served, but you will have to wait until the dishes are cleared away and the dessert has been set out.

And at all these functions it will be the responsibility of no fewer than eight nor more than fifty persons to comment on how their preacher loves to eat. They will take pride in it as though they created this need in him to constantly fill himself with tuna noodle casserole, shredded chicken sandwiches, cherry pie, green beans with ham chips, lasagna, and iced tea.

Nine out of ten Methodist ministers I have known in my life are fat. Is it any wonder?

I would not call myself svelte, but I have managed to keep things, well, manageable—love handles notwithstanding—by taking small portions and picking at them. And I drink a lot of iced tea and coffee. And I do sit-ups and I walk whenever I get a chance.

So, of course, there was no saying no to Marie Wisdom's invitation to eat with the family.

I was a Methodist preacher. I would eat. It was as simple as that.

I didn't want to eat. I wanted to get out of there and go talk to Les.

No, that's not true either. I didn't really want to talk

to Les. Ray wanted me to talk to Les, and I wanted to get it over with. And I wanted to find Naomi. And I wanted to go home and put a fire in the wood burner in the living room of the parsonage and pour a large shot of Black Jack and put my feet up and think about serious, theological issues that don't really make any difference to anybody but preachers. And then I wanted to talk about them out loud and have Naomi ask me questions and let me explain them to her, not so much for her understanding as for my own.

That's what I wanted.

What I got was tuna noodle casserole. And pie. And coffee laced with chicory so bitter it threatened to grow hair in my mouth.

It started to rain as we ate and the house grew cold. Charles threw some coal into a wood burner and lit it as the house got dark. We talked and listened to the rain on the tin roof and we all got very sad together.

Bethabelle took the kids home to her trailer for their afternoon naps. Charles and Marie drifted away in each others' arms, and I was left with Charlotte, reading her Bible again, and Mother Cleopha.

Mostly I listened and Cleopha talked. I lit my pipe, ignoring the disapproving scowl of Charlotte, and said, "U-huh" and "M-m-m," when it seemed appropriate, and in truth, my mind wandered a bit as she talked. I didn't really know what to say. It was all very sad.

It was sad how this woman and her husband, in their ignorance, had thought that beating their children was the way to show them love.

It was sad how poverty had trapped this whole family and chained them to the coal mine and the slow death that it promised.

It was sad that the only escape from this hard,

miserable life on the mountain was to throw yourself into a bottle, as Big John had, or into religion, as Charlotte had, or at men, as Bethabelle did.

I realized, with a start, that I wasn't saying "U-huh" anymore because Cleopha had stopped talking. She was asleep in her rocker and Charlotte had slipped out, probably back to her half-finished cabin that would, now, never be finished.

I ran through the rain to my veedub, cursing myself for not getting my winter clothes out of storage earlier and cursing Ray for making me promise to talk to Les Eastman. I got in the car, started it, and nearly got stuck getting out of the hollow and back out onto the road.

Twenty-five minutes later, following a map Ray had drawn for me, I was parked in front of Les's trailer. The cans were still piled around the outside, his truck and ORV were parked in back, a ribbon of smoke rose from a soup-can-size chimney in the roof, and the windows were dark.

I knocked at the door, holding my suit coat over my head as though it would protect me from the rain. There was no answer.

"Les?" I called out, knocking again. "It's Pastor Thompson. I thought I'd stop by and see how you were doing." Still no answer.

Screw it. He was gone, out catting around with R. D. Miles, probably. Or up at R.D.'s watching television. Well, Ray, I tried, but he wasn't there.

I got back into the VW and had started the motor when I remembered the jar of corn shine under the seat. Well, it would help him keep the chill out of the trailer, out of his bones. I reached under the seat, pulled it out, and thought of Tanya.

Don't ask me why I thought of her, she just popped

into my mind. Sometimes that happens. Some preachers call it divine inspiration, some call it the subconscious mind. Whichever it was, I nearly dropped the jar of shine, so immediate and clear was the recollection.

I don't remember her last name. I may have never known it. But that afternoon, sitting in the car with the motor running, I remembered her face. She had been sixteen years old, and I had been a freshly graduated seminarian doing my pastoral care training in a large urban hospital. She had been blond and pretty in a cheerleader outfit from one of the local high schools, and I had been in a clerical collar and a lab coat with "chaplain" sewn over the pocket.

She had been dead, on a table in the emergency room, and I had been standing with her parents, holding her mother's hand.

Earlier that night Tanya had been celebrating her school's football victory over a long-standing rival. She had been at a party. She had been drinking with all the other cheerleaders and a couple of the football players and she had passed out on the floor of her friend's family room while her friends got so drunk, they didn't notice or care about what she was doing.

What she was doing was throwing up as she lay passed out on her back on the floor.

She aspirated, choked to death, on her own vomit.

Sitting there in the rain, I remembered the hungry, desperate look in Les's eyes as he tried to answer Ray's questions. And I remembered the smell of the place and Les's dash to the cabinet under the kitchen sink as we left.

The ORV and the truck were parked out back. Smoke was coming out of the chimney. But there were no lights on in the trailer.

I decided to make sure that Les Eastman was not lying on the floor of the trailer aspirating on his own vomit.

The door popped open when I turned the handle and the stink rolled out as it had earlier in the day, only this time it was accompanied and intensified by the heat of a wood-burning stove working overtime.

And it was coal-black dark inside.

11

HAD IT NOT BEEN RAINING, THERE STILL MIGHT HAVE BEEN enough light from the sun to filter through the dirty windows into the trailer, but as it was, I could only make out dim shapes and the outlines of objects in the shadows. The rain sounded like cannon fire hitting the metal roof.

I took a breath of fresh air and stepped inside, fumbling for a light switch next to the door, found it and flipped it several times before I realized that the power was out. Not uncommon this far up the mountain. Les had no doubt jury-rigged a line from a nearby pole, pirating his own electricity. The rain or wind or a falling tree branch had knocked down the line.

A faint glow came from a corner of the tiny living space between the kitchen and the bedroom, and I realized after a moment that it was the wood-burning stove. Les had removed the old gas burner and replaced it with this small, antique, cast-iron wood burner and a coal bucket full of firewood scavenged from the woods. The stove was so hot that it glowed in some areas around the door and where the metal had become weak and thin.

Much hotter and the damned thing would burn up the trailer. Campers like this one were no less flammable than the big luxury models. They were all made of plywood and would burn to the ground in just a few minutes if not watched carefully. Les was taking his life into his hands using a wood burner. But it was cheaper and easier to supply than a gas stove or furnace, and Les was broke.

I knocked on the wall and called out again. "Les? Anyone home?" And got no response.

The smell of old beer, whiskey, cigarette butts, and body odor was nearly a solid presence in the hot trailer, and if Les was okay, or not home at all, I wanted to be out of the place as quickly as I could.

I made a quick circuit of the living area and kitchen, stumbling over chairs and trash that seemed to be thrown around with no concern at all for where they fell. A pile of paperback books, not a stack, a pile, stood beside a leg of the kitchen table. I walked on what felt like a stack of old magazines. Dirty dishes, pots, and pans seemed to be everywhere—the table, the countertops, the floor.

Jesus! How could he live like this? Poor was one thing, but filthy was quite another.

He wasn't passed out at the table or on the floor of the kitchen, so that left the other end of the little trailer. A short hallway led to a single bedroom with a closet to the left and a bathroom—a commode closet, really—on the right, both their doors slid shut. God only knew what kind of mess those two offered. An almost visible cloud of stench gave a very strong hint, however. I decided to check the bedroom first, feeling my way down the hall, tripping over discarded clothing and old shoes.

It looked like he had stood at the foot of the little bed, held his arms out to his sides, and fallen backward across the mattress like a child making snow angels. His arms were straight out from his shoulders, his legs spread wide. That's all I could tell, the room was so dark.

The smell of alcohol was stronger, like alcoholic breath, and I was sweating in my wet summer suit. Now the smell of whiskey vomit attacked me, and even from the bedroom, I could tell that the toilet, a few feet away down the hall, wasn't working any better than the lights. My head began to ache and my stomach rolled from the stink.

"Jesus, Les," I said aloud as I knelt on the side of the bed. First I wanted to see if he was on his back or his stomach. His features weren't discernible in the dark. Then I wanted to check for a pulse, or at least see that he was breathing.

It was easier to check for the pulse first since his wrist was right next to my knee, so I reached down and tried to pick it up. That was my first inclination that things were even worse than they seemed. His arm wouldn't move.

The wrist was bound by what felt like cotton clothesline rope. Nearly blind in the dark, I followed the rope to the corner of the bed and down to the metal leg where it was tied securely. Quickly I knelt back on the bed and reached for his chest to shake him.

"Les! Les!" I shook his chest and he barely moved.

My hand came back wet and my stomach rolled over again.

What in God's name was going on?

I laid my hand back on the wet chest and felt for a pulse. Nothing. His chest felt soft and spongy, and I knew the sticky wetness covering my hand was not whiskey vomit, but blood.

What to do? Get out of here? Call Ray? Les didn't have a phone. And Ray was in Perry doing paperwork. Call the Carmack brothers! Get the ambulance up here. Find someone who knew what they were doing, fast!

I backed my way off the bed and realized, my head spinning and my ears starting to ring, that I still wasn't sure it was Les in that bed. It was someone with Les's build. And that someone was dead. But I wasn't sure it was Les.

I took my disposable lighter from my pocket, swallowed hard, and knelt one more time on the sagging mattress. I extended my hand above where the head was, readied myself to look, and flicked my Bic.

I'm a pipe smoker, so I keep the flame turned up high. There was more than enough light. I wish there hadn't been so much. I wish I hadn't seen so clearly, without some shadow to soften the impact.

What I saw was one yellow, rheumy eye buried in what used to be Les Eastman's face. Had it not been for that eye, I might still have doubted the identity of the corpse, but the eye gave it away. As for the rest of the face, there was nothing left to identify. It had all been turned to a pulpy, bloody mess. Like beefsteak pounded tender with a butcher's meat hammer.

Something in my mind must have registered that the smell I had identified earlier as the bathroom was, in reality, coming from this very room, because it was to the bathroom that I stumbled, my hand cupped over my mouth. All that cake and cobbler and ham and tuna casserole I had eaten at Pitchfork Hollow was now coming back up.

With my other hand I groped in my pocket for my smelling salts. I could not, would not, faint! The thought of lying on the floor in this stinking trailer with Les's corpse in the other room was more than I could handle.

The sliding door to the bathroom was shut and I took my hand from my mouth, stuck my fingers into the recessed handle, and pulled hard. Please, God, let the toilet be working!

It groaned and slid open about two inches.

I got the palm of my hand against the edge and pushed hard. It held for a moment and then gave, sliding into the wall with a crash. I nearly fell, caught myself, and realized in that slow-motion way that you do in times of extreme stress that I was not alone.

Someone was standing in the bathroom.

And he hit me.

I felt his fist slam into my nose, felt my nose break, felt my head hit the wall and bounce me back into him as he tried to slide past me and get to the door.

Funny how a broken nose can make you forget about puking and fainting. Now all I could think about was the blinding pain in my head and the difficulty I was having breathing. And, out of desperation, I hit back.

He was trying to get by me and we were nearly pinned in the hallway shoulder to shoulder, shoving and pushing at each other, so I pulled my left arm forward and shot my elbow back into his middle. The air went out of him with a whoosh and a grunt and he doubled over. That was all it took to break us free of the tight hallway.

Carried backward by the momentum of my elbow, I reeled back toward the bedroom and grabbed a handful of hair to keep from falling. He cried out in pain and came up swinging. My hand wrenched free of his hair and we were face-to-face, but I could still only make out his shape and form. Two blows caught me on the shoulders and hurt but didn't do any damage, but a third glanced off my broken nose, sent pain raining through my head and set my eyes to watering again.

I reached out blindly and grabbed what felt like bib overalls, but he pulled away and I felt the fabric tearing until I was falling forward with nothing but air in my hand. I heard his footsteps move quickly toward the front of the trailer, and I tried to see what he looked like as he moved toward the door, but my eyes were blurred from the pain in my nose. I couldn't crawl fast enough to catch him, which was stupid. I should have just lain there. Played dead.

He must have seen me crawling toward him, because he stopped before he got to the door, and I heard him walking back toward me. Then all I heard was the sound of my own skull banging against my brain as he hit me on the top of my head with something big and hard.

In the movies people get hit over the head and they just fall down. Plop! But having been on the receiving end of one of those hits, let me tell you that it doesn't work quite that easily. Not nearly that easily.

It felt like someone had driven a pike down through my skull, into my shoulders and spine, all the way to the small of my back. My neck compressed and the muscles seemed to explode, my head felt like my brain would explode out of my ears, and my forehead seemed to fly off into space.

Everything started going around in circles. Bright lights flashed. A loud popping sound went off in my ears. I threw up. And then I fell, slowly from my knees to the floor.

I remember thinking, "Now he'll dump me in the crapper. I'll die just like Big John Wisdom. Covered in lime and shit."

And then there was just the briefest flash of clarity and I realized that I had stumbled on something that might help Ray find the killer, if only I could think of what it was.

But I didn't really care. I just wanted to sleep.

Light flashed, exploding into the core of my brain.

It was raw and persistent, burning through my eyelids and setting off a bomb between my temples each time it went off.

"Mother, for God's sake! He's comin' around again. You want him to be blind?"

It was Ray's voice and I tried to open my eyes again just as the light exploded, setting off a rocket that ricocheted through my skull, landed behind the bridge of my nose, and settled there to burn itself out. I must have groaned.

"There! He's hurtin'. You happy now?" Ray again.

"He's fine," May June said, petulantly. "Just got a bad knock on the head and a broken nose. Doc says he'll be up and about by tomorrow mornin'. I'm done anyhow. I got to get these to the camera shop before they close. Pete said he'd have 'em back by tomorrow if I got them in tonight."

I heard her walk across the floor and go out the door.

"Is it safe to come out?" I asked, my eyes still closed. Each word seemed to echo inside my head, and I sounded like I had a head cold.

"Come on out," Ray said. "She's gone."

I opened my eyes slowly and looked around at the antiseptic hospital room. Perry Memorial Hospital, Perry, Kentucky. It was a D.O. hospital, most of the doctors trained at Ohio University in Athens, Ohio, especially to practice medicine in Appalachia. I'd always shied away from D.O.s in the past, preferring M.D.s. I assumed they were the real thing.

But the osteopaths in Perry were the best, most gentle, cheapest, most dedicated doctors I'd ever come across. They practiced medicine for the love of it. It was still an art for them. Most of them were younger than me, and nearly half were women.

"How you feel?" Ray asked. He was standing between the bed and the door of the room, smiling.

"Like shit," I said, meaning it. "Can I get a drink of water?"

He upended the blue plastic pitcher by my bed, and about a teaspoon of water dribbled into the glass. "Nope," he said, looking at it. "Guess I drank it all."

"Was it good?"

He shrugged. "It was somethin' to do. Tell you what. You sit here and rest and I'll run down to the cafeteria and get you some more, then I'll explain how you got here, and you explain why. How's that sound?"

"Peachy."

He smiled without showing his teeth and walked out the door. Just beyond the door he told someone, "He's awake and talkin'."

The door flew open and Naomi flew in.

Up until that moment my head and neck hurt, my

hair was shaved on the top of my head, and I could feel a bandage up there. My nose and cheeks were covered with a bandage, and my entire face ached. My arms, shoulders, and ribs were tender, I had to pee, and I was nauseated. Magically, at the sight of her, it all disappeared.

We both spoke at the same time: "I'm sorry . . ."

Then she was sitting on the edge of the bed, touching me, caressing me, gliding her fingers gently across my bandaged face, crying, and I started to cry, too. Part of it was the pain and the fatigue and just feeling sorry for myself, generally. And part of it was my relief at seeing her okay.

"I was camping," she sniffled. "I couldn't bear the thought of you being mad at me. I needed to get away, to think about things."

"I tried to apologize," I interrupted her. "I tried to call you about a thousand times."

"I've decided, Dan. I don't want to lose you. I'll do whatever you want. You want to get married? We'll do it. Tonight!"

God, how I loved this woman. She meant what she said. She'd do it if I said that's what I wanted. But her camping trip had given me some time to think, too. And John Wisdom's funeral had had a funny effect on me.

"That why you're so wet?" I asked. "Camping in the rain?"

She looked down at her damp clothes, ran her fingers through her wet hair. "I was just coming in the cabin when my phone rang. It was Ray saying you were on your way here." She took my hand in both of hers, held it tightly.

"Dan, I meant what I said. I will . . ."

"You'll work for your daddy and take care of him

and his boys as long as he needs you. Then we'll get married and have a bunch of little preachers," I said, using Ray's favorite expression for my future children.

"But I thought—"

"I was horny and tired and an asshole," I said.

Yes, she would do it. And when her daddy finally did die, she would always wonder if it was her leaving that sent him to an early grave. Her daddy didn't hate me, but he didn't have much use for me either. No doubt he thought she could do better, as all fathers thought of the men and boys their daughters brought home. No, let her take care of her father. He had maybe a year, eighteen months to live. "We have a whole lifetime ahead of us," I said. "Give Hebrew what he needs."

If it was possible for her face to soften more than it had upon seeing me in the hospital bed, it did then. And then, as quickly, her eyes brightened and she reached under the covers. "I was thinkin' maybe of givin' you what you need . . . Reverend Thompson."

Hospital gowns are amazing things. Usually I complain about them being immodest and humiliating. At the moment, it was merely convenient. The opening in the back was spread open and she snaked her hand under it and explored across my chest and down my stomach. "Thought maybe a little therapy might be in order," she said, huskily. "That is, if you're feelin' up to it."

Her hand grazed my pubic hair and began to delicately explore farther south. Oh, yes, I was, in spite of the other problems with my battered body at that moment, up to it. So to speak.

So, naturally, the door crashed open.

"Hope I'm not interrupting anything important," said a tall, attractive woman in a white lab coat with a stethoscope hanging from the pocket. "You checkin' his pulse, there, Naomi?"

Naomi turned scarlet and pulled her hand quickly from under the sheet. "Hi, Dr. Markle," she said.

"Oh, Lord God," the doctor said, taking my wrist in one hand and watching her watch with the other. "We go to grade school together, we play Barbie dolls together, we date the same boys in school, and she won't even call me by my first name." She looked at Naomi. "You gonna introduce us or do I have to do everything in this hospital?"

"Reverend Dan Thompson," Naomi said to me, then turned to the doctor. "Dr. Louise Markle."

"Lu," the doctor said, dropping my wrist and shining a light into my eyes. Her eyes were green and I could see red hair trying to escape from the scarf she had tied around her head. Her complexion was like milk and she had a cute overbite. "How you feel?"

I told her I felt awful, and she said that's to be expected after what I had been through. She also told me that there wasn't much they could do for me that I couldn't do for myself at home. A broken nose, she said, would give my face more character, and the orange-size lump on my head would go down in a few days. "Whoever hit you should choose his wood more carefully. From the splinters in your skull, I'd say it was pine. Oak or hickory woulda done more damage. Come back in about a week and I'll take the stitches out," she said. "Or May June can do it. Only took half a dozen, and May June's about the best granny woman in the county."

Fifty years ago granny women had mixed fundamentalist religion, mountain superstition, and herbal remedies, treating everything from broken bones to depression, with mixed results. May June was of the new breed of granny women who had forgone the fundamentalist religion and superstition, improved the herbal remedies, and took midwifing and first aid courses at the hospital. Her granny bag, as she called it, could damned near outfit a complete surgical theater, and she had delivered more babies than most city obstetricians.

Lu Markle asked me my name, address, and my mother's maiden name. She asked me how many fingers she was holding up and if I had insurance. When I got all the answers right she winked at Naomi.

"Fit as a fiddle. We'll keep him overnight and you can take him home in the morning. Keep him quiet for a few days, he'll get dizzy easy. Other than that, he'll be fine. Nothin' important is broken."

She patted me gently on the shoulder and breezed out of the room as quickly as she had come in.

"Ain't she somethin'?" Naomi asked. "She was always the smart one in school. She was a year ahead of me and I wanted to be just like her, but I wasn't smart enough to be a doctor."

"You'll do fine," I said. How Naomi Taylor could want to be like anyone but Naomi Taylor was beyond me. "Besides, I like your examination better than hers."

"Oh, really?" she said, the gleam coming back into her eyes. "Well, maybe we should—"

The door flew open again and Naomi sighed.

LeRoy Whiteker, tall, dark, and handsome as ever, walked in wearing a safari jacket and khaki pants. To the extent that Perry could be called urban, LeRoy was Perry's yuppie. He was also the sole proprietor of Whiteker Funeral Home, a doting father of three, and so in love with his wife, Andrea, that he wouldn't even talk about other women, much less look at them. Of course, with a wife like Andrea, who would? She was nearly as tall as her husband's six feet, blond and as regal in bearing as she was loving in manner. A former Miss Eastern Kentucky, she wore miniskirts like most of the men in the county wore bib overalls—comfortably and unself-consciously—as though she were born in them.

LeRoy took out his key ring, fumbled with it for a moment, and came up with a small tape measure. He walked directly to my side and extended the tape across my shoulders, down my legs, up my side, smiling like a maniac.

"Put that away," I told him. "I'm not dead yet."

He looked up in mock surprise. "Oh, hell. And I thought you were going to be a paying customer. I got the wood ordered, and Marcus is ready to start sawin' and nailin' as soon as I call him with the measurements."

"Just put my golf clubs in it," I said. LeRoy had spent most of September trying to teach me how to play golf, and it had been like trying to teach a cat to bark.

"Too late," he said. "I already burned 'em."

We both laughed, I winced with the pain it caused, and we laughed harder.

"Are you guys talkin' about a coffin?" Naomi asked, unbelieving. "Are you? I don't believe this. He nearly died. It ain't nothin' to joke about!" She rounded on LeRoy. "What is this, some kind of sick mortician humor?"

"Funeral director," LeRoy corrected her, and we both managed to control our laughter. "How you feelin' there, big guy?" he asked me.

"I break out tomorrow," I said. "Soon as I prove I've got insurance."

"Good." He looked to Naomi. "You need any help gettin' this no-account back home?"

She shook her head.

"Okay, then," he said. "I guess I better run. I understand they brought a payin' customer in with you. Can't keep him waitin'." He headed for the door and I stopped him.

"How much?" I asked him.

He looked down at the safari jacket and shrugged. "L.L. Bean catalogue. Summer clearance."

"How much?"

"Hundred and a quarter. I got jungle boots and a bush hat, too. But Andrea says that's overkill. What do you think?"

"I think it looks like you overdosed on testosterone," I said, smiling.

He smiled back. "Good. That's the look I was tryin' for. Andrea can't keep her hands off me when I wear it. You want me to order one for you?"

"What, and have Andrea climbing all over me, too? My woman's broad-minded, but not that broad-minded," I said, winking at Naomi.

"Your loss," he said, without missing a beat. "See ya." He stepped out the door and was gone.

"You'd like that, wouldn't you?" Naomi said, leaning down and resting her chin on my chest. I didn't have the heart to tell her it hurt like hell.

"Like what?" I asked, innocently.

"Havin' Andrea Whiteker climbin' all over you," she said, smiling.

"The woman does have a way of generating male fantasies," I said wistfully. "If only there were something we could do. That crack on the head, I guess. We need to find something to straighten me out."

Naomi giggled and reached under the sheet again. "Oh, I think I can straighten you out."

The door flew open yet again and Ray walked in with two blue plastic pitchers.

"Visitin' hours is over. Sorry, Naomi, but we got business to attend to here. The game's afoot."

Naomi said, "Shit," and withdrew her hand from the sheet as she stood. "We could get more privacy on the square in front of the courthouse." She gathered her purse, keys, and denim jacket. "We'll pick this up later," she said, and left.

Ray watched her go. "Did I interrupt somethin'?" he asked me when the door eased itself closed.

"Ray! In a hospital room? With me in the shape I'm in?"

He looked around the room innocently. "I don't know. Hospital rooms ain't so bad. One time me and May June—"

"Ray, I don't think I want to hear this."

"Yeah? Well, okay. Guess we better get down to business." He poured us both a glass of ice water and took out his notebook. "Okay. Now, you tell me everything right up to the part where you got knocked out, and then I'll take it from there."

I sipped my water and began talking. There was something. Something I needed to tell him. Something I had thought of just before I lost consciousness.

But I couldn't remember what it was.

12

It took about twenty minutes to tell Ray what had happened up at Les Eastman's trailer. At least what I could remember of it. He didn't talk, just sat there listening, smoking, writing in his little notebook, and drinking ice water.

When I finished, he nodded his head and dropped his cigarette into the bottom of a Styrofoam cup with several others, soaking in water. "Sounds about right," he said, closing his notebook. He got up and poured us both some more water. "I gotta pee," he said, walking into my toilet room. "You didn't get a good look at the guy?" he called out over the sound of his cascading water.

"It was dark and he was beating the shit out of me, Ray," I said, to answer his question.

"How big was he?"

"Big enough to beat the shit out of me," I said. "We were both crowded into the bathroom and the hall. He seemed about my size, but I don't know. He could have been bigger or smaller, a little either way."

The toilet flushed and Ray came out of the room, zipping up his fly. He sat down again. "Well," he said, beginning his cigarette ritual again. "It was R.D. what found you. Said he was comin' down to check on ol' Les. Says he knew Les was drinkin' more and more and wanted to make sure he was okay. He says he saw your car there and the door to the trailer bangin' open and he came in and found you. Found Les, too. Put you in the car and drove you to Baird. May June looked after you until Gilbert and Gaylord could get you into the unit and get you here."

"Tell May June I appreciate her help," I said, meaning every word. Granny woman indeed.

"She said to tell you the same thing," he said, smiling. "Says them pictures of you with your head all caved in is just what she'll need to get the Administrative Council to give some of that money toward startin' a medical clinic in Baird." He chuckled and shook his head. "That woman is a pistol."

"You check out R.D.'s story?" I asked.

Ray nodded and drew on his cigarette. "Yup. Checks out according to his wife, and she didn't seem to be lyin' so's I could tell. Says he was up to the house gettin' underfoot, and she told him to go check on Les. Says he left the house about five-fifteen. Found you and Les and arrived in Baird about five-fifty. Couldn't do it much faster, so he's tellin' the truth."

I sighed and sank back into the bed.

"Yeah, me too," he said. "I was kinda hopin' this thing would be wrapped up by now. I figured it was Les what done in Big John."

"What happened to Les?" I asked. "I know he's dead, but what exactly?"

"Someone tied him to the bed and beat him to death with a piece of kindlin' wood from the coal bucket. He wasn't as lucky as you. They used hardwood on him. Then they ransacked the trailer and set the wood burner to cookin'. Probably planned to burn the place down and hide their trail. Wouldn't have been enough left of ol' Les to pick up with a Kleenex if they'd done it." He smiled and looked at the bandage across my nose. "Looks like you got there just in time."

"Whatever I can do to help," I said.

"Heard you pull up and hid in the crapper. You surprised him and he coldcocked you and got away. You figure you marked him any in the tussle?"

I probed my cheeks and nose with my fingers, wincing. "I think I tore his overalls. The front pockets on the chest. That's about it. He may be bruised in the chest area. I got in a good lick with an elbow."

"Well, torn overalls don't narrow it down much," he said. "And I can't ask every man in the county to drop his pants and open his shirt so's I can check for bruises." He stood to leave.

"Wait a minute," I said, trying to sit up and feeling dizzy with the effort. "What's next? Where do we go from here?"

"Well," he said, leaning against the door. "You go to sleep and then home tomorrow morning and lay in bed for a couple of days. And I go talk to Mr. Leather, Price Deaver, and his pals. Elias and a couple of the other deputies is lookin' for him right now."

"The guy who was up on the mountain ORV'ing on Sunday," I said, remembering. Adam had told me about him.

"Yeah. Big John met someone up there, I'm bettin'. And I'm also bettin' it was Price Deaver."

"Why?" was all I could think of to ask.

"Well, Elias says they been suspectin' Pricey boy of dealin' pot for some time now, but they can't pin anything on him on accounta his daddy's on city council here in Perry and they need about a truckload of hard evidence to put away the son of a councilman." He smiled. "See, city council sets the salaries and what have you of the sheriff's deputies, there bein' no city police in Perry."

"You think Big John was selling pot to Price Deaver?" I asked. My eyes were getting heavy and all this talk was beginning to wear me down.

Ray nodded. "An' Price was bringin' it into town and sellin' it. It's a big mountain. Lots of things could be grown up there and no one would ever know."

"But what could it have to do with Les? Why kill Les?"

Ray shrugged. "And why torture him first? And why ransack his trailer? What were they lookin' for and why? What did Les know and how?" He sighed. "This things got more questions than Dear Abby, don't it?"

"I want to go with you, Ray," I said, feeling myself dropping off to sleep. "I want to see Price Deaver face-to-face."

"You think you'll know if he's the one whipped your ass?"

"Can't hurt to try," I said.

"Well, we'll see when we find him and how you're feelin'—"

The door burst open and whacked Ray in the back, and a little, bony black woman in a white uniform came in. Her name tag said Ruth Lee, LPN. "Raymond Hall! What are you doin' here? Don't you know it's after visitin' hours?"

"I'm not visitin', Ruthy," Ray said in his own

defense. "I'm an officer of the law and I'm conductin' an investigation."

She strode over to the tray table beside my bed and picked up the Styrofoam cup, made a face. "And smokin', too! In a hospital room. My Lord, my Lord, just who do you think you are? What'd you take the policy book home and study it so's you could break all the rules in one visit?"

"I had to talk to him—"

She grabbed his arm and ushered him out of the room. She, the bony little black lady, ushering big Ray Hall out like an errant schoolboy. "Now, you go on home before I call May June and tell her what you been up to and she puts a whippin' on you."

Ray winked at me and disappeared out the door. She continued to mutter and sputter as she took my temperature, blood pressure, pulse, and looked into my eyes. "Big, full-growed man like that ought to know better. Messin' with my patients. Why, I never seen him act this way before. Gettin' awful uppity since they give him that badge, you ask me. How you feelin', darlin'?"

It took me a moment to realize she was talking to me. I yawned. "Tired. And I have to pee."

"Well, it's no wonder. Get all beat up the way you are and then him in here a-botherin' you, drinkin' ice water by the pitcherful. Can you make it to the bathroom by yo'se'f?"

I said that I could and did. The dizziness wasn't there every time I moved now. When I came out of the lavatory she was still puttering around the room, touching things, straightening and talking. The bed looked like no one had ever been in it.

"I'll have to wake you up every hour or so just to

check on you," she said. "I'm sorry, but that's the way it is with head trauma."

"I'll be fine," I said, climbing into the bed and starting to drift off as soon as my head hit the pillow.

"'Course you will. Ruth Lee, LPN, be lookin' after you now." And she was gone, flipping out the lights as she went.

And, of course, I couldn't sleep.

I was so tired, my eyelids felt like anvils, but I couldn't sleep. Too much had happened. What was it I wanted to tell Ray? I couldn't remember, and the more I tried to remember, the further it seemed to elude me. I let it go, hoping to catch a glimpse of it as it danced out at the edge of my mind.

Les came to mind. Poor Les. Broke, drunk, and then beaten, tortured to death in his own home. Dirty and stinking and awful as it was, it was his home. His castle. I wondered what would happen to it now. Did Les have kids who would want it? Probably not. No kids, or if he did, they sure as hell wouldn't want it. No one wanted anything to do with Les. No one except R.D., his boyhood friend. R.D. seemed to understand him, wanted to protect him when everyone else had given up.

Once, when I was doing a stint in youth ministry right after seminary, I took a group of high school kids to New Mexico. We worked at an Indian reservation for a week, repairing the roof of an adobe house. A shack, really. It belonged to a family of six named Ironjaw.

The father, Clarence Ironjaw, sat in the yard and smoked and drank and watched us work on his house and never lifted a finger to help, never got out of his chair, never moved, even to say hello.

One evening the kids in my work group were talking about it. How could Clarence just sit there and let us work on his house and do nothing to help? Why wasn't he working? Why didn't he go out and get a job to help get his family off welfare?

One of the work camp coordinators, a born-again college kid, answered some of their questions: Clarence had worked at construction for several years, traveling around New Mexico with a crew. Then he had fallen off a roof and broken both his legs. While he was laid up with his legs in casts, the crew replaced him and moved on. He had tried to get work since then but had failed.

The coordinator explained about prejudice and broken promises, but his explanations fell on deaf ears. The wealthy white kids from my church couldn't comprehend it. Why didn't he get a job at McDonald's or something? How could he just sit there?

"Why don't you ask him?" the coordinator said. "I'll be Clarence. Go ahead, ask me."

So they asked him, role-playing the game. And they got nowhere. Every time they made a suggestion about how Clarence could better his lot in life, the coordinator, playing the role of Clarence, came up with an excuse. Some were good, some were obvious pretext.

The kids got mad. "You're just lazy," one of the boys spat out, feeling full of his own righteousness and the American Dream that still lay spread out before him.

And then one of the girls said something so beautiful, so sensitive, so unbelievably right, that I heard in it the voice of God. "No," she said to the boy, her eyes full of sudden comprehension. "Don't you see? You're treating him like his problem is that he's broke. That's not his problem. His problem is that he's broken."

I nearly cried from the beauty of it.

That was Les. He hadn't been broke. He had been broken.

Oh, Les. What did you know? What did you see or have or hear that they wanted it so bad, they would do that to you?

Throughout all of this, Ruth Lee, LPN, came into the room twice more to check my vital signs and leave. She did so quietly and efficiently, and I pretended to be dozing on my right side, my back to the door. I probably did doze a little, but it was a brief and fitful kind of sleep.

Now she entered again, and I, once again, ignored her. I didn't feel much like talking. Let her do her work and leave me in peace.

I felt her hand, cooler this time, on my forehead. Then she picked up my left wrist and held it a moment. She must have been tired, because she sat or put her knee on the side of the bed and I could feel the mattress shift.

That's what I had done at Les's trailer. I had put my knees on the bed to feel for his pulse. While someone waited in the dark bathroom . . .

The weight shifted again and I realized that Ruth Lee, LPN, was much too small to make the bed shift that much. And why was her hand so cold this time? Was it the same hand?

I let my eyes drift around the side of the room, seeking out something I could use as a weapon. Nothing. Maybe the telephone. I had seen a man in the emergency room of a hospital, once, who had been beaten nearly to death with one. But I couldn't reach it quickly enough. In my condition, quick action was out of the question.

I felt hot breath on my neck and ear, and sweat broke out on my forehead. Whoever it was was moving in close, no doubt trying to keep me quiet.

"How's the patient doing?" a voice said into my ear.

"Jesus! You scared the shit out of me!" I flopped over on my back.

Naomi jumped back a little and then reached her hand out to cover my mouth. "Sh-sh-sh!" she said, holding a finger across her lips. "There are sick people in this hospital and it's after midnight. You want to wake everyone else up?"

"What are you doing here?" I asked, still surprised to see her. "And how did you get in?"

She reached under the covers with her left hand and started unbuttoning her shirt with the other. "I got ways," she said, mysteriously. "Besides, it's time for your therapy." Her hand found what it was looking for and I sprang to attention. Suddenly I wasn't tired anymore.

I reached up and tried to help her unbutton the shirt. She wasn't, I noticed, wearing a bra, and her nipples were straining the fabric. I longed to feel those nipples pressing against my chest. "I'll do it," she whispered. "You just relax." Now both of her hands were busy, one with me, the other with her buttons.

I nodded toward the door. "What about . . ."

"Don't worry," she said. "This won't take long."

Now, I know that the possibility of being caught is supposed to be a big turn-on for a lot of people, but for a minister, it is a nightmare. Ministers don't only put on their best clothes to go out in public, they put on their best characters. Ministers do not pass gas, belch, tell dirty jokes, smoke, or drink in public, much less do the big dirty. And while a hospital room isn't exactly public, it's far from private.

Naomi slipped out of her shirt and blue jeans—clean and dry, I noticed—leered at me, and ducked her head under the sheets. She found me with her mouth and I gasped.

I kept my eyes on the door and—give the girl her due—there came a minute there when I no longer cared if Ruth Lee, LPN, came in and caught us. Hell, I didn't even care if my entire congregation, the Durel County Sheriff's Department, and the Perry High School band all marched in together and caught us.

By the time she slithered up out of the sheets and straddled me, rocking gently back and forth, I was oblivious to everything outside of my bed. I pressed the button that raised my head and kept it pressed until my face was buried between Naomi's breasts.

My broken nose complained bitterly once or twice, but I didn't care. Naomi's rocking became more like bouncing and she gritted her teeth to keep from crying out, as did I. When we both finally came it was in the middle of a fit of giggles from her and groans from me.

The mixture of pain and pleasure was, well, interesting to say the least.

She rolled off me, ran into the lavatory, and came back out almost as quickly. "Ray says you may go with him tomorrow," she said, slipping on her blue jeans and shirt. She kissed me on the cheek and headed for the door. "Be careful. Price Deaver's a dick."

No sooner had she left than Ruth Lee, LPN, came in, flipped on a night-light, and I breathed a sigh of relief. Timed perfectly, I thought. Now I really was drowsy.

The little black nurse checked all my vital signs again, looked into my eyes with a little flashlight, and walked around the bed, tucking it in and talking the whole time under her breath. I kept my eyes half-closed, watching her all the time.

Finally she stood back, her hands on her hips, and surveyed the room around her. She looked down, stooped, and when she stood back up again she was holding a pair of women's panties. She shook her head, wadded the panties into a ball, and stuck them in her pocket.

"I thought that child was never gonna leave," she said. Then, as she turned off the night-light, "You think you be able to finally go to sleep now, Reverend?" And she, too, was gone.

I'll be damned.

Ray was shaking my arm, making my head rattle and my face hurt. "Dan! Dan! Come on, boy. We got that little fucker."

"What time is it?"

"Ten after six. Come on. We got him."

"Got who?"

Ray went to the closet and started throwing clothes at me. They weren't the tan suit I'd been wearing when I came in. "Where'd you get these?" I asked, still trying to wake up.

"May June went over to your place and picked them up. Come on, will ya? Elias and the boys tracked Price Deaver down. He's at his girlfriend's place over on Railroad Street."

"By the tracks?" I asked. "What's a rich kid doing with a girlfriend from The Tracks?" The Tracks was a notorious stretch of shacks and shanties along the railroad on the west side of town. It was Perry's version of a combat zone, slum, high-crime area. It was the Dodge City of Durel County.

"Who knows? Maybe he's flauntin' her poverty in front of his daddy. Maybe she's a powerhouse in the sack. Maybe he likes her. Who cares?"

I pulled on my pants and started to put on my shoes. I was moving slowly, trying to keep the dizziness from coming back.

"Put them on in the car!" Ray said, grabbing my arm and propping me up. "Come on."

"Coffee."

"In the Jeep."

"I gotta check out," I protested. "Pay the bill."

"I already took care of it," he said, dragging me down the hall. "We'll settle up later."

Elias Knowly was the big, military-looking deputy sheriff in charge while Sheriff Fine was out of town. Elias had gone to school with Naomi and they had dated. He had been captain of the football team, she was captain of the cheerleaders. She had gone off to college and he had gone to the state police academy and come home and married the first girl who fell in love with his uniform. He was a nice guy but a little slow between the ears. He introduced me to Deputy Merchison, who looked like he was about sixteen years old, and Deputy Karn, who looked like she should have been slinging hash at a truck stop. All three of the deputies wore starched, no-nonsense, Smokey the Bear–style uniforms.

"So, what have we got?" Ray asked.

Deputy Karn reached into her shirt pocket and produced a joint. "Genuine article," she said, smiling.

"Boy I busted said he bought it from your friend in there about four hours ago. I been sittin' on this place since I called you, and ain't no one been in or out."

"How many inside?" Ray asked.

"Price Deaver and his girl. Another girl and two other guys. His buddies and a tramp they picked up at the Star Bar, probably. My source says that's where they were earlier." I got the impression that Deputy Karn enjoyed using police talk. My source. That kind of thing.

"Okay," Ray said. "I guess we got probable cause, so we don't need a warrant."

Deputy Merchison reached in his shirt pocket and pulled out a piece of paper, waved it in front of Ray. "I woke up Judge Peeler, just in case."

Ray smiled and sipped his coffee. "Okay. What we got here is a simple pot bust. I don't want nobody shootin' nobody. Y'all got that?"

Elias looked hurt. "We done this before, Ray. You don't have to treat us like we's children."

"I know, Eli. I just want to hit 'em hard and fast. I got to talk to that Deaver boy and I don't want him dead. He's probably asleep with his pants around his ankles anyhow." Ray reached into the Jeep and pulled the old single-shot shotgun out from under a blanket with his tools and spare. He broke it open, slid a shell into the breech, and held two others in his left hand. The other officers checked their revolvers. "Everyone ready?" They nodded. He turned to me. "You stay out here until we call you." I nodded. This was way out of my league.

Ray told Karn and Merchison to cover the back. He and Elias would take the front door. They would go in first and call out when the two deputies were to enter.

I sat in the Jeep drinking coffee and smoking my

pipe. The cool morning air was clearing my head, and it was easier to move without getting dizzy. I took the packing out of my nose and reduced the bandage down to a neat little patch. My cheeks were still tender and swollen, but not as bad as last night. The bump on my head was already shrinking. The human body is truly an amazing thing.

Ray and Elias waited a few minutes for the deputies to make it around back and then Ray hit the door of the little house with his size-fourteen foot. The door caved in and the two big men followed it. I could hear them screaming as they went. "Police! Everybody stay where you are! Get down!" Then another door crashing in, Deputy Karn, no doubt, and more voices, but I couldn't make out what they were saying.

Then, as I watched the house, something moved at the side of the building like it was falling and I heard an "Oomph" as it hit the ground. It was human. Someone had slipped out a side window.

I scrunched down in the seat as far as I could and watched the figure move furtively from one car to the next, making his way from the house. In a minute he would be next to the Jeep. Light reflected off the hardware on his chest, and I realized he was wearing bib overalls without a shirt or shoes. No leathers, but then he wouldn't sleep in leathers, would he?

I tried to look closer, but it was too dark. Was this Price Deaver? Was this the same man I had met in Les Eastman's trailer? No way to tell. He was big, but he was also doubled over, trying to avoid being seen. He was wearing overalls, but I couldn't tell if they were torn or not. Was there a little flap hanging down in the front?

No matter. He had come from the little house and he was getting away and no one seemed to know about him. I reached under the blanket in the back of the Jeep and fumbled around until I found what I was looking for. A tire iron.

Slipping from my seat in the Jeep, I put my sneakered feet quietly onto the gravel and crouched down, duckwalking to the rear fender. He came at a dead run, almost fully erect, no doubt thinking he was far enough from the house to not be seen.

I swung the tire iron like a baseball bat right at where I figured his stomach would be. But he wasn't fully erect yet. The iron bar hit him across the chest and knocked him flat on his back. He grabbed his chest and began to roll around, on the ground, groaning and moaning, gasping for the breath that I had knocked out of him.

I tossed the bar back into the Jeep and stood too quickly and let my imagination start thinking about what it must have felt like to get smashed in the chest with an iron bar, and I started to get dizzy again. I slid down the side of the Jeep and leaned against the wheel, feeling frantically for my smelling salts. Nothing. Clean clothes. I gulped the night air and shook my head. It helped a little, but he was still groaning there, and that wasn't helping at all.

"Here he is," I heard Deputy Karn call out. "Looks like the reverend got him." She stepped over me, handcuffed the man on the ground, and said, "Well, Pricey, you oughta watch where you're goin'. Looks like you run inta somethin'." Then I felt her hand on the back of my neck and the other hand pulling my knees. I pivoted on my butt and the next thing I knew, I was lying down in the gravel and my feet were up on the Jeep. "There you go," she said cheerily. "Gotta keep that blood runnin' to your head. You was lookin' a little peaked."

Thirty minutes later we were sitting in the sheriff's office, drinking his coffee. Elias and the deputies were booking the crowd from the railroad shack, and Ray and I were smoking and watching the sun come up over the mountains.

"How you feelin'?" Ray asked.

"Like I got out of bed at six o'clock to smash some guy's chest," I replied, testily.

"You didn't break nothin'," Ray said, chuckling. "His overall pockets was full of grass. All you did was knock the wind outa him." He chuckled again.

"I could have killed him, Ray," I said. "Wouldn't that look great on my résumé. 'Methodist Pastor Beats Councilman's Son to Death in Drug Raid.' "

"Hey," Ray said, ignoring me. "That just reminds me. You know how they're always sayin' that on television during football games? How someone got the wind knocked out of him? Well, I heard this ol' boy once say that's because they can't say shit on television. So when they say wind, what they really mean is shit. How about that?" Ray affected a deep announcer's voice. "No, Dick, he's not hurt bad, he just got the wind knocked out of him. That's right, Dave, in this high Denver altitude the players have to struggle not to lose their wind too early in the game." He chuckled again.

"Well," he said, draining his coffee cup. "Let's have a talk with our boy."

13

The Durel County courthouse sits dead center in the town of Perry, the county seat. It's a big, pre–Civil War, three-story brick building with white pillars, and it stands in the middle of a park complete with cannons, war memorials, picnic tables, park benches, sycamore trees, and old men telling lies to each other.

It has a different kind of beauty each season of the year, and I'm always taken with it. Norman Rockwell would have loved it.

The Sheriff's Department is on the first floor in the back end of the courthouse, near the parking lot and the county garage where they store and service the cruisers.

The county jail is upstairs from the sheriff's office. It was remodeled from its Civil War state, not a minute too soon in 1980. The six cells are modern in every way except for the bars themselves, which are the same ones that came with the building. There isn't an interrogation room as such. The muster/meeting/conference/visiting room stands in on those few occasions when someone has to be interrogated, which Ray says is about once every ten years.

Mostly, people in Durel County are proud of their crimes. The only interrogation that takes place is something like this: "Okay, Bubba, you wanna tell us what the hell happened?" Usually that is enough to send the suspect into a torrent of explanations and rationalizations about why he was perfectly justified in shooting, stabbing, burning down, robbing, and/or beating the hell out of something or someone else.

Price Deaver was not so forthcoming.

He was sitting in one of the molded plastic chairs in the visiting room, trying to get the ink off of his fingers with a moist towelette when we walked in. Looking at me, he sneered, threw down the paper, and pointed at me.

"I don't know who you are, mister, but you're a dead man," he said, pulling his chin down and rolling his eyes up. He had seen Malcolm McDowall in *A Clockwork Orange.*

Ray chuckled and pulled out a chair across from Deaver. "Well, Pricey, this here is the Reverend, that is the Late Reverend Mister Daniel Thompson. He's the fella what clotheslined you."

Deaver's eyes sprang open in surprise. "Goddamn! What kinda preacher'd do a thing like that? Look what you done to me!" He pulled the front of his bib overalls down and showed an ugly bruise about three inches wide that ran across the middle of his chest. "You coulda killed me." The overalls, I noticed, were not torn at the top.

"Well, he's sorry, Pricey. He really is. But then you shouldn'ta taken off like you done. What'd you do, hop out the crapper window?" Ray took out his notebook.

"Fuck you, pig. I don't have to talk to you."

This kid either didn't know Ray Hall or he had the biggest set of balls in the county.

Ray shook his head and smiled. "The last youngun said that to me, I had to straighten him out a might."

"Fuck you. You lay a hand on me and my daddy'll cut your pecker off."

"Elias Mirandize you, did he? He tell you your rights?"

Deaver smirked. "I don't need some redneck cop to tell me my rights. I know what my rights are, and right now I got the right to tell you to go fuck yourself. I got nothin' to say to you."

Ray licked the point of his pencil and examined it like it was the most interesting thing in the world. He was holding it in his right hand. Without taking his eyes off the pencil, he shot his left hand out, across the table, and slammed the heel of it into Deaver's bruised chest so hard, it knocked him off his chair. Price Deaver screamed and grasped his chest while I hurried around the table and helped him back into his chair. I shot Ray a look that said I didn't approve, and he rolled his eyes and shrugged his shoulders in a way that said he didn't give a shit.

"That was to get your attention," Ray said, still examining the end of his pencil. "No, you don't have to talk to me. All you got to do is listen. After I said my peace, you might decide to change your mind. Maybe not."

Deaver boiled and pouted and clutched his chest. But he listened.

"Now," Ray went on. "What we got here is a bust for possession of a controlled substance with intent to sell. We also got possession and sale. We also got you playin' tickle butt with a minor girl. Oh, you didn't know she was a minor? Well, you do now. You been dippin' your wick in that, you're gonna be in more trouble than a one-legged man in an ass-kickin' contest."

Deaver was still pouting and rubbing his chest, but he looked a little worried now. Not so defiant.

"What's your daddy gonna say he finds out you been stickin' it to some little white trash whore only sixteen years old? And not a condom in the place. Ain't you never heard of AIDS, boy? Jesus.

"But that ain't the best, or worst, of it. The pot, the dealin', the screwin'. That's bad, but it ain't the worst. What we also got is this right here." Ray reached into his shirt pocket and pulled out a little cellophane packet and tossed it on the table. Some of the white powder in it escaped onto the table. "Now, I don't know much about drugs, but I'll bet a month's pay that when I take that little bag over to Doc's in a few minutes, he's gonna tell me it's cocaine. You want some of that bet?"

Price Deaver's face had gone completely white. Sweat was popping out on his upper lip. Pot, even dealing pot, and screwing an underage hooker were problems, but nothing that couldn't be worked out with a handshake between some good old boys. Cocaine was another thing entirely. Cocaine scared the hell out of people in these mountains. Cocaine was hard time. And Price Deaver did not want anything to do with hard time.

"That ain't mine," he said, his accent strong now, Kentucky mountains creeping back in. "It's her's. I told her it was trouble, but she's hooked on it."

"Make her horny, does it?" Ray asked.

Deaver looked away, and it was enough of an answer to satisfy Ray. "Well, it don't matter. Thing is, I found it in the cabin and you was in the cabin and if I say it's yours then it's yours and there ain't diddly shit you or your daddy can do about it. How you like the idea of spendin' the next five or six years in a cell with a big hillbilly with no teeth and tattoos on his arms pinchin' your butt and callin' you darlin'?"

Deaver was sweating all over himself. "What do you want?"

"Where you get the grass you sell?" Ray pounced.

"Around. Lots o' places."

"Name some."

"I can't remember all of 'em."

"How about up on Mount Devoux?"

"Yeah, sometimes. There's some old boys up there grows more than they need and I buy it off 'em."

"One of those old boys wouldn't be Big John Wisdom, would it?"

"Yeah, couple of times I . . . Oh, shit. Wait a minute, you don't think I killed Big John Wisdom, do ya? Are you crazy?" Deaver pushed his chair back from the table and started to stand. I put my hand on his shoulder and pressed him back down. As I did so, I took a measure of him. It could have been him in the trailer. Maybe.

"You ever have a run-in with Big John, Price? You two ever get into it?" Ray asked, sitting back in his chair.

"Sure. Everyone who came around Big John got into it with him sooner or later. He loved to kick ass. All he was good for."

"So what happened, Price? He short-weight you on the grass you bought from him?"

"What grass? I ain't bought any grass from him in near a year! What the hell you talkin' about?"

"Well, I'll tell ya. We know you was up there on the mountain on Sunday evening. Got us a witness," he lied. "You and your friends in there were up there drivin' your ORVs around, and the way I figure it, you met Big John after they all split up to race into Devoux. Big John sold you some grass he probably had stashed somewhere. You paid him and you both went your separate ways.

"But when you got into the grass you found out old John had short-weighted you. Ripped you off. Be just like him to do that. But you'd had enough of his shit. He figured you for a pussy, wouldn't do anything about it, but you were gonna show him otherwise.

"You snuck over to Pitchfork Hollow and hid up in the trees until dark and you waited and watched, and directly here comes Big John and you go down and confront him. Say you want your money. But he says fuck you. So you coldcock him and throw him in the shitter. Then you—"

Price Deaver started laughing.

It began as a giggle, then became a titter, then exploded into a full bray. He was laughing so hard that tears began to form in the corners of his eyes. He shook his head and held up his hand. Finally he was able to talk.

"Oh, Christ. Ray, that's great. I wish I woulda done it, I really do. I hated that big fart, and he short-weighted me more than once. But you got this one comin' outa your ass."

"I'm waitin'," Ray said, quietly.

"I wasn't anywhere near Mount Devoux on Sunday. Christ, I wrecked my ORV over a month ago. Daddy was gonna get me another one, but we haven't been able to find one we like."

"That ain't much of an alibi," Ray said, still looking intently at Deaver.

"Oh, that. Yeah. I was at home all day and all night." He smiled at some personal recollection. "Haven't you heard? Daddy's runnin' for reelection. He had a football party out at the house. I had to be there for it. You know, being the fair-haired boy. Afterward we had a barbecue out on the patio. Party went on past midnight."

"You sayin' your daddy can provide you with an alibi for Sunday night?"

Deaver smiled broadly. "Nope. Not Daddy. Not just him, anyway. Him and every upstanding citizen in Perry. The mayor, the treasurer, the county trustees, the school board, everyone. They were all there. And they all saw me. See, I got kinda drunk. Daddy said I made an ass of myself in front of the whole town. Me, I don't remember it all that well. Sorry I can't help you, Ray." His smile stayed plastered to his face.

Ray stood quickly, pushing the table away from him as he did. It slammed neatly into Price Deaver's chest and the smile melted. Ray looked at me and nodded to the door. "Come on," he said, picking up the cellophane packet from the table.

A small cloud of white powder drifted up from it and settled on his shirt as he stuffed it into his breast pocket. I stared intently at the little cloud of dust. There it was again. Something I should have noticed or did notice but couldn't recall. Something that had occurred to me just before I lost consciousness in Les Eastman's trailer. Damn it. If only things would slow down for a minute so I could think. If only my head would stop throbbing and my nose and face would stop aching. If only I could get a good night's sleep and clear my mind.

"Hey, Preacher!" Ray snapped. "You comin'?"

"Yeah, yeah." I needed a cup of coffee. And maybe some breakfast.

"I'll have Elias check out his story, but I suppose it'll stand up. It's too elaborate to be made up." Ray was sitting at his usual stool in the diner, back in Baird. It had taken nearly an hour to get back home, and neither of us had spoken a word on the road. A couple of extra-strength Tylenol had dulled the ache in my head to a mild roar. Now we were eating cold biscuits with strawberry preserves and drinking coffee and talking.

"So now what do we do?" I asked.

Ray shrugged. "We gotta take a fresh look at it. There's too much goin' on. Too many people lyin'."

"They can't all have murdered Big John and Les," I said, wondering if it was true.

"Nah. Hell, everyone lies. They all got their reasons. Some of 'em are good reasons—to keep from hurtin' people, like that. But someone's lyin' because he murdered two men, and it's pissin' me off."

"Why," I said, not a question. "If we knew why, we'd know who."

"Well, Les is easy," Ray said. "Les saw somethin' or knew somethin' that made him a liability. What I don't understand is why they tore up Les's trailer like that."

"Maybe they wanted to make sure he wasn't hiding evidence. A note or something," I offered.

"Yeah, maybe."

"The problem with Big John is that everybody in the county had reason to kill him."

"Yeah." Ray's head came up. "Except they didn't kill him. Not on purpose, I mean. Maybe it was an accident. Maybe they only intended to coldcock him, an' throwin' him in the crapper was to teach him a lesson. Maybe they didn't intend to kill 'im."

It was my turn to say, "Yeah, maybe. But Big John wasn't the kind of guy you piss off on purpose."

"So if it wasn't Price Deaver met Big John up there on the mountain, who was it? And why? And why did Eugene lie about no one bein' up there?"

"Because he's trying to protect his older brother's reputation?"

"Shit," Ray said.

"That's fine talk. And him bein' a preacher, too." May June and Naomi came in the front door and let it slam behind them. "I got the pictures," May June said, and tossed the packet in front of me on the counter.

Naomi sat down next to me and kissed me on the cheek. "How ya doin'?"

"Better," I lied. "Tired."

"Your mother called," May June said. "Wanted to know how you was doin'."

"Why doesn't she ever call me to find that out?" I wondered.

"'Cause you won't tell her the truth," May June said.

"You didn't tell her the truth, did you?"

"'Course not. No need to get her all worked up." She smiled and fanned the pictures out in front of me on the counter.

There I was in all of my black-and-blue glory. Blood covering my shoulders and ruining my tan suit. Nose spread all over my face. Then some others with me in the hospital, still unconscious.

May June beamed. "I show these to the Administrative Council and tell 'em how close you were to dyin', maybe we'll get that medical clinic up here."

"I wasn't close to dying," I said. Though I did look like it.

"They don't know that," she said, defiantly. "And I bet you didn't know that either, lyin' there with your head and nose all beat in."

I smiled and shook my head. "I thought I was a goner. I remember I could hardly see because my eyes were tearing from my nose getting broken and we scuffled in the hall and he broke loose. I thought, he's getting away, but I had trouble getting to my feet. But he wasn't getting away, he was coming back. He hit me over the head with something—"

"Piece of that kindlin' wood just like he used on ol' Les," Ray interjected.

"I felt like my head was caved in. I thought, now he's going to throw me in the crapper and I'm going to die like John Wisdom, covered in shit and lime." I stopped abruptly. That was it. Something about shit and lime. My face must have betrayed me, because Naomi took my hand and shook it.

"Dan? Dan, what is it?"

It was a piece of a puzzle. I knew it was a piece and I knew it went to the puzzle I was working on. Only I didn't know what the puzzle was supposed to look like, so I didn't know where the piece went.

"Ray," I said, trying to think and talk at the same time. "Ray, why do they put lime in outhouses?"

Ray shrugged. "We just always have. Mother, you're the granny woman. Why do we put lime in the crapper?"

May June looked blankly back at me. "Well, I don't know what it does, chemically, I mean. It's a purifier. Mostly it's supposed to neutralize the smell, or at least control it."

"So whenever someone uses the outhouse, he dumps lime in it?" I asked, trying to move the puzzle piece around, slide it here and there.

"No, maybe once or twice't a week. Once a day if it's a big family."

"Whataya got, Dan?" Ray asked, seriously.

I couldn't put it together, so I just laid it out randomly. "There was lime on John Wisdom's body. We both saw it. Not much but just a little, right?"

Ray nodded. "I just figured that after Cleopha done her business, she musta dumped some in before she saw Big John."

I looked at May June. "Maybe," she said.

"No," I said. "You had Doc check the lime ladle for prints and it came up clean, right? And remember the smell? No crapper could smell that bad if they were using lime regularly."

Ray nodded again, something dawned in his eyes. "Right. So it couldn't have been Cleopha who dumped the lime on John. It had to be someone else. Someone with enough sense to wipe it clean."

I shook my head again. It was coming together. "It doesn't figure, Ray. Someone sneaks up on Big John and hits him over the head for some reason. Either he means to kill him or he doesn't. Either way, he dumps the body in the crapper."

Ray nodded. May June stopped thumbing through

the pictures and looked up at me. Naomi squeezed my hand.

I plunged ahead. "He figures Big John will sink to the bottom, but he doesn't. The muck is too thick. He floats there. So why would this guy take the time to find the lime bucket in the dark, dip in and get a couple of scoops of lime, and dump them on Big John? And then put the bucket back in exactly the same place without getting lime all over everything in the dark? It doesn't make sense.

"Besides, we know Big John came to for a few seconds and floundered around down there before he died. I'll bet whoever dumped him down in there was long gone by that time." I heard Naomi groan under her breath. She hadn't known exactly how the man had died.

"So how did the lime get on him?" May June asked, stuffing the pictures back into the envelope.

"It didn't," Ray said, looking at me.

"Well, of course it did. You just said you saw lime powder all over him when you looked down—"

"It weren't lime powder, was it, Preacher?"

I shook my head. "I don't think so," I said, and pointed to the traces of white powder still clinging to his shirt pocket.

May June was getting impatient. "Well, what was it that—"

"And it weren't marijuana that was bein' bought and sold on Sunday evening, was it?" Ray asked me, as much for his own sake as mine.

I shook my head.

"Come on," he said, grabbing his jacket off the back of his stool. "You too, Mother."

"Me? Why me? What do you want me for?" May

June took off her duster and took an old raincoat off a hall tree by the door on her way out. "Drag a person off and don't even tell her what for. Naomi, dear, will you mind the diner while I'm gone? There's bologna and onions and eggs if someone wants lunch. The special tonight is chicken and dumplin's."

"And call the Carmacks," Ray hollered into the store from his Jeep. "Tell 'em to meet us at Pitchfork Holler with the honey dipper. And tell 'em to bring their buckets."

I looked at Naomi and shrugged. She wrapped her arms around my waist and pressed her breasts into my chest. "How about dinner tonight?" she asked. "I'll cook."

"And miss May June's chicken and dumplings?" I teased. "What will the parishioners think?" I asked, about half-seriously.

"We'll start early. I'll leave at a respectable time. They know we're stuck on each other, Dan. They don't expect us to stand at arm's length. Besides, they think we make a cute couple. The ones who aren't jealous of me gettin' you do, at least." She kissed me under my chin and I felt her tongue dart in and out.

"I may be late," I said, my voice cracking.

"I'll keep it warm," she said, and giggled. Ray honked the horn on the Jeep and she pushed me away. "Go on. I'll call Gilbert and Gaylord. You enjoy your treasure hunt."

14

"WHAT THE HELL DO YOU WANT?" EUGENE WISDOM CAME off the porch of the big house and toward us before we could even get out of the Jeep. He was wearing bib overalls that looked like they must have belonged to one of his brothers. They hung off of him in folds. His T-shirt was used-to-be white. "You catch the man what killed my brother?"

"We're workin' on it, Eugene," Ray said, ignoring him and walking toward the outhouse.

"I'll just go on in and see Cleopha," May June said, and waddled toward the porch. "You call me."

"Charles ain't here. He's at the mine," Eugene said, following Ray like a yapping dog. "What're you gonna do? Beat me up again?"

"Maybe," Ray said. "You don't stay outa my hair." Something had come over Ray driving over Mount Devoux to Pitchfork Hollow. He had gotten quiet and he seemed to be getting angry. The back of his neck was flushed and he had forsaken his cigarettes for a cheek full of Beechnut.

Eugene started to say something else, pushing his luck, I thought, but the Carmacks crashed down off the road and onto the gravel drive that led into the hollow, air horn blasting. I could see them both in the cab, bouncing around and smiling like they had just arrived at a church picnic. On the side of the cab, hand-lettered with what looked like a felt-tip pen, it said, CARMACK SANITARY DISPOSAL, and their phone number. Then, like an afterthought, CHEEP RATES, with *cheap* spelled wrong. The truck looked like a normal tanker except that it was smaller than a semi and there was a giant vacuum cleaner right behind the cab. Several buckets were tied along the side of the bed along with rope, a ladder, and two shovels.

"You gonna dip out the crapper?" Eugene asked, unbelieving. "What the fuck you doin' that for? You think the guy that killed my brother's in there? Jesus." He stormed off back to his trailer. As he went in, Bethabelle came out. She was wearing a tight leather miniskirt and a white blouse with a big ruffle on the front. She approached slowly, taking advantage of every step.

"Hey, Ray," she said, looking at me the whole time. "Hey, Reverend."

Ray helped Gilbert and Gaylord get the hose uncoiled from the truck and slide the outhouse along its tracks, exposing the muck-filled hole. "Hey, Beth," was all he gave her without even looking up.

Had he looked up, he would have been rewarded for the effort. The ruffled blouse was as sheer as nylon and she wasn't wearing a bra. Out of the corner of my eye I saw Gilbert elbow Gaylord and raise his eyebrows up and down several times.

"You know them things I was talkin' about with you the other day?" Bethabelle said to me, trying to use her eyes to flirt. It wasn't working, but with that blouse, who cared? "Well, I ain't even had a chance to try them out yet. What do you think I should do, Reverend? I mean, if a girl was to try out somethin' like that with you, without any warning or anything, would you think she was, like, too fast?" She was standing about three inches from my arm, looking up at me and batting her eyes. It would have been pitiful if it hadn't been for those great boobs.

I cleared my throat. "Not if she was my wife," I managed to say. "I'd be flattered."

She leaned forward and her breasts pushed against my bicep as she reached up and gently stroked the bandage on my nose. "Gosh, I bet that hurts, don't it?" Up to then I hadn't been able to smell a thing, but her perfume, something really sweet, was managing to wake up my poor broken nose. She must have just put it on with a fire hose.

"It's sore, yeah," I said, trying to edge away.

An engine turned over behind her trailer and roared to life. "Is Eugene goin' somewhere?" I asked, trying to change the subject, and immediately realized that it was the wrong thing to say.

"I don't know," she said, sweetly. She took my arm in her hands. "Why don't we go see?"

"Bethabelle, for God's sake," Ray said, coming out of the outhouse cabin. "Can't you see we're trying to clean out this shit hole? This ain't no place for a pretty little thing like you. Go make us some coffee, why don't you." He pulled her away from me and pushed her toward the house, swatting her on that great ass of hers. "Go on, now. About a third chicory, okay?"

She put on one of her classic pouts. "Oh, Ray." And stormed off.

Ray watched her go for a moment, then said to me, "That may look like pussy, but it ain't. It's trouble. Stay away from it. Eugene already don't like us."

"I'm trying to stay away from her, Ray, honest to God. But she's like a leech."

"And I bet you got a fish she can latch on to," Ray said, and laughed. The Carmacks, who had finally finished fiddling with their truck, laughed, too. "Come here and look at this," Ray said, walking back into the outhouse cabin.

I followed him in and he was standing at the seat, holding the hinged top up, looking down at the grass under the cabin where we had rolled it aside. One of the top boards, the front one, wasn't part of the hinged top. It was about three inches wide and formed a lip at the front of the seat. Another one ran across the back and was the foundation for the hinges. The front lip board was grooved so the lid fit down against it and was supported by it.

"I was lookin' around here tryin' to figure out where that white powder come from." He reached under the front lip and felt around. "There. Right there. Reach under there and see if you can feel it."

I reached under the lip and felt around until my hand fell on a small metal eyebolt. I looked up at Ray, let my face ask the question.

"Four of 'em," he said. "Two in front and two in back, one in each corner. Perfect hiding place for drugs. Watch." He took a long cord of twine from his pocket, wadded his bandanna around a rock, and tied the four corners of the bandanna to one end of the cord. "One bag on each end," he said, showing me the other end of the cord. "Then you thread the cord through the eyebolts." He reached under the front lip of the seat and brought his hands out empty.

"Big John hung his drugs from the bottom of the crapper seat," Ray went on. "One on each end of the string, hangin' just above the shit. Then he put the lime in here, but he didn't use it. Didn't want to neutralize the stink. No one's gonna spend too much time lookin' for drugs in here. If the cops come unexpected, all you got to do is reach under here and cut the string. The bags fall down in the shit, the rocks carry 'em beneath the surface, and you fish 'em out later with a long pole and a hook. Son of a bitch was smart. Gotta hand it to him."

"So who killed him?" I asked.

"Someone who wanted his drugs. Find the drugs, we find the killer."

"So why are Gil and Gay dippin' out the pit?"

"Insurance. Proof. There was cocaine on John's body down in the pit. The boys hosed it off when they got 'im out, thinkin' it was lime. But the onliest way there coulda been dust on him was if one of them bags broke. Now, the only way one could break was if there was a struggle, which there weren't or Big John woulda won, or if it was knocked loose when Big John was dumped in there."

"And," I finished for him, "if he was hiding it the way you just demonstrated, the one that didn't break is down in the pit floating around somewhere."

Ray didn't smile. He just nodded to Gilbert Carmack, who shouted to Gaylord, who engaged the big vacuum pump and started, very gently, scooping up the mess.

It took them less than an hour to find it. A bag about

the size of my pipe tobacco pouch with a baseball-sized stone tied to it and a long length of twine tied to the other end. The bag was plastic and filled with white powder. "Get May June," Ray said to no one in particular. Gilbert ran off toward the house.

A few minutes later May June Hall was bent over the bag on the hood of the Jeep. "Shew! Smells like it came out o' the privy!"

"It did," Ray said. "Whataya think?"

"Well, give me a minute," she said, removing a barlow knife from her raincoat pocket. She made a neat little slit in the bag and brought some of the powder out on the blade, ran it gently under her nose, moistened her finger and took a little bit, ran it over her gums. Nodded. Said, "M-m-m."

"Mother, for God sake!"

"I just wanted to be sure."

"Well, are you?"

"Well, I ain't Crockett ner Tubbs and this ain't 'Miami Vice,' but I'd say what you got here is street-grade cocaine, cut with—" she ran her tongue over her teeth and gums "—confectioners' sugar and maybe talcum powder."

"Goddamn," Ray said, anger beginning to burn in his eyes. "You're a fine granny woman, Mother."

"'Course I am," she said, winking at me.

"Granny women know drugs?" I asked, not quite believing. "Street drugs?"

"They do now'days," May June said, proudly. "Gave a course down to the hospital on first aid for overdosed drug users. Said if we was to give first aid, we had to know what kinda drug was bein' used and they showed us how to identify it. I just took to it kinda natural. I guess it's a gift."

"What was he doing, do you suppose?" I asked Ray. "Buying it or selling it?"

"Both, probably. Too much for personal use."

"Who to and who from?"

"I don't know," Ray said. "But I sure as shit know the one's gonna tell me." His jaw was set and the crimson splash on his neck was working its way up to his jawline. He started the Jeep, and while it warmed up, he tied the bag of cocaine into his handkerchief.

May June grabbed my arm with a viselike grip. "Go with him, Dan. Gil and Gay will drive me back. Don't let him do nothin' stupid. He gets crazy where hard drugs is concerned. Watch over 'im."

I jumped into the Jeep and held on for dear life as we skidded up the driveway and onto the road. I hoped Ray knew where he was going. I had no idea.

Back over Mount Devoux, down Route 3 to Route 42 and all the way back through Baird, Ray said nothing. The red flush receded back down below his collar, but his jaw remained set and the speed of the Jeep told me he was close to the boiling point.

Finally he leaned over and yelled his question: "How'd you figure it out?"

"Figure what out?" I asked. I hadn't figured anything out. I didn't even know where we were going.

"The cocaine," he said. "How'd you figure it out?"

Oh, that. "I didn't. It just seemed wrong that it was lime. It didn't occur to me that it was coke until it did to you. I wasn't sure until May June confirmed it."

That seemed to satisfy him. I don't think he liked the idea of a preacher being better at police work than a constable.

"I still don't get it," I said, trying to yell over the

roar of the wind. "Was he buying or selling? Who to and who from? And why did they kill him?"

Ray shrugged. "I'm not sure myself, but I figure it's gotta be pretty much the way we figured. Price Deaver figures into it somehow. I'm bettin' he was Big John's buyer."

"But he wasn't on the mountain Sunday. His alibi is solid."

"Then Big John wasn't sellin'. Whoever he met on that mountain was his source. He was buyin'."

"How could he carry the coke back to the hollow without the other guys noticing it?"

"Didn't have to," Ray shouted. "It was delivered there. That's why he was in the crapper. Taking delivery or making sure it was made. He set it up on the mountain during the race to Devoux and took delivery that night. Or it was delivered and he was checking on it."

"You think whoever sold him the drugs killed him and ripped him off?" I asked, trying to figure out who in Durel County had balls that big.

"Or he tried to rip them off and they got pissed. That's more likely."

He swung the Jeep onto the Baird-Towne Road and headed up Clark Mountain. For just a second it seemed like we were tilting on two wheels. I grabbed for the roll bar and hung on for dear life. Ray shifted gears and his face never changed. If he were a cartoon, smoke would have been coming out of his eyes, nose, and ears.

"Ray," I yelled, as we sped up Clark Mountain. "What are you so mad about?"

"I'm not mad," he shouted back, slamming down the clutch and slapping the gearshift into second to take a hairpin curve.

"Bullshit! You look like you're ready to eat nails and you're driving like a maniac. Who are we going to talk to?"

He let the Jeep slow down to sixty. "You said Adam was gonna go up on the mountain on Sunday."

"Yeah, but he didn't. He stayed at home all day. His daddy and his brothers will vouch for him. Probably Naomi, too."

He gave me an I'm-sure-they-will look.

"I believe him, Ray. I watched his face and eyes when he told me. He had no reason to lie. And he's kept his nose clean ever since the Bertke girl."

"I believe him, too," Ray said. "Adam's a good boy. Why didn't he go up on the mountain with his ORV?"

"Because Price Deaver was going to be up there and—"

"But Pricey boy wasn't up there," Ray corrected.

"He thought Price was going to be up there," I said. "That's why he didn't want to go."

"Price never had any intention of bein' up there," Ray said. "Why did Adam think he was gonna be up there?"

I thought for a moment, trying to recall the conversation. Then it came to me. "Benny told him," I shouted. "He and Benny Kneeb were going to take the trails, and Benny said Price was going to be up there and they better not—"

"Right," Ray said. He slammed the gearshift into third and took the Jeep back up to seventy on a short straightaway. "Benny knew damn well there wasn't gonna be no Price Deaver on that mountain. The onliest one on that mountain besides the Wisdom boys and their two friends was Benny Kneeb. He didn't want Adam goin' with him, fuckin' up his dope sale."

"Benny?" I asked, incredulously. "Benny Kneeb is the connection?" Benny was a big country boy. Nearly as tall as Ray and maybe thirty pounds heavier. He had taken to wearing a scraggly beard and a Merle Haggard cowboy hat. Bib overalls were the only pants that fit him without going to a king-size store. He wore shit-kicker boots and tattoos on both of his arms. As much as I hate to admit that Naomi's father could be right about anything, I had to admit that his assessment of Benny Kneeb was probably right on the money. Benny was trouble. Anyone who went to the pains Benny did to look like a dick probably was one. The only problem was that he had the look but he didn't seem to have the smarts to be a cocaine dealer.

Ray nodded as he slammed the Jeep to a stop and backed into an almost invisible cutback going up the mountain. "And he should be along any minute," he said, lighting a cigarette.

Benny Kneeb's coal truck was one of those bigger-than-life monster trucks with tires nearly six feet tall. Benny had his name painted proudly on the side of the cab amid camo designs and a death's-head skull. Most of the coal drivers for Hebrew Taylor named their trucks, usually after their wives or girlfriends—Janine, JoAnn, Mary Louise, Beatrice. Benny's truck didn't have a name on the door under his own. It just had the letters BFT. I asked Adam Taylor, one time, what the letters stood for, and he just laughed and shook his head. "Big Fuckin' Truck," he said. That Benny! What can you say?

It was nearly five o'clock before Benny made his appearance coming up the mountain. We had sat there for nearly an hour, waiting, watching other trucks, and smoking, and I didn't know if I was happy or sad to see him coming. The truck looked bigger than ever, and I didn't like the look in Ray's eyes when he saw it coming.

Ray ground the ignition and the Jeep coughed to life. He shifted into first and let his hand rest on the stick, patting it, waiting patiently. Then, just as the big truck approached our hiding spot, Ray shot out onto the road in front of it.

Normally, going downhill or on a straightaway, with the truck loaded to overflowing with coal, you don't mess with one of these big dudes. They get paid by the load and they own the road. You get out of their way because they take no prisoners. You get in a road fight with one and you will always, always lose.

Deadheading back to the mine, as Benny was, empty and going uphill, was a different story, however. The truck was going no more than thirty miles per hour when we jumped out in front of it.

All Ray did was slow down.

And slow down.

And slow down.

Benny must have been furious. He was grinding gears and blasting away on the air horn. I could even hear him shouting and cursing. The slower he went, the slower he had to go. There was no way for the big, heavy truck to pick up any momentum going up the mountain behind us. Not as long as we were going uphill. If he didn't stop before we got to the top, however, we would be in trouble.

I didn't look back. I bit down on my pipe hard enough to bite it in half, hung on to the roll bar and the side wall, and waited for the impact every time we slowed down.

Then, finally, mercifully, I heard the sound I had been waiting for. The sound of air brakes being applied. Benny had come to a complete stop. Ray must have heard it, too, because he slammed the Jeep into first, popped the clutch, killed the engine, and was out of his seat and running back to the cab of the truck before I could climb out.

Benny was coming down out of the cab as fast as Ray was coming toward him. "What the fuck do you think you're doin'? You tryin' to get someone killed, you silly motherfucker!"

He jumped the last few feet and must have recognized Ray, because he said, "Oh, Christ. What the fuck's the law—"

But he didn't finish it.

Ray hit him. One, two, three, four quick punches. The first to the face, two and three to the huge gut, and four back to the face again. The punches drove Benny back but didn't knock him down, which was, no doubt, what Ray had hoped would happen. Ray had always said, "When you fight a bigger man, anything's fair. Put him on the ground and keep him there. And don't get down there with him where he can use his size against you."

But Benny Kneeb wasn't going down on the ground. He charged Ray like an enraged grizzly bear. Obviously the big truck driver was used to fighting people who were intimidated by his size and appearance. I would have been. Seeing this huge, bearded animal charging at me with his arms stretched out above his head, blood coursing out of his lips, and screams roaring out of his mouth would have sent me in the opposite direction as fast as I could go.

And that, of course, would have been the wrong thing entirely. Ray, of course, did the right thing. He stepped inside those great reaching arms and brought his knee up so hard into Benny's crotch, he nearly toppled himself backward with the effort. I heard it crunch and squish.

Then he followed the knee with a series of punches that wound all the way around Benny's big body. Stomach, side, kidneys, back, kidneys, side, stomach. For a big man, Ray could do some really amazing bobbing and weaving.

Benny seemed to fall in slow motion, crumpling up from the knees all the way up to his head, which was the last to hit the ground. He lay there in the middle of the road, bleeding and moaning, and I wasn't sure what it was I was supposed to do. So I did nothing. I didn't really seem to be needed here.

Ray walked quickly back to the Jeep, took the shotgun out of the back end, and gave it to me. He handed me three shells and said, "If he makes a move to get up, kill him." He turned and started climbing up into the cab of the truck.

I walked over and stood over Benny as he moaned and groaned on the ground. He wasn't about to get up, and for that I was eternally grateful as I had no intention of killing him if he did.

A shower of debris began to fall on Benny from above. Cardboard coffee cups, McDonald's wrappers, cigarette cartons, girlie magazines, a lunch box and a thermos, clothing, rags.

"Where is it, Benny?" Ray hollered down from above.

Benny continued to moan.

"Come on, you little shit. You didn't sell it all. You kept a taste for yourself. Where d'ya keep it?"

More stuff rained down. A pair of boxer shorts. Two pairs of women's panties. A box of condoms. A four-pack of beer and two empties. I thought, Lord,

Benny, what do you do in that truck? It must be even bigger in that cab than it looks!

Two coats. A small toolbox, open, the tools crashing around us.

Now Ray was screaming. "Goddamn you, Benny, I'll beat it out of you if I have to. Where the hell do you keep your goddamn stash?"

I tried to think of where the stash might be. I didn't want Ray beating anything else out of Benny, who was now throwing up on the road. I also didn't want to get hit by any of the falling debris. Where would Benny hide his stash? Somewhere safe, where you wouldn't expect people to look. Somewhere where you could get rid of it quickly if you had to. I let my eyes roam over the side of the truck and saw it almost immediately.

The gas tank. Or one of the gas tanks. The big silver cap was right there in plain sight. I felt around it and found the thread, held it tight and unscrewed the cap with my left hand. Clever, Benny. If you didn't know the thread was there, you'd just unscrew the cap and the stash would fall down to the bottom of the gas tank. You could drain the tank and get your stash later. A problem, sure, but not like getting caught with coke.

I tugged gently on the thread and the bag popped out of the gas tank. It was three bags, really. Triple-sealed against leakage. Couldn't have cocaine leaking into the gasoline or vise versa. Most street coke was cut with baking soda, talcum, or powdered sugar. That last one would make a mess of your truck if you let it leak into the gas tank. There was a rock in the bag, too, to make it sink if it was loosed into the tank.

I held it up in front of my face. "Ray?"

Stuff continued to rain down on us.

"Ray?"

"What?"

"I found it."

His head poked out of the door.

"In the gas tank."

"Son of a bitch," was all he said. He came down the side of the truck, grabbed it out of my hand, rolled Benny over on his back, and sat on the big man's chest, his crotch right on his chin, before I could make a move to stop him.

"How's the jaw, Benny?" Ray asked, casually, slapping Benny lightly on his face. Ray had broken that jaw just over two months ago, and I doubted that it was completely healed yet. "You and me have to talk, big guy."

I wouldn't have thought it possible, but Benny replied by arching his chest and trying to throw Ray off. Poor Benny. Not a good idea.

Ray reared back and punched Benny in the face, a quick, sharp pop that broke his nose. My own eyes watered in memory and a sharp pain shot through my forehead.

"No way to treat an officer of the law, Benny. Now, talk to me. Where'd you get it?"

"Fuck you." But there wasn't much force behind it.

Ray used his middle finger and flicked Benny hard on the nose. The big man moaned. "The next one's two fingers. Then three. Then I use my fist again. By the fifth time there won't be enough of that nose left to sew back on."

Things were getting out of hand. "Ray," I said. "It's a clean bust. Don't you think Elias—"

Ray shot me a look that said, *Stay out of it, Preacher.*

He leaned down over Benny and flicked his nose

again, this time with two fingers. Benny tried to bring his hands up, but they were pinned by Ray's knees.

"Benny?" Ray asked.

"The coal train," Benny said, through tears. "The brakeman on the coal train. Name's Kramer something. Or something Kramer. I don't know. I sell him shine, that's how he knows me."

"Now, that's more like it," Ray said, sitting up straight. He reached into his pocket and flipped his notebook and pencil to me. I wrote down, "Kramer—coal train."

"How much?" Ray asked Benny.

"Couple o' pounds a month. Not much. Never know when. He gets it when he gets it. Oh, Christ, I can't breathe."

Ray let him turn his head to the side and spit. Blood was running from his nose down into his throat. Benny gagged and spit and tried to raise his chest again, but this time all Ray had to do was raise his hand.

"How much did you sell to Big John on Sunday?" Ray asked.

Nothing.

"Benny, I don't have all day. You wanna keep your nose, you better—"

"I don't know what you're talkin' about, damn it. Big John Wisdom? I ain't never sold no coke to him."

"Boy, don't you bullshit me. I know you was up on that mountain on Sunday and I know you met with Big John when they all separated and there was cocaine on his body when we found him. What he do, cut the price on you? He refuse to pay you? Or maybe he decided to cut you out altogether. Maybe he decided to make the pickup himself. That why you killed him?"

"No! I never killed nobody! Christ! Especially not Big John."

"Yeah, well, we'll see," Ray said, starting to get off of him. "You got the right to remain silent, you got a right to an attorney. . . . Anything you say can and will be used against you—"

"It was Eugene! I met Eugene on Sunday!" Benny was nearly pleading. "I didn't kill nobody!"

Ray stopped short. "Eugene?"

"Yeah! It was his idea to meet up there. He was gonna start the race. He said they'd all split up. He was scared to death Big John would find out we was dealin' coke and kill us both. Said he'd tell 'em he got stuck in Stinkin' Creek. We threw mud all over his ORV."

"How'd he get the cocaine back to the holler without them seein' it?" Ray asked.

"He didn't. I did." Benny sat up and pulled a bandanna out of his back pocket and held it up to his nose. "Oh, Jesus. Look at this." I didn't know if he was talking about his nose or the trash lying all over the road.

"You took it to the holler?" Ray asked.

"Yeah. Eugene paid me and said he'd stall 'em for a while. Get them drinkin' at the store in Devoux or somethin'. I went back over the mountain in my ORV. I was supposed to wait until dark, but when I got back to the holler, there weren't nobody around, so I went on down and hung it in the crapper just like he said."

"And then you waited until Big John come out and—"

"No! I got the hell outa there. I didn't want to be there when Big John got back. I had my money; why would I hang around? I got back home about eight o'clock. Daddy was watchin' that home video thing on TV, that's how I know what time it was. I ain't seen none of the Wisdoms since. I swear to God, Ray."

"How'd Eugene know you wouldn't just run off with his money and not leave the dope in the crapper?" I asked.

"What?" Benny had forgotten I was there.

I asked my question again.

"Run off? Where? What else am I supposed to do with cocaine? This ain't New York City. You can't just sell it on the streets of Perry. I figured I was lucky to get anyone to buy it."

"You still got the money?" Ray asked, moving toward the Jeep. Benny stayed sitting in the road.

"Nah. I spent it on tires for this fucker," he said, pointing at the truck.

Ray opened the bag of dope and stuck his little finger into it. He put it on the tip of his tongue and walked toward the truck. Finding the open gas tank, he dumped the contents of the bag into it.

"Aw, Christ on a fuckin' crutch," Benny groaned. "Whataya doin' that for? Didn't I tell ya ever' fuckin' thing you wanted to know?"

Ray picked up the shotgun from where I had leaned it against the fender of the Jeep. He pointed it, one-handed, at Benny, who cringed. I held my breath.

"Benny, up till now you just been a pain in my ass. Moonshinin', growin' pot, gettin' in fights, runnin' cars off the road with this monster, just generally fuckin' up. I let you get away with most of it because you was young and I figured you'd smarten up with time. But all you did was get dumber.

"Now you ain't just a pain in the ass no more. Now you're a dope dealer. You're a big boy now, Benny. Now you gotta do time. You're big and you're dumb, so you'll probably come out just as dumb and twice as bad as you are now." Ray's voice dropped to nearly a whisper. "But by God, you're gonna do time. And you be thankful I'm not the judge that's gonna sentence you. 'Cause if I was." He cocked the hammer on the single-shot shotgun.

"Hey, Ray. Come on. I come clean, didn't I? I'll do my time, come on." Benny was holding his arms in front of his face.

Ray pulled the trigger and the hammer fell with a click. Benny screamed and tried to bury his head into his shoulders.

Ray broke the shotgun open and laid it in the back of the Jeep. "I'm gonna call Elias Knowly and tell him where to pick you up. They don't give me handcuffs with a constable's badge, so I'm just gonna have to trust you to stay right here."

Benny nodded his head. "I'll wait right here," he said.

"That's good, Benny. 'Cause I don't want to have to come lookin' for you, and you don't want me to. Do you?"

We didn't hear his reply. Ray started the engine of the Jeep and we lurched around in a three-point turn and headed back down the mountain toward Baird.

"Eugene?" I said, letting it be a question. I held up the three shotgun shells he had given me. None of them had ever gone into the gun. "You have me all figured out, don't you?" I said.

Ray shook his head. "Dan, I reckon you're about the onliest thing in this whole mess I do have figured out."

"We going after Eugene?" I asked.

He just watched the road and gripped the wheel. His hands were snow white, so hard did he grip it.

15

May June and Naomi were waiting for us on the porch of the diner, bundled up against the October chill in big, baggy sweaters. May June's was an old college letter cardigan I had seen up at the thrift shop, Naomi's was a turtleneck big enough to fit Ray. Her hair was pulled back in what she called a George, and she looked fresh-scrubbed and good enough to eat.

"Well, it's about time," May June said, rising from her rocker. "You two round up the bad guys and make Durel County safe for law-abidin' citizens again?"

Ray grumbled and walked past her, and she watched him go into the diner, past his office, and up the stairs to their apartment. She looked worriedly at Naomi and they exchanged something with their eyes. Naomi hugged her, and when they separated May June just stood there rubbing her hands together, looking into the diner. Finally Naomi leaned down and spoke to her, and May June followed Ray into the diner and up the stairs.

Naomi watched her go and came down the steps to me. "Ready for some of May June's chicken and dumplin's?" she asked, coming into my arms.

"I thought you were going to cook," I said, not at all disappointed. May June makes chicken and dumplings, like the ones they eat in heaven.

Naomi smiled and snuggled in under my jacket. "I don't even try to compete with May June," she said. "Come on. Dinner's over to the parsonage. All we gotta do is nuke it and eat. Got some apple cobbler and Cheddar cheese, too. And fresh cider and rum."

It sounded good. In fact, it sounded like Ray's favorite meal. I looked into the diner, but there were no answers there. It was empty, the few dinner patrons long since gone.

"What was that all about?" I asked, nodding toward the screen door.

Naomi said, "Later," and took my hand, leading me toward the parsonage.

Yes, the entire church knew that Naomi and I were sweet on each other. You might even call us an "item," though they wouldn't. They still used words like "sparkin'," or "courtin'," or "stuck on each other." And yes, most of my parishioners would have found nothing scandalous or even remarkable about my steady girlfriend fixing me a homemade dinner in my own home.

So why, you ask, did we walk from the front of the diner to the back and down the dirt road behind Aunt-tiques and the two visitor dorms of the Mountain Baptist Children's Home to the back of the church? And why, you will want to know, did we sneak quietly in through the back door of the church, through the sanctuary, through the sacristy, into my office and on to the parsonage?

And you will find your answer to these questions when you follow us into the church sanctuary, and find, there, draped over the pulpit, a large turtleneck sweater. And you may still be curious even then, but your curiosity will begin to be satisfied when you find, below the worship table, a small pair of high-top tennis shoes and a pair of blue jeans. And by the time you reach the door of the sacristy and find my jacket and shirt, you will, no doubt, have your answer.

Ministers are, by definition, passionate people. We have to be. We believe passionately, we preach passionately, we minister and lead passionately. If we didn't, we wouldn't last long in the profession. So why are you people always so shocked when you discover that your pastor loves passionately as well? And not just in that safe, detached, impersonal sense wherein we care deeply about all humankind, but in the intense, personal, physical, erotic way, too? What is it that's so shocking?

Well, be done with those illusions, oh faithless generation, and know that this pastor's passions are not reserved exclusively for the faceless masses. This minister of the Gospel had passion enough and more for those wretched souls with plenty left over for one particular, beautiful, sexually charged woman with whom he was hopelessly in love.

The parsonage was cold. I had expected to be back earlier and neglected to turn up the oil stove in the living room before I left yesterday, reasoning that the house would heat up with the day's sunshine. But I had been detoured to the hospital and a cold front had followed the rain and the stove hadn't gotten lit and the place had never warmed up.

The bed and the microwave were the only two pieces of furniture in the house that had not been borrowed from the Mountain Baptist Children's Home upon my arrival in August. The microwave I bought in Perry shortly after I realized that the closest I would be coming to having to cook would be reheating stuff I brought home from the diner. The bed I bought the day after Labor Day when I realized that I was completely and hopelessly in love with Naomi Taylor.

We lay in that bed under two quilts and a comforter, naked and spent, the chicken and dumplings still sitting on the counter in the kitchen. I looked at the ceiling and thought how good my pipe would taste, and Naomi snoozed under the crook of my right arm, her breasts pressed against my side, one of her nipples, erect from the cold in the room, trying to arouse my spent passion as it brushed back and forth against my ribs.

"Ready to eat?" she said, coming awake and smacking her lips.

"What, again?" I asked. She yanked some of the hair on my chest, an excruciating torture, and I cried out.

"What would June Ann Crabtree say, you talkin' like that?"

"Boy, you know how to destroy an erection, don't you," I said, trying not to form a mental picture of the woman I had lambasted at the Administrative Council meeting two nights earlier.

"What?" Naomi asked, all innocence. "June Ann? I think she's cute. She's just run this church for so long, she doesn't know what to do about a competent minister. She wants to assert her authority, that's all." She stretched and rolled over, nestling her perfect rear end against my hip and pulling my arm around and placing it on her breast.

"You heard about the meeting?" I asked.

"I heard you lowered the boom on her," she said. "Not too nice, for a preacher."

"Yeah. Preachers should be weak, ineffectual, nerdy little guys who you can walk on and wouldn't say shit if they had both hands full." I wasn't liking the way this conversation was going.

"I don't think so," she said, wiggling her butt. That was better.

"You think I was too hard on her?" I asked, really interested.

"No. I just think you should bury the hatchet now. Go over and apologize—"

"Kiss her ass," I interjected.

"Yeah. What difference does it make? You made your point, and I doubt she'll ever bring it up again. But she's a force in the church and you need her."

I hate it when someone tries to tell me how to do my job and then turns out to be right.

"I'll think about it," I said.

"Well, think about the organ while you're at it," she said, yawning.

"The organ?"

"Yeah. Bernard Weems was over to the diner lookin' for you with a catalogue full of organs."

"Oh, hell." Bernard Weems, of Weems Hardware in Perry and Weems Sawmill, lived right down the road from the church. The richest man in Baird, he had gotten it in his head to donate an organ to the church, which had never had one. Mostly we got along with

Dora Musgrove banging out the hymns on an old, out-of-tune upright piano. "Who's going to play this organ?" I asked.

She shrugged, which felt very nice. I'd have to ask her more questions that she didn't know the answers to.

"Dora plays by ear," I went on. "She can't read music and she sure as hell can't play the organ. And besides, he went to some mall in Lexington, and a salesman has damned near sold him on some electronic synthesizer organ that you have to be a rocket scientist to play."

"Whataya gonna do?" she asked.

"Avoid him and hope he loses his enthusiasm. Bernard's like that. Next week it'll be something else. I hope."

She didn't answer. I wondered if she was going back to sleep.

"What was that business back at the diner?" I asked.

"What business?"

"Between you and May June when Ray came storming in. She looked like she was afraid of him. I've never seen either of them act like that before." My right arm was starting to go to sleep, so I tried to shift it and she nestled further into me, making it impossible to even want to move. I kissed my right hand good-bye.

"She is, kinda," Naomi said.

"What, afraid of him? Why? I can't believe Ray would ever—"

"No, nothing like that." Her voice was different. Almost sad. "It's their son."

"Their son?" I had only heard Ray mention his son once. They had a room in the back near the store that had been their son's. Naomi had been nursed back to health in that room after a car wreck last summer. When I asked who the room belonged to, Ray had said, "It was our son's. He died in the war." That was all I'd ever heard of him.

"He died in Vietnam, didn't he?" I asked.

"Yeah. Only there's more to it than what everyone thinks. That's why May June is so worried." Now Naomi rolled over and sat up. The blankets fell away from her breasts, but the expression on her face was so serious, I had no thoughts beyond what was on her mind. "May June told me about it tonight. She was so worried, she could hardly cook. Finally I guess she just had to talk to someone. She said I could tell you. Probably should. But she just couldn't. She said Ray would have a fit if he thought anyone knew."

I didn't say anything. I could have. I have a whole bag full of good, psychologically correct, response-eliciting questions that I can whip out at a moment's notice. They just didn't seem necessary.

"They were informed of Junior's death in 1971. That was his name, Raymond Junior. I guess they got the news the same way as everyone else. Said he was killed in action. That was all. I guess they nearly died from grief. Ray drank. May June ate. She said she gained all her weight back then. Over a hundred pounds in three months. Ray never left the building in all that time. He just sorted his letters and drank. That was before he was constable. He was just postmaster then. And they had the diner and the store.

"Anyway, one day Ray just stopped drinkin', took a shower, and went into his office. He drank coffee and he ate sandwiches she brought him for three days, and all that time he was readin' Junior's letters that they had saved.

"May June thought it was his way of rememberin', you know. Goin' back over the letters and all. But that isn't what he was doin', rememberin'. He was writin' stuff down. Names and cities and stuff. When he came out he had a list of the names of the boys in Junior's unit, the ones who had come home. Said he was gonna find out what happened."

"Dear God," I said. The grief must have been crushing. Ray no doubt figured the only way to get out from under it was to know the whole story so he could put it to rest. No more questions, wondering, imagining.

Naomi nodded her head. "He was gone for over a month. May June got Darnell to help her around here while he was gone. When he came back, he went into his office for a couple of hours without sayin' a thing, came out, and started sortin' mail. He never talked about it.

"May June asked questions. Begged him to tell her, and all he would say is that she didn't want to know the details, and let the dead bury the dead, and how the truth can't bring back their son. He just wouldn't talk about it.

"Finally she snuck into his office one day and went through his notes and found some phone numbers and stuff and started calling the folks Ray had visited until she found the truth. When she confronted him with it he was really mad for about a couple o' hours and she thought he was gonna start drinkin' again. But he didn't. After he calmed down he took her to bed and they made love and told stories about their son and remembered him together when he was a little boy. And they cried and made love some more and they agreed never to say anything about any of it ever again 'cept to each other."

I wondered if she realized that she had left out the most important part of the story, but I didn't ask. I could no more ask her to violate a confidence than I would if she asked me. She sighed, crawled back under the covers, and snuggled up to me again, as before, shivering.

"He was a junkie," she said. "He died of an overdose while on leave in Melbourne, Australia. The army sent him there to dry out, but he found some dope somewhere, or someone smuggled it into the clinic to him, and he OD'd. The army covered it up to spare their feelings."

"Jesus Christ," I said. Poor Ray. Poor May June. I have seen much sadness in my years as a minister. I've sat in emergency rooms of hospitals and I've stood in funeral homes and beside deathbeds and tried in whatever ways I could to comfort those who grieve. And I have learned this one thing more certainly than any theolgoical truth: There is nothing sadder or more painful than surviving your own child. And there is no word that can comfort those who do.

Ray and May June had not only survived their son and grieved over his loss, but they had done so in silence, their secret kept between them in a place where secrets and gossip were among the most valuable means of social exchange. Constantly afraid, terrified that someone would find out. "They sent him to do his duty for his country," I mused. "He was a fresh-faced, rednecked mountain boy. Sergeant York."

"And he died like any junkie on any city street," she finished for me. "They'll die if it ever gets out, Dan. They'll just die."

"That's why he took the constable job when it was

offered, isn't it?" I asked. "It wasn't the two hundred dollars a month or the badge. It was the drugs. That's why he's such a maniac about hard drugs."

Naomi nodded. "May June says he does what he can about the pot an' the shine, but he just won't tolerate hard drugs. He can't, she says."

I pictured Ray mashing Benny Kneeb's nose, forcing him to tell us about the drugs. I thought about May June's warning back in Pitchfork Hollow that Ray got crazy when it came to drugs. I pictured that shotgun pointed at Benny and the hammer falling on an empty chamber. Had Ray known that the chamber was empty? Was he sure? I wondered if Ray had remembered to call Elias or if Benny was still sitting out there in the middle of that road.

I thought about all of these for a long time and I was glad that Ray was too tired to go after Eugene tonight. I hoped he would cool off some by tomorrow morning. But cooled off or not, I knew Ray Hall well enough to know that two things about tomorrow were certain. One, he wouldn't call Elias for help in bringing in Eugene Wisdom for the murder of his brother and various drug charges. And two, I knew I would be with him. To save Eugene if I needed to. And maybe to save Ray Hall, too.

My stomach growled and I tapped Naomi on the butt. "You ready to eat?" I asked.

She looked up at me and smiled. "What, again?"

That's the great thing about microwave ovens. They don't care how long the food has been sitting on the counter.

I woke up Friday morning in a panic. The clothes in the sanctuary! What if someone came in? What if . . .

Naomi was gone. My clothes were folded neatly on the chair in the corner of the bedroom. Protecting my honor. Was this woman great or what?

Breakfast was a three-egg omelet, thick bacon, honey-fried toast, and coffee. I ate it at the diner, sitting at my usual place at the counter, watching May June's big butt move back and forth from the refrigerator to the griddle to the waffle iron and back again. She managed to do it like a ballerina, graceful, purposeful, and never missing a beat—cracking eggs, whipping them in a bowl, buttering toast, frying bread and butter on the griddle, pouring coffee—all the time keeping up a constant stream of chatter.

Finally, a little after eight in the morning, the breakfast rush stopped and she brought her mug of coffee over in front of me and refilled mine. "She told you?" she asked, not looking at me.

I sipped my coffee. "Yeah."

May June nodded. Thought for a moment, her face pinched with the effort it took. "He's a proud man, Reverend. He can't stand the thought of someone knowin' about our Junior. Dyin' the way he did."

In the two or so months I had been in Baird, May June Hall had called me Reverend only in public or in front of other members of the church. She thought that calling me by my first name might show that I was closer to her and Ray than to other members of the church and get me accused of favoritism. The fact that nearly two thirds of the active members in the church also called me Dan had somehow escaped her.

In private, she always called me by my Christian name. Except on three occasions: once when she came to inform me of a death of a member of the church, once when she asked me to explain a point of theology that she had never been able to understand, and just now. Using my title was, for May June, a signal that she was talking to her pastor, not her friend.

So I put on my best pastoral expression—serious, concerned, caring, supportive, strong, and a little world-weary. And I said nothing.

"I don't know why I told Naomi," she said. "I just couldn't stand it. I was so worried about you two. I saw the look on his face when it turned out to be drugs down there in Pitchfork Hollow."

"He really has a thing about drugs, doesn't he?" I asked, more to prod the conversation along than anything else.

She nodded enthusiastically. "It's a fixation with him. That's why he took the job when the sheriff, his cousin, offered it to him." She took my arm in her strong hand. "He's a good man, Dan. I don't have to tell you. He's as fine a man as ever come outa these mountains. But he's gonna kill Eugene Wisdom if that boy gives him half a reason. He'll look at Eugene and all he'll see is a drug dealer, and he'll kill him. I'm just worried sick."

"I know he's mad, May June. But he's been constable for, what, five years? He's never killed anyone yet, has he?" I wasn't sure I believed this myself, but it sounded reasonable.

She shook her head. "But he come close. The Taylor boys, Naomi's brothers? He like to beat poor Joshua to death with his bare hands. Jacob's still got a knee that ain't right. And they didn't resist arrest. They come along peaceful."

So that was it. I had heard the stories of Ray's arresting Naomi's two oldest brothers and how their father had never forgiven him for it. I thought it was for the arrest, for sending his boys to prison. But jail time was often worn like a badge of valor in the mountains. It wasn't the prison that had embittered the Taylors against Ray, it was the beatings and the humiliation.

"Why didn't someone report him?" I asked.

"It's not Hebrew Taylor's way to ask the police or a judge to settle scores for him," she said. "Besides, he said if he had known about what they were doing, he would have given 'em that beating hisself. He's mad because Ray took it on himself to do it instead of tellin' Hebrew about it and lettin' him deal with his family."

"And Naomi?" I asked. "Where does she fit into all of this? Why hasn't she ever said anything to me about it?"

May June shook her head and slapped my arm. "She was away at college. She never heard anything about it until it was all over and them boys was in prison. All she knew was that Ray arrested 'em and put 'em away. And that's what he done."

"Only he meted out a little Ray Hall justice before he turned them over to the state," I added.

She nodded again.

"What do you want me to do, May June? I'm a preacher. I'm not a cop. Shouldn't we call Elias and get some of the deputies up here? Maybe if they're all here, we can bring Eugene in alive."

"No," she said. "You done enough. You been beat up and stepped on already. I'm just as glad you didn't go with him this morning. I just wanted you to know. Pray for him. He's got the mood on him and he took his shotgun and I—"

"He's gone?"

She looked puzzled. "Why, yes. He left a few minutes 'fore you got here. I thought you knew. He said you were out of it now. Wouldn't do for a preacher to get mixed up—"

I ran as hard as I could for my Volkswagen. He had a thirty-minute head start on me and I would lose more time trying to baby the VW across the mountain, but it was the best I could do.

The motor fired the instant I turned the key, but then it sputtered and coughed. I prayed a quick prayer that it would at least get me to Pitchfork Hollow, slammed it into reverse, and backed out onto the road in front of a huge, green Ford LTD.

Naomi honked the horn and leaned out the window. "Hey, where you goin'? Where's Ray? I thought I'd come over and sit with May June while you two were out chasin' bad guys . . ."

I pulled the VW back into the parking lot, hopped out, and jumped into the passenger seat of her car. "Ray's gone. He left half an hour ago. How fast can you get me to Pitchfork Hollow?"

She left a black teardrop on the road as she spun the car around, and we passed three coal trucks before we got to the cutoff at County Road 3, heading up Mount Devoux.

16

"HE BEAT ME UP! LOOK WHAT HE DONE TO ME!" Bethabelle Wisdom sat on the porch of the big house crying. A large bruise was starting to form on her left cheek, and the corner of her mouth was bleeding. I could imagine that there were a couple of loose teeth in there as well.

Marie Wisdom, Charles's wife, sat next to her, dabbing at the cut mouth with a wet cloth, stroking the younger woman's hair. "That's nonsense," she said. "She went after him with a kitchen knife and he took it away from her's all. She didn't get no more'n she deserved."

"He's gonna kill my Eugene!" Bethabelle screamed. She began crying hysterically. Marie patted her back.

"Can you tell us what happened, Marie?" I asked. "When did Ray get here?"

Marie dipped the cloth in a bowl sitting at her feet

and wrung it out. "He got here about forty minutes ago, maybe eight-thirty or so. He drove his Jeep right through the yard over to Eugene and Bethabelle's trailer and commenced poundin' on the door."

"I got younguns!" Bethabelle sobbed. "He coulda shot one of 'em."

"Hush now!" Marie said to her. "Fine time for you to start carin' about them younguns of yourn. They was never in any danger from Ray Hall." She looked up at me. "He called out for Eugene to come out. If he'd asked, we coulda told him we ain't seen Eugene since yesterday when you all dipped out the privy. He took off in that ORV o' his an' we ain't seen him since."

Naomi brought a first aid kit from the trunk of the LTD and knelt to apply some ointment to Bethabelle's mouth and jaw. "What happened?" she asked Marie.

Bethabelle looked up suddenly and took in Naomi with her eyes. She looked at me and back at Naomi and back at me again. Oh, her eyes seemed to say. So that's how it is. She pulled her bathrobe, which had fallen open, revealing most of her breasts, tight around her waist.

Marie looked at Naomi and simply smiled. The birthmark on her neck and face seemed to fade a little when she smiled. "Well, Beth here started bad-mouthin' the constable. Cussin' and swearin', and he told her he was comin' in to search the trailer, and when he did she come at him with a kitchen knife. A wonder he didn't shoot her." She shook her head.

Bethabelle began to sob again. "He was doin' it for me! He told me he was just tryin' to get us enough to get off this stinkin' mountain. He wanted to be able to buy me nice things."

I looked at Marie and let my eyes ask the question.

"The drugs," Marie said. "She knew about it all along. We never knew until she told us just a bit ago. Said she was gonna run off with Price Deaver. Told that to Eugene." Marie couldn't seem to shake her head enough. "Told him she was leavin' him for a rich boy who would buy her nice things, so he worked up this deal to sell drugs that he bought from that Benny Kneeb. Ended up sellin' 'em to the Deaver boy. When you all found them drugs in the privy he just took off."

"Where did he go?" I asked both of the women.

Marie looked at Bethabelle, but Beth was having none of it. She had talked once, but she wasn't about to talk again. "I hope he kills that big old bastard. He took his gun with him and I hope he fuckin' kills him for what he done to us. Now I'll never get off this mountain." She was screaming now. Hysterical. "I hope he gutshoots him and—"

The screen door to the big house slammed, and in an instant Bethabelle was being lifted off the porch by her hair. She screamed and found herself facing her mother-in-law. Old Cleopha drew her hand back and slapped the girl so hard, I felt my own teeth rattle. Bethabelle screamed from pain and shock and Cleopha hit her again and she stopped screaming just as quickly.

Cleopha's voice was quiet but commanding. "This here is a preacher," she said, nodding to me. "He's here to try to save lives, not take 'em. Your husband done killed his brother and his friend and God knows how many other folks with that poison. And he done it all because he couldn't stand to see you twitchin' your butt in other men's faces like a bitch in heat." She tossed the girl back down onto the porch like a rag doll. "Now, you tell this man what he wants to know and you be quick about it or so help me, Jesus, I'll beat you like your husband shoulda."

Bethabelle collapsed into a pile of snot, blood, and tears. "The cabin," she said, just barely loud enough to hear. I looked at Marie and Cleopha and their faces were blank.

"What cabin?" I asked.

"On the trail," she sobbed. "On the ORV trail to Melrose. It's the cabin he used to meet Price and sell the stuff. They were supposed to meet last night. He said he would warn Price and they would get outa the county together."

Thank God. Ray might have been too late. Maybe Eugene and Price Deaver had met and already taken off for the low country. Maybe the highway patrol or the sheriff's office could pick them up and Ray wouldn't have to bring Eugene in dead or alive.

"When were Eugene an' Price gonna leave?" Naomi asked, reading my mind.

Bethabelle was drying her tears, getting back some of her sass. The robe had fallen open again and she left it, staring right into my eyes. "They ain't left yet," she said, almost defiantly.

"How do you know?" Cleopha demanded.

"'Cause one or t'other of 'em woulda come for me." She looked defiantly at Cleopha. "An' I don't rightly care which one it is."

I thought that Cleopha would be on top of her again, yanking hair and smacking her around, but she just stood there shaking her head. "Child, you got a lot to learn," she said. "You think you got the onliest one in the county?"

Knowledge dawned slowly but certainly in Bethabelle's eyes. *"No!"* she screamed. "They wouldn't leave me! They love me! Both of 'em! They told me they did!" She started to cry again.

Cleopha sat down on the porch and took the girl in her arms. "Most men will lie for a piece o' tail," she said, stroking Bethabelle's hair. "And many a man will kill for one. But ain't many willin' to die or go to prison for one."

I leaned close to Marie. "Where is the cabin?" I asked. "We've got to get there."

She pointed vaguely beyond her trailer, parked next to Eugene and Bethabelle's. "Yonder. It goes up and over the mountain to Melrose. From what she said, it's about six or eight miles over the mountain."

I looked at Naomi. "We'll find it," she assured me. But I wasn't so sure. My eyes roamed over the big LTD. On the road the big V-8 had eaten up the miles like a Tasmanian devil. But on a mountain trail it would be worthless. Ray's Jeep, on the other hand, would have had no trouble with the ruts and boulders.

Marie's voice penetrated my thoughts. ". . . Charles's ORV behind the trailer. It's gassed up and the keys are in it. I don't reckon he'll mind. I got to call him at the mine anyway. He'll want to come home and help us deal with all o' this."

Naomi and I ran across the yards, jumped the creek, and found the ORV behind the trailer just as Marie said it would be, gassed up, the keys in it. It being little more than a souped-up Volkswagen, I took the wheel.

The ORV trail was just that—a trail. It wasn't anything like a road. There were no tire tracks or ruts to follow, just a wide path through the trees sloping along the side of the mountain. Other trails intersected it, and twice we turned when we shouldn't have or went straight when we should have turned. Each time the trail we were on ended abruptly in a cluster of trees or just petered out.

Tree roots and boulders jutted up out of the ground, and I began to realize why the guys usually wore helmets when they drove these things. And I realized how Les Eastman rolled his ORV on the way to Devoux. Several times we bounced up on two wheels, nearly toppling over. Other times we would go over a sudden drop in the trail and the entire car would be airborne.

There was no speedometer on the thing, so I couldn't tell how fast I was going, but the look on Naomi's face told me it was plenty fast enough as far as she was concerned. Probably forty or fifty miles per hour, but it felt like eighty.

I didn't see Ray's Jeep until it was too late to stop. We rounded a sharp curve and I was struggling to keep the ORV upright. Sunlight sprayed through the trees and blinded me just long enough so that when we were back in the shade, my eyes didn't adjust to the dark quickly enough. We hit the Jeep's rear end with a loud smack that would have thrown us both over the front bumper had we not been wearing the shoulder harnesses.

The Jeep, of course, didn't move an inch. The front end of the ORV smashed into it, under the rear bumper, bent the front end all to hell, and killed the motor instantly.

It was then that we heard the gunshots.

There were four of them, loud and explosive, but not the deep boom of a shotgun. More like a *crack.* Four of them, pulled off in rapid fire. *Crack . . . crack . . . crack . . . crack.* A handgun. Probably a .22 or something about that size.

Then nothing.

In the woods they seemed to be coming from all around us and we dove out of the ORV and crawled behind Ray's Jeep. I peeked over the side just enough to see that the keys were in it but the shotgun wasn't.

"Can you tell where the shots came from?" I asked Naomi as I hunkered down beside the Jeep. I wondered if we shouldn't crawl under it.

Naomi shrugged, then pointed over the Jeep. "On up the mountain, I think. That makes sense. Most folks build uphill from the road if they got a choice."

I looked at her. Really?

"That way if it's rainin' or snowin', you can slide on down to the road without gettin' stuck. Get to work or to town if you have to." She shrugged again and smiled. Just another little bit of mountain wisdom you city preachers wouldn't know about.

I peeked over the Jeep again and swallowed. I did not like the idea of walking into a gun battle, but if the sound was a handgun, it meant that Ray wasn't doing the shooting. It also meant that Eugene had given Ray his excuse. If May June and Naomi were right, one of those men would kill the other very shortly. Either way, Ray would be the loser. I had to try to stop him, stop it from happening. How, I had no idea.

I knelt back down beside Naomi and started to say, "You stay here," but before I could get the third word out she said, "Bullshit," and took off up the mountain, running zigzag like a trooper.

I followed.

A hundred yards up I was winded and leaning against a tree when three more shots rang out, followed by a voice shouting something I couldn't make out. Still no shotgun blast.

I wondered if Ray was okay. He must have been or

Eugene wouldn't be shooting. But why wasn't Ray shooting back? Another twenty yards up the slope, Naomi motioned that we should keep moving. I sighed and followed her.

Fifty yards farther and I could see the cabin. It wasn't a cabin, really. More of a shack. It was snuggled into the side of the mountain, its back wall pressed tight against the red earth. Rough-cut pine boards were nailed together with gaping holes between them. Two windows, probably scavenged from other old buildings, had been set into the walls on either side of the door, but all the glass was broken out of them. The door was painted red and had obviously come from another shack, probably just like this one.

I crawled up next to Naomi and we crouched behind a big white oak tree. "What's going on?" I asked. "Can you see anything?"

She smiled and pointed.

I followed her arm, and there, not thirty yards away, parallel to us, in front of the cabin, was Ray. He was sitting behind another big oak, leaning against it smoking a cigarette. The shotgun was lying, broken open, across his legs. Naomi giggled.

"Looks like he's okay," I said, relieved.

"Hell. It looks like he's squirrel huntin'. Look at 'im. Just sittin' there smokin' like he's got all the time and not a care in the world."

I took off my cap and waved it back and forth trying to get his attention. Nothing doing. Whatever he was thinking about, he was thinking hard and not about to look up.

"He's in his own world," Naomi said. Then she stuck two fingers in her mouth and whistled a sharp blast that nearly deafened me.

Ray looked up with a start, saw us cowering behind the tree, smiled and waved. Naomi smiled and waved back.

What the hell was wrong with these two? Here we were, hiding behind trees being shot at by a lunatic, and they were waving and grinning at each other like they had just arrived at the church social.

Three more shots rang out and Naomi and I hit the ground, trying to get as small as possible. Ray looked over his shoulder at the shack, then stood and, without so much as a crouch, walked to where we were shivering on the ground.

"You didn't bring any coffee, did you?" he asked as he sat down and leaned his shotgun against a tree.

"Jesus, Ray!" was all I could make myself say.

"I didn't think so. What'd you think, I was gonna kill that poor boy?" he asked, nodding toward the shack.

"It crossed our mind," Naomi said, still smiling.

Ray began his cigarette ritual. He nodded. "Mine, too. Matter of fact, that's what I come up here for this morning."

"But?" I asked, hoping desperately that there was a "But . . ."

"But I've been doin' some thinkin' here the last hour or so." Four more shots rang out from the cabin, but Ray didn't so much as cringe. "Don't worry. He can't hit shit. He's all loaded up on cocaine. Thinks he's James Cagney. Top o' the world, Ma!"

"Fuck you, lawman! Fuck you! You hear that? I said, fuck you!" Eugene's voice rang out clear but nearly hysterical from the cabin.

Ray shook his head sadly. "Lawman. You ever hear such nonsense?"

"Where'd he get the coke?" Naomi asked. "I thought you guys found his stash in the bottom of the crapper."

"Price Deaver," Ray said, drawing on his cigarette. "This here's Price's clubhouse. Probably kept a stash here or brought some with him."

"Price Deaver's in there?" I asked.

Ray nodded. "Sure is. Or was. Dependin' on how you look at it."

"Whatdaya mean, dependin'?" Naomi asked. But I knew what he was talking about. Sadly.

"He means that Price is dead," I said, looking at Ray for confirmation. He nodded. "Eugene kill him?" I asked.

He nodded again and sighed. "Yeah, I reckon. Thought Price was gonna run off with his woman."

"I thought Price was in jail," I said. "What's he doing up here?"

Ray shrugged. "Price's daddy is rich and a member of city council in Perry. Probably bailed him out no more'n the door locked."

"How do you know he's dead?" Naomi asked.

Ray leaned out around the tree and pointed. "That's his jacket, ain't it?"

I looked, and sure enough, a black leather jacket was lying on the ground beside a big tree stump. It looked wet.

"Gene threw it out there a while ago when we were talkin'," Ray said. "That's blood on it."

"You've talked to Eugene?" I asked.

"Nothin' but talked," Ray said. He ground his cigarette against the sole of his shoe. "He told me some of it; I figured out the rest."

"The rest of what?"

"Of what happened." Ray stretched out his legs and leaned back around the tree. "You okay in there, Eugene?" he yelled.

Three shots rang out. "Fuck you, Hall!"

"He's okay," Ray said, sitting back up. "What I figure is he went out to get his stash from the crapper where Benny hid it and Big John caught him. He got scared and coldcocked John and dumped him in the crapper. He was panicked and forgot to get the stash first and it went in with Big John. He came back out and saw Les headin' off for the woods. He probably seen Eugene kill Big John. Anyway, I figure he killed Les to cover his tracks."

"But why did he torture Les?" I asked. It sounded plausible, but something didn't track quite right.

"Les was probably blackmailin' 'im. Gene was just makin' sure ol' Les didn't have nothin' written down. When he didn't find nothin' he decided to burn Les's trailer just to make sure. Or maybe he figured Les had the stash, had gotten it before Big John came into the picture. Who knows?"

I didn't know what to say.

"Funny thing is," Ray said with a sigh, "she ain't even that good-lookin' aside from the tits and ass. You see her teeth? Looks like she's been eatin' Oreos for about a month and never drank her milk."

"What?" Naomi said. "Who are we talkin' about here?"

"That wife of his," Ray said. "He done it for her. Said she was gonna leave him if he didn't get them enough money to move. Said she would leave with Price Deaver, who, by the way, she was screwin' in this here shack. Romantic, ain't it? Price'd meet Eugene here to buy his dope and then double back and screw Eugene's wife right here in the same cabin."

"Wait a minute," I said, suddenly realizing what was wrong with the story. "Charles said he got home at midnight and Les and R.D. were gone already. John didn't die until after one in the morning."

Ray chuckled. "Charles lied," he said. "I knew he was lyin', but I had it wrong what he was lyin' about. I talked to his wife this mornin' and he didn't get home until nearly three in the mornin'."

"But why lie about it?" Naomi asked.

"The union! That spit and whittle group he was with was plannin' a wildcat walkout. That's why he lied. He didn't want anyone knowin' what the union was plannin' to do. Afraid the company would take action. Charles's livin' in the nineteen twenties. He still believes the company will call in the Pinkertons if they find out about a strike."

"So it was Eugene who broke my nose in Les's cabin?" I asked, not believing it. He was such a skinny little fart. It hurt my pride to think he had bested me in the trailer.

"Sure. He took off after the funeral and came over to Les's house by way o' this here path. Probably took him about thirty minutes. Parked his ORV in the woods and beat the shit outa you and Les. Lucky you startled him or he woulda burnt down the place and we'd have no evidence."

"He told you all of this?" I asked.

"Some of it, I told you. Some I figured out. Why, Preacher? You don't like the sound of it?"

I didn't. Something was still wrong. Something we had both seen or hadn't seen that made the story a little hard to swallow. But, again, I couldn't remember what it was.

"Anyway," Ray went on, directing his story at Naomi. "Eugene and Price was supposed to have a meet up here and Price was gonna buy the dope from Eugene. Only the dope was in the crapper and then we had it, and Eugene figured his goose was cooked. So he come up here, and when Price walked in, Eugene shot him. Three, maybe four times.

"He may not be able to hang on to dope, but, by God, he was gonna hang on to his woman."

"Hey, pig fucker!" Eugene's voice shot out of the cabin. "Why don't you leave me alone and go find the fucker that killed my brother?"

Ray stood and brushed his butt off with his hands. He picked up his shotgun. "It's the drugs talkin'," he said. "Trouble with cocaine is it makes you think you're perfect, invincible, smart, and everything else under the sun. What I'm afraid of, he'll think he's bulletproof and come chargin' outa that cabin with guns blazin'. I'll have to shoot him in self-defense."

"I thought that's what you come up here for," Naomi said, winking at me.

"Oh, I did," Ray said, smiling. "I surely did."

"What changed your mind?"

"Well, we been sittin' here, talkin' and yellin' back and forth at each other, and it just occurred to me, he ain't dangerous, he's pitiful. No merit in killin' a man as pitiful as him."

"No," Naomi said, agreeably.

"I guess May June told you 'bout our trouble," Ray said without looking back at us. "Or else why would you come all the way up here?"

Our silence was enough of an answer.

"I thought so," he said. "Well, don't worry, I ain't lost my marbles yet." He loaded a shell into the shotgun and held two others in his left hand. "Well, I guess we better get him outa there before he does some real damage with that peashooter he's got." He shot a look over his shoulder as he moved away toward the cabin. "Naomi, you get yourself a handful o' rocks and crawl over yonder away from the door. You wait until I whistle and then you start throwin' rocks at the cabin and screamin' your lungs out. Try to draw his attention toward you, but stay down outa gunsight. Anything happens to either of us, you hightail it back to a phone and call Elias and tell him what I told you just now. Tell him to get up here with everything he's got."

He looked at me and then back at the cabin. Two more shots rang out, more for effect than for accuracy. "Well, come on, Preacher. Let's see if we can flush this sinner out of his hiding place."

17

"He's crazy but he ain't stupid," Ray said after Naomi had moved off toward the other side of the shack. "He never empties the gun. Shoots three or four rounds, then stops. He may reload or he may not, no way to know. He must have a whole box o' shells in there."

"So how we gonna flush him out, Rambo?" I asked, not at all excited about Ray's including me in his plan.

"Well," he said, standing and leaning behind the tree. "First we try to talk him out." He cupped his hands to his mouth and yelled, "Eugene! Okay, boy, it's time to stop fuckin' around here. We had a nice talk and ever'thing's settled. Now, put down that gun and come on out and let's finish it up. I promise not to hurt you none."

The silence seemed to go on forever, though it was probably no more than a minute. Then, *crack, crack,*

crack. "Fuck you! Ain't nothin' settled. You don't know shit!"

Ray blew out through puffed cheeks, took off his cap, and ran his hand through his hair. "Goddamn drugs." He reset his cap and looked at me. "Well, we ain't gonna talk him out."

I followed Ray from tree to tree, walking slowly, slightly crouched, until we were within twenty feet of the corner of the cabin. Unless Eugene looked directly out the window, he couldn't see where we were. The only two windows were in the front on either side of the door. The ends of the shanty were completely boarded over.

Ray nodded toward the end of the house and we both ran to it and flattened ourselves against the wall. He put his fingers in his mouth and whistled a loud blast and immediately a hail of fist-size rocks started pounding the opposite end of the cabin. Naomi was screaming and hollering from somewhere behind a tree and hurling the things like a Gatling gun.

Ray waited until he heard the shots and then he moved like a rocket. *Crack!* He was around the corner. *Crack!* He was under the window on our side and moving toward the door. *Crack!* He slammed against the door with his shoulder and it caved in. *Crack!* He was standing in the shack pointing his shotgun at Eugene.

By the time I got inside the cabin, Eugene was still pointing his pistol out the window toward where the rocks were coming from, but he was looking, startled, at Ray. He hadn't shaved, but what little beard he had just made him look dirty around his mouth. He was wearing the bib overalls he had worn in Les's trailer, the pocket on the bib torn and hanging by one corner.

The place was a mess. The only furniture was in the center of the cabin, a table and two old kitchen chairs. On the table was a Coleman lantern and a piece of mirror with two neat lines of cocaine laid out on it. A razor blade and a small plastic bag half-full of powder were beside it. A small ghetto blaster was sitting in one corner of the room, and some girlie magazines were thrown here and there. An old red Coca-Cola cooler was pushed under the table. The whole place smelled like beer, pot, cigarettes, and unwashed bodies. And blood. I looked around for Price Deaver and saw him in the darkest corner of the building. He was propped up against the wall, his legs out in front of him, crossed at the ankles, a joint hanging from the corner of his mouth. He was wearing leather motorcycle chaps over blue jeans and a sleeveless undershirt. There were a dozen little red dots on his chest, and each had a line of red running down from it. The blood had pooled under him and begun to coagulate. I tasted bile in the back of my throat and swallowed hard as I looked away. It wouldn't do to start throwing up here. I felt in my pocket for my smelling salts. Not there, of course. I'd left in too big a hurry to bring them.

"Just drop the gun outside the window," Ray said in a low, firm voice. This was not a request.

Eugene didn't move, but he smiled. It was a drug smile. Ray's fear was becoming reality. The coke was making Eugene feel invincible. Did he think he was bulletproof as well?

"Eugene, goddamn it, boy, I don't want to hurt you, but I will. Drop that goddamn gun right now." Ray cocked the hammer back on the shotgun.

Eugene began to giggle. "Big fuckin' cop. Big fuckin' hillbilly, thinks he knows ever' goddamn thing. You don't know shit, Mr. Constable."

"Why don't you put the gun down and educate me, Eugene." Ray stepped forward. The barrel of the shotgun was not more than four feet from Eugene's chest.

"Eugene! Eugene! Jesus, you sound like Momma and Charles. Big John never called me Eugene. Said it sounded like a sissy name. He called me Gene." He rested his arm on the windowsill, but the gun stayed in his hand.

"Okay, Gene," I said, trying my luck. "We do have some questions. Maybe you could help us fill in the blanks. It wouldn't hurt things a bit if we could tell the county attorney that you were cooperative."

"That's right," Ray said, nodding. "He don't have to know about any of this here stuff."

"Big John woulda killed me if he saw me like this," Eugene said, looking down at the table and the coke. "He didn't like drugs."

"That why you killed him?" Ray asked. "He catch you with the drugs and try to whup you?"

"No! Goddamn, you're stupid. Think, will ya? Big John was down in the shit and piss in the crapper." He brought his empty left hand up and wiped sweat from his face. He was coming down from the cocaine. In a minute he would start to feel persecuted, hounded, paranoid, and he might panic.

Ray looked at me and rolled his eyes. Yeah, right. "How about Price here?" he asked. "He tryin' to steal your woman?"

Eugene spit a large gob toward Deaver's body. "I shoulda never got mixed up with him, the little faggot. Swishin' around in them leather pants, gettin' me fucked up on this damn shit. He was fuckin' her right here. Right here in our shack. Don't that beat all? She said she was gonna leave me and go with him.

"Him, the little shit. He comes up here thinkin' he's gonna buy some more dope from me and then fuck my wife while I'm on my way back to the holler. Well, fuck him!" He spat again.

"And Les?" I asked him.

"Hey, Preacher," he said, as if seeing me for the first time. "You throw a pretty good punch for a preacher. Sorry about the crack on the head, but . . ." He didn't finish. What could he say? Sorry I nearly crushed your skull, but you caught me torturing a man to death, and a man has to do what a man has to do.

"Why?" I asked. "Why, Les?"

"Hell, I figured he had my stash! And besides, he knew—"

"Jesus, what are you all gonna do, talk all day?" Naomi walked through the front door and I turned, realizing that it was a mistake. Everything seemed to happen in slow motion then.

I saw Naomi's face smiling as she looked at Ray and me. Then her face turned serious and paled as her eyes widened. As I turned my head to see what she was looking at, I noticed that Ray had turned to see her come in, too, and now he, too, was turning back toward Eugene.

Eugene brought his hand back into the window, faster than I would have thought he could move, as strung out as he was. But the hammer on the revolver caught on the crosspiece of the window and made him hesitate for a split second. That split second saved my life.

By the time I was completely turned around, the .22 revolver was pointing straight at my face. Yes, it was only a .22, but from my vantage point it looked like a howitzer. And it was so close, I could smell the cordite from all the shells he had fired. It smelled like death.

Eugene's first mistake had been not dropping the gun when Ray told him to. His second was pointing it at me instead of Ray. Ray was the immediate threat, not me. But I was the first one in line as he brought the gun around, so I was the one he pointed it at. And the decision to shoot the preacher was his last mistake.

Ray shot him.

The .410 shotgun is not very big or powerful by shotgun standards. It is so little, in fact, that it's just about worthless for birds. It's a varmint gun, mostly. The shells are too small to fill with anything but BBs. No double-ought buckshot for this gun. And Ray's was a single-shot. You fired it, broke it open and ejected the shell, reloaded, popped it back together, and fired again. It was slow, inaccurate, and not very powerful.

But at four feet—three by the time Eugene turned around toward me—it was plenty big enough. The force of the blast picked Eugene up and all but threw him through the window. It was a small window, not more than two feet by two feet, but Eugene went most of the way through it, back and ass first.

He was dead before he hit the wall. His chest was a mass of mangled bone, muscle, and flesh. I yelled in fear and surprise, Naomi screamed, and Ray just stood there, holding his shotgun with both hands and looking at Eugene's body.

Finally the smoke cleared, the ringing in our ears stopped and our hearing came back, and Ray stepped out of the cabin. "Goddamn drugs," he said. "Goddamn drugs!"

* * *

We took Ray's Jeep back to Pitchfork Hollow and called Elias, Doc, and the Carmack twins from there. It would take them over an hour to get to the hollow, so we sat with the family and told them, as best as we could, what had happened at the cabin.

Bethabelle became hysterical and ran to her trailer, Charlotte following after her, quoting her Bible and admonishing her to be strong in the Lord. I guess Charlotte figured that she now had a kindred spirit in Bethabelle, both of them being widows and all. Yeah, right. Fat chance.

We didn't tell them what we thought had happened on Sunday night because we still weren't sure ourselves. No, that's not right. Ray was sure. I wasn't. I prevailed on Ray to say nothing until we had a chance to talk, and he agreed, reluctantly.

Elias and Doc and, surprise, Deputy Karn arrived, and it was well past noon by the time we had finished making our statements and they had finished taking pictures, measuring, and gathering evidence. Gilbert and Gaylord brought the bodies down the mountain in body bags in the back of Ray's Jeep, the trail being too narrow for the unit.

The big deputy sheriff was still sweet on his old high school sweetheart, Naomi, and it was kind of cute watching him question her while trying to be gentle and polite. With me, the guy who was dating and planning to marry his old girlfriend, the guy who was a good sixteen years older than him and his ex-girlfriend, he was polite but abrupt. With Ray, he was as awestruck as ever.

"Christ A'mighty, Ray," Elias whined. "There's over a hundred twenty-two shell casings in and around that cabin. What'd you two do? Have a war up there?"

"He did," Ray said. "Not me. He was full of drugs and shootin' at anything that made a noise."

"An' Price Deaver's got more 'n fifteen holes in him. Eugene had to reload his gun twice to shoot him that many times. That's a right smart o' hate."

Ray just nodded.

Elias shrugged. "Well, the sheriff ain't gonna like this, I can tell ya. He ain't gonna like this one bit. All you have on him, really, is his unsubstantiated confession and the dope. Sheriff Fine ain't gonna like it."

Ray sighed. "Elias, the fucker is dead. He tried to shoot the preacher here and I shot him. I got two witnesses who'll verify that. Now, what the hell is there not to like?"

"Well, what about John Wisdom and Les Eastman and Price Deaver? What about the three of them? How do they fit into this picture?" Something dawned suddenly on Elias. "Oh, shit! With the sheriff outa town, I'm gonna be the one has to tell Mr. Deaver his boy's dead. Oh, shit!"

Ray patted him on the shoulder. "That's why they pay you them big bucks, boy," he said. "Can we go now?"

Elias visibly swelled when Ray asked him for his permission. At least there were some benefits to being the chief deputy. Ray Hall showed you respect. "Yeah, go on," he said, going easy on us. Lettin' us off with a warning. "But I want your report on my desk by noon tomorrow."

We stood to leave, Ray, Naomi, and I, and Ray shook his head and grumbled, "Don't push it, Elias."

When we got to Naomi's LTD I got behind the wheel and Ray leaned into the window. The muscles in his face sagged with weariness and sadness, both in equal measure. "So you gonna tell me what's on your mind about what happened Sunday night?" he asked.

I looked out through the windshield at the crapper in the side yard. The privy, the outhouse, the Taj Mahal, the Trump Tower, the Empire State Building, the National Cathedral of crappers. Something. Something about it was still sitting uncomfortably on my mind. And something Eugene had said was scratching at that discomfort, trying to open it, make it bleed.

"Tomorrow," I said. "Brunch?"

Ray looked at me and shook his head again. "Brunch my ass."

I should have gone home. I should have worked on my sermon and tried to put the events of the last four days out of my mind. I should have made myself a mug of strong tea and a shot of Black Jack and tried to get some sleep.

But that's why I'm the pastor of a little hillbilly church up in the mountains where they still shout "Amen" during the sermons and they call potluck dinners "pitch-in's." Most men and some women who have been ordained as long as I have are in big suburban churches with nice split-level parsonages filled with kids and dogs and new furniture. But that's because they know what they should do and they do it. That's always been a problem for me.

My mother says it's a character flaw. Something about rebelling against authority. Mom took a course in psychology once. I don't know what it is. Maybe she's right, most of the time. But not that day.

That day I didn't go back to my house and work on my sermon like I should have because I had just seen a man blown in half with a shotgun. I had seen another who had been shot fifteen times lying in a lake of his own blood. I had heard Bethabelle Wisdom's scream of despair when she learned that her only two chances at freedom had been killed. I had seen the look of despair and sorrow on Charles Wisdom's face, and I had heard Marie Wisdom's sweet, clear voice singing "Amazing Grace" as we drove from the yard of her mother-in-law's home.

There was no way I was going to go home and sit alone and try to write a sermon, and I knew that if I cracked open that bottle of Black Jack for one drink, I would climb right down into it and not come out for two days.

So what I should do entered my mind for about three seconds, flitted around, found no welcome, and left as quickly as it came. What I wanted and needed took its place and snuggled in for the evening.

What I wanted and needed was to go home with Naomi and sit with her in her hot tub under the balcony and look out over the gold and red and orange October mountains. I wanted to drink a glass of cheap, sweet wine and feel it warm my chest on the way down. I wanted to rest my head between Naomi's big, warm breasts and listen to her heartbeat and be assured that life really was stronger than death. And I wanted to make slow, tender love on her big featherbed under the quilts that her grandmother and mother had patiently stitched just for her and her future family.

So I went home with Naomi, and we sat in her hot tub and we drank hot applejack because she was out of wine, and we crawled slowly, wearily, into her bed just as the sun was going down and we gave each other ourselves. Slowly, tenderly, peacefully, touching, kissing, fondling, exploring, embracing, joining, moving, and, finally, crying out together. And then drifting, sleeping, entwined in each other's arms, afraid to let go, to be alone for even a moment.

Except I couldn't sleep.

I dozed and woke, dozed and woke.

"You awake?" Naomi asked, running her fingers through my hair, playing with my ear. My head rested on the crook of her arm, my chin on her breast. We had, I realized, reversed roles. Tradition said it was the woman who was supposed to lie in the man's embrace. At least that's the way they did it in all the movies. Screw the movies. And screw Sigmund Freud, too.

"Yeah," I said. I didn't want to break the mood.

"It's ten o'clock and we haven't had anything to eat since breakfast," she said. "I'm hungry."

"How about an omelet?"

"With Swiss cheese and bacon? And an English muffin?"

"I'll cook," I said, getting slowly out of bed. My clothes were on the floor, and I realized, for the first time, that Eugene Wisdom's blood had somehow made it onto my flannel shirt. I went to the closet and found a pair of corduroy slacks I had secreted there with a big, hooded pullover shirt my mother had bought in Mexico on one of her senior citizen tours. I pulled on a pair of Naomi's big, woolly sweat socks.

"I'll help," she said, getting out of bed and throwing on a terry cloth robe.

We cooked in silence, enjoying the closeness of her tiny kitchen. Touching, patting, holding each other as we moved back and forth. Naomi brought a comforter out of a closet and spread it in front of the fireplace and lit the gas burners, while I slid the omelets onto two plates, buttered the muffins, and refilled our mugs with applejack and cinnamon sticks. In a moment the fire was crackling and she shut off the gas. The room was warm and comfortable and I never wanted to leave it. I didn't give a damn what the people of the church thought or said.

"So what is it?" she asked, a few minutes later, setting her empty plate aside and sipping at her mug of jack.

"Well, in the past three days I've seen four dead bodies, gotten beat up and nearly shot," I said. Wasn't that enough?

She laid her hand on my neck and massaged the muscles there. "But there's somethin' else," she said. "You're not scared now. You were earlier, but you aren't now. You're thinkin'. I can tell the difference."

I rolled my head back, enjoying her massage. "Pretty perceptive," I said.

She continued the massage, moving around behind me, pulling my head back against her.

"He confessed to killing Les and Price Deaver. He even confessed to beating me up," I said. "But he didn't confess to killing his brother. Not outright, like the others. It was more like he was teasing us."

"Ray said he did," she said, not arguing, just bringing it up. "He said he killed him, but he never said why."

I nodded and sat up, looking into the fire. "Ray asked him if he killed Big John because he caught him with the dope. And he said no. He said Ray was stupid. Big John was down there in the shit and piss."

Naomi moved around beside me to where she could see my face again. "But if he didn't kill him because of the dope, then why did he kill him? And what does being down in the outhouse have to do with it? Was that some kind of message? The shit and piss?"

"Why?" It was haunting me. "Why would he kill his brother? And why put on such a show about catching whoever did it and being so angry and all? If it wasn't the dope, what was it?" My applejack was getting cold, but it still warmed my chest on the way down and it was making me drowsy.

We sat there in silence for a few minutes, both of us running the whole thing through our minds over and over. Sunday night. Eugene at the cabin talking like a crazy man. Ray asking him questions. His answers.

"Dan? Dan?" Naomi was shaking me. I must have dozed off, sitting in front of the fire. Or maybe I was lost in thought.

"What?"

"Tell me again. What exactly did they say?"

I closed my eyes. "Ray asked, 'Is that why you killed Big John? Because he caught you with the dope?' And Eugene said, 'No! You're stupid. Big John was down in the shit and piss.' Or something like that."

Naomi bit her lip in thought. "So you and Ray thought that when Eugene said 'No,' he meant, 'No, that's not why I killed him.' "

I nodded.

"But what if he didn't mean that at all. What if he meant, 'No, I didn't kill him.' What if he meant that Big John's bein' in the outhouse proved that, if only you'd think about it?"

So I thought about it.

And, of course, she was right. It was right there, had been all the time. Ray and I had even seen it and forgotten that we'd seen it. But things had been so crazy, and people kept dying. No wonder we'd missed it.

I kissed Naomi and called Ray. I told him who had killed Big John Wisdom, and how and why, and he agreed to meet me the next morning at the address I gave him.

And he said, "Tomorrow I want you to kick my ass for me for bein' so blind and cussed."

"I think I'll leave your ass kickin' to May June," I said.

He didn't laugh, but I could almost hear him smile through the phone. "Naw, she'd like it too much. I let her get near my ass and next thing you know, she's got ideas."

I hung up the phone and smiled at Naomi. Now I had ideas. We fell into bed, not giddy, not even happy, really. There had been too much pain and death in the past seventy-two hours for much happiness. But we were content. Content and comforted and safe in each other's arms.

Sometimes that's as good as happy.

18

R. D. MILES WAS SITTING ON HIS PORCH DRINKING COFFEE and smoking a cigarette when we pulled up in Ray's Jeep. The first frost had come the night before and the shady spots in his tiny yard were still white. The rain from two days before had knocked some of the leaves off the trees, but they were still beautiful and the sun was bright enough to take the edge off the morning cold.

R.D. offered us coffee and we both accepted. Ray took his black and I doctored mine with milk and sugar, as always.

Back out on the porch, Ray took a slat-board rocker and I sat in the porch swing. R.D. took a tulip-shaped metal lawn chair. We all lit smokes and I realized that this was the first time I had been to R.D.'s house. I had seen him several times and he had even pulled me out of Les's trailer and taken me to Baird, maybe even saved my life. But this was the first time I'd seen where he lived.

It was a little two-bedroom frame house, white with fresh paint, and a yard that would have been well tended if grass would have grown in the sandstone and clay. His ORV sat beside the house, half under the porch which stood on stilts only a few yards off the road. Anyplace else in the country he would have been considered poor. Here he was solid middle class.

"I heard about Eugene and the Deaver boy," R.D. said. "I'm sorry for you, Ray. I know you don't take no pleasure in such things."

Ray nodded and sipped his coffee. Any smile that might have been on his face as I talked to him on the phone the night before had long since moved on. He clearly didn't like being here, doing what he was doing. "Loretta and the children?" he asked.

"They went off to see Loretta's mother over to Middletown for a spell," R.D. said. "I sent 'em in the truck." He started to sip his coffee, but he just looked into the mug instead. "I allowed as how you'd be here sooner or later. Sooner what with what happened yesterday."

Ray threw his cigarette butt into the road and sank back in his chair with a sigh. "I don't take no pleasure in this, R.D. You know that."

"I know you don't, Ray. Nor you, Reverend," he said, nodding to me. "I appreciate your comin' along. It's a comfort." He looked back at Ray, then at me again. "You got it pretty much worked out?"

I nodded.

"How'd you figure it?"

"Drag marks," I said. "There weren't any drag marks. One man couldn't have carried Big John

Wisdom into the outhouse and thrown him in. It had to be two men or there would have been drag marks. Doc's report said he weighed two hundred eighty-four pounds when he died."

"Maybe he was already in the crapper," R.D. said without much enthusiasm, just to be talking.

I shook my head. "He had plumbing, R.D. There wasn't any need for him to use the crapper. Cleopha said he never used it. And he was hit on the back of the head. Someone had to have snuck up on him."

"You never did know about the drugs, did you?" Ray cut in. "You and Les never knew."

R.D. shook his head. "Not until later. I sort of figured it was somethin' like that, Eugene killin' Les the way he did. But I didn't know for sure until last night when I heard about what went on down to the holler. What was it exactly, Ray?"

Ray started his cigarette ritual and I relit my pipe. "Well, Benny Kneeb was sellin' cocaine to Eugene Wisdom, who was sellin' it to Price Deaver, who was sellin' it to white trash kids in town."

R.D. nodded as though he'd known it all along.

"Eugene never got stuck in Stinkin' Creek on Sunday," Ray went on. "He met Benny there and paid him and told Benny to hide the drugs in the crapper, hangin' from a string under the seat, and that's what he done. Eugene figured to go get the stuff after you all were gone or passed out drunk Sunday night."

R.D. shook his head. "We fucked up his drug bidness, didn't we? Me and Les surely fucked up his drug bidness. Just like we fucked up ever'thing else."

"They all said you left early," Ray said, prompting R.D. He knew that the only proof we would ever get would be a confession, and he wanted to get R.D. in a talking frame of mind.

"And we did," R.D. said. "Lord, Ray, it was awful. Big John was ridin' Les all day. John always did pick on Les, but it was worse than usual. He just wouldn't let it go. The football game, Les turnin' his ORV over, the race. An' Les just kept drinkin' and stewin'."

"Ain't a good thing for a man to let his feelin's stew," Ray said. "Especially when there's anger in 'im."

"Well, that's what he done. After me and Charles broke up the fight after the ball game, ol' Les, he just kept it all in, bidin' his time. So after we got back to the holler, after the race, we all sat around drinkin' beer and shootin' the shit. Finally I can't stand Big John's mouth any longer an' I says to Les we oughta get goin' before it's dark." He smiled and shook his head. "Hell, like we was scared of the dark or somethin'. Shit, I woulda figured Big John to take off on that. He knew damn well that we grew up on this mountain. Me and Les, we coulda drove them ORVs home blindfolded in a fog and a twister if we wanted. But Big John, he let it go by, and I figured it was time to cut an' run."

R.D. pulled his cigarette pack out of his shirt pocket and found it empty, wadded it and threw it off the porch. Ray offered him one of his Camels and he took it and lit it with an old Zippo.

"So we take off and get about a half mile into the woods," R.D. went on. "And Les says he don't feel so good. Says he's drunk too much beer and he's gotta puke. We pull up an' he gets out and walks around a bit, but he ain't pukin'. What he's doin' is lookin' back down the trail toward the holler.

"I'm thinkin', 'Oh, shit.' And I'm tryin' to talk him outa doin' somethin' dumb, you know. But he's drunk and his pride, what little he's got left, is hurtin'.

"Finally he says, 'I'm goin' back. Me an' Big John still got a score to settle.' An' he starts walkin' back down the path, me followin' tryin' to talk sense to 'im.

"Well, hell, Ray. I mighta just as soon tried to talk sense to that big sugar maple yonder." He puffed the Camel, inhaling short drags. He was used to low-tar cigarettes, and the Camel was making him a little woozy, I think.

"Well, by then it was pure dark and we got back to the holler and Les just sits down on them logs by the crapper there and says he'll wait. Sooner or later, he says, Big John'll have to leave his mother's house and walk on over to his own place, and when he does Les figures on callin' him out.

"Now, I'd been drinkin' beer, too. Not like them other boys, but I guess I drunk my share, and after a while I had to take me one killer of a piss, and seein' as how we was right there by the crapper, I stepped inside to use it. Well, I no sooner got my fly unzipped than I hear voices outside.

"Big John, he come outa Cleopha's place staggerin' like a sailor—he's a mean drunk, let me tell you—and Les stands up and calls him out, says somethin' about whippin' his ass for him." R.D. tossed the cigarette into the road. "Goddamn, what was wrong with him? What made him think he could whip Big John Wisdom's ass? Even drunk he shoulda knowed better.

"Well, Big John, he thinks that's the funniest thing he's ever heard, and I can tell he ain't gonna stop at whippin' Les's ass. Big John was drunk and mad and in a bad mood, and like as not he woulda killed Les. So I eased outa the crapper there, and I picked up the first big stick I could find and I just stayed in the shadows and walked around behind John and I coldcocked him right upside the head." R.D. stood up and walked to the railing of the porch.

"He fell like he'd been shot," he said, wonder in his voice. "Me and Les, we just kinda looked at him and at each other and I guess we panicked. We thought I'd killed him, and we panicked and figured we'd better hide the body. Les took his legs and I took his arms and we grunted and groaned and hauled his fat ass up into the crapper and dumped him in."

He stopped then. He stood, staring out across the road at the mountains. I hadn't noticed before, but there was a beautiful view of the mountains from R.D.'s porch.

"But he wasn't dead," Ray said, quietly. Prompting, I suppose.

R.D. shook his head. "Oh, Christ Jesus." His voice was breaking. The memory must have been haunting him all week. "He came to, no sooner than he hit bottom. Gruntin' and cussin' and threatenin' us. An' gaggin' and pukin', too.

"I guess I panicked again. I took off. I hit that door and I didn't stop runnin' again until I was standin' beside my ORV up the trail. I don't know what I was more afraid of, that I'd killed him or that I hadn't. I knew that if he ever got outa there, he'd kill us both, and I was flat scared, I'll tell ya.

"Les come walkin' up the trail about a half hour later. He said he tried to help Big John outa the crapper, but he was too fat and his hand kept slippin' away. He said Big John was cussin' and gaggin' one minute and the next he was dead, just floatin' in the shit. We figured the whop on the head finally caught up with him."

Ray shook his head and looked at me. Ain't this the pitifulest goddamn thing you ever heard, his eyes seemed to say. "Nah," he said aloud. "It was the fumes. Weren't no oxygen for him to breathe down there."

"Well," R.D. said. "Whatever it was that killed him, he was dead and we was to blame. We powered up our ORVs and took off back home as fast as we could in the dark. Then we just waited to see what would happen. It weren't nothin' like we figured, was it?"

Ray stood and walked up next to R.D. They both leaned on the railing and looked out at the mountains. "The way we figure it," he said, "Eugene was comin' to get his drugs when he saw Les leave the crapper. He must not have seen you leave. Anyway, his drugs got knocked down into the shit while Les was tryin' to get Big John outa there, and bein' so dark in there, Les didn't even know it had happened, but Eugene didn't know that. He saw Les come out, and after Les was long gone, he went in and his drugs was gone and Big John was dead and he figured Les had the drugs."

"So he tortured Les to death tryin' to get him to tell where the drugs was when Les didn't even know there was any drugs," R.D. said.

"Yeah. Damn near broke ever' bone in that poor old man's body," Ray said. "I guess he finally figured out that Les didn't know anything about the drugs and then he got really pissed and just kept flailin' away at him with that stick of kindlin' until he'd beat him to death. Preacher here got there just in time to keep him from burnin' down the place to cover what he'd done. You got there just in time to save the preacher."

"What about the Deaver boy? Why'd Eugene kill him?" R.D. asked.

"Price was screwin' Bethabelle, or she was screwin' him," Ray said.

"Oh, that."

"You knew?" Ray asked, not shocked, but a little surprised.

R.D. shrugged. "I thought ever'one did."

Ray just shook his head. He sat back down in the rocker and looked at his coffee. It was long cold, so he didn't try to drink it. We all just stood and sat there, smoking and looking at the mountains.

"It was an accident, Ray," R.D. finally said, not turning around. "I mean, I never meant to kill him. I just meant to put him down. I was afraid for Les and it looks like I got him killed just the same." He was crying and he didn't want us to see him. He bowed his head and his hand went up to his face.

"Only a fool wouldn't be afraid of Big John Wisdom," Ray said. "And you did save the preacher here."

"You think that'll go in my favor?" Some hope in his voice.

"It might. It might." Ray looked at me and raised his eyebrows. I nodded. Yes, I'd testify that R. D. Miles's quick thinking and infinite compassion had saved my life. Why not? Big John Wisdom was a bully and a prick. No friend of mine or anyone else's I could name, except maybe his mother, and even she had grown weary of him. She loved the memory of him, the image she kept of him as a child, more than she loved the man he had become.

"Well, I guess we better go tell all o' this to Elias," R.D. said. "It won't take long. I've got it all written down." He walked into the house and returned a few minutes later with a fist full of yellow legal pad paper. He handed it to me and smiled. "You really a Methodist preacher?"

I nodded as I put the papers in my jacket pocket. "I sure am," I said.

He smiled again. "I ain't never heard a preacher call it a crapper before." Then, as he walked down the steps to Ray's Jeep, he chuckled to himself. "What would your momma say?"

Epilogue

R. D. MILES WAS TRIED FOR THE DEATH OF JOHN WISDOM and found guilty of manslaughter. He was defended by Percy Mills, who was older than anyone in Durel County could remember and still one of the best lawyers in the state, not to mention the personal attorney of Hebrew Taylor, my future father-in-law. I testified, Ray testified, and believe it or not, Charles Wisdom even testified in R.D.'s behalf, and the judge pretty much agreed with my assessment of Big John Wisdom, although he put it in more delicate terms.

R.D. was given a suspended sentence and probation, with Ray as his probation officer. He was still out of work, but at least he was free.

Charles and Marie Wisdom brought Cleopha to church several times that autumn, but then, as the pain of that October began to heal, they fell away again. It was a forty-minute drive, at least. Marie still sings in the choir during holiday seasons and Cleopha comes to hear her, but that's about all I see of them.

Eugene Wisdom was buried up at the family plot, but I didn't do the service. The Reverend Clyde Harland of the Melrose Pentecostal Holiness Church of God had that honor. No, Eugene had never been saved, but it seems Bethabelle had trod the sawdust trail herself just the day before the funeral and "accepted Jesus Christ as her personal Lord and savior." So I guess the Reverend Harland softened his stance somewhat. Funny how he wouldn't soften it for the husband of tall, homely Charlotte. You don't suppose those big eyes and that sexy pout and that apple-shaped ass and those great boobs had anything to do with it, do you? Or am I just being cynical? Or maybe a little jealous? Naomi says neither. My mother says both. Ray just shakes his head and smiles.

Benny Kneeb spent three thousand dollars getting the powdered sugar and cocaine cleaned out of his truck engine. With everyone involved in the drug deal dead, the county attorney didn't think Ray's case was very strong and he let Benny go. Ray said he didn't mind. Benny, he said, had suffered enough, what with the sugar in his engine and having to sit in the middle of the road all night. Ray had forgotten to call Elias to come pick Benny up, and the story is that Benny was so frightened, he sat right there in the middle of the road until dawn and was almost run over by Kramer Poston, who was driving his own truck to work.

May June's picture ploy worked, sort of. The pictures of me with my nose encased in plaster and my head swathed in bandages didn't create enough guilt to get a complete medical clinic from my parishioners, but we do have a small medical office in the basement of the Mountain Baptist Children's Home now. Twice a week Ruth Lee, LPN, drags one of the resident D.O.s from the hospital up to Baird and they check out the babies, give shots, give out medicine samples that salesmen leave, free of charge, at the hospital, and raise hell with all of us about our smoking, drinking, and eating habits.

We also got the steeple fixed so we could ring the bell on Sunday mornings. That was the faction that won, in the end. The put-it-in-the-bank faction gave them a good run for the money, but church bells usually win out in that kind of a contest. It's an image thing.

I had every intention of following Naomi's advice and kissing June Ann Crabtree's ass. I drove over to her place and was invited in and was just about ready to apologize over coffee and apple pie when she blurted out how sorry she was! So it wasn't so much an ass kissing as it was an exchange of apologies, and she loved it and I felt better and I left with a homemade apple pie on the seat of my VW. She is now one of my strongest allies and most ardent defenders in the church. Go figure.

Hebrew Taylor, Naomi's father, is still alive and, if anything, in better health than ever. It's not that I wanted him to die, please try to understand. It's just that Naomi simply refuses to leave him until he does. And life is so complicated and promises to get no less so until, I am convinced, we are happily married.

So we continue, as we have been, sneaking around.

I often think about what R.D. said about Bethabelle and Price Deaver's affair when Ray asked him if he knew about it. "I thought everyone did," R.D. said.

I wonder how much these folks really know about Naomi and me. I don't think I want to know. So we try to be discreet.

Ray never did tell me the name of the guy in Perry who rented and sold the pirated videotapes, and I never had the guts to ask him. When I broached the subject with Naomi she giggled. "You wanna watch a dirty movie so bad, why don't we just make one of our own."

Is it any wonder I'm so in love with that girl?

And, I know, Mom—Discretion! Discretion!!